THE
SWORD
OF THE
GOLEM

By the same author

THE THOUSAND DOORS
THE HEIRS OF CAIN
THE SONG OF DAVID FREED
THE OTHER MAN'S SHOES

THE
SWORD
OF THE
GOLEM

Abraham Rothberg

The McCall Publishing Company

NEW YORK

Published simultaneously in Canada by Doubleday Canada Ltd., Toronto.

Library of Congress Catalog Card Number: 71-134477

SBN 8415-0078-9

The McCall Publishing Company
230 Park Avenue
New York, N.Y. 10017

PRINTED IN THE UNITED STATES OF AMERICA

Design by Tere LoPrete

To all who have searched the past of the Golem and questioned his meaning; but most of all to the great Leivick, who breathed new life into the Golem's clay.

For
JACOB BEHRMAN
and
ANDREW AMSEL
friends in deed

THE
SWORD
OF THE
GOLEM

I

The winter night was dark and moonless, a storm threatening. Distant and blinking, the few stars were occasionally revealed through the drift of heavy clouds that blotted the towers of Prague from sight and hung like rotten clusters over the silver Moldau. As the three men made their way quietly through the sleeping city toward the river, a mist rose from the cobblestones and hid their feet. Why, Rabbi Low wondered, does my heart quake with fear? What gives me pause? Did not the Lord reveal what I was to do and His dreams command me to save the community? *Thou shalt mold a Golem of clay who shall be your David against the new Goliaths and Philistines.* It promised that this time at least they would be saved by the Lord's intercession. Why, then, was he so uneasy?

Jacob Nissan's passionate "We have been victims long enough" rang in his ears, and behind him he felt the weight of the *Judenstadt* heavy as his years bowing down his shoulders. There are more ways to be a victim than to be cut down by the sword. Is not he who cuts down with the sword an even greater victim? He who lifts up the sword is worse by far, for he loses his share of the world to come. But he lives, he lives, his heart cried, and he who is cut down is dead.

The river bank was empty. In the tangled shrubbery a chill wind blustered, then was still. Behind him, Isaac Hayyot in a shuddering voice exclaimed, "Rabbi, I am afraid." Jacob was silent, glowering in the dark. "There is nothing to fear," Rabbi Low reassured them. "We carry out the Lord's commandment that our people shall be saved, not slain." Yet he felt the weakness of his bones, the quivering of his loins.

As if of their own volition, as if a hundred times before they had beaten a path there so that they were familiar with every ridge and gully, his feet led him to the clay pit only a stone's throw from the river's brim. "Here," he heard himself announce, "right here." Carefully, he placed them around the edge of the pit, proclaiming, "We shall make a golem. For this act of creation, we must have four elements: fire, water, air, and earth. You, Jacob, are the element of fire, and you, Isaac, are water. I myself am air. Together, with the Lord's help, out of the fourth element, earth, we shall shape a golem."

Jacob lighted the torches and anchored them in the clay. With outstretched arms, as if he were blessing the clay and the river, the bank and the shrubbery, Rabbi Low intoned, "We have prayed and have sanctified ourselves to be ready for this great moment. But if we are not pure at heart, if we are not free of every base ambition and sinful thought, then we shall be in danger of our very lives, for we shall have used the holy name of the Lord in vain. We shall have desecrated the name of the Almighty."

In the flickering torchlight, their eyes fixed on the clay beneath their feet, they chanted together:

How manifold are Thy works, O Lord!
In wisdom hast Thou made them all;
The earth is full of Thy creatures. .

Thou openest Thy hand, they are satisfied with good.
Thou hidest Thy face, they vanish;
Thou withdrawest their breath, they perish,
And return to their dust.
Thou sendest forth Thy spirit, they are created;
And Thou renewest the face of the earth.
May the glory of the Lord endure forever;
Let the Lord rejoice in His works!

The torchlight wavered over the pit, Jacob and Isaac chanted Psalms, and Rabbi Low bent to his task.

The clay was thick and shaped itself only reluctantly to his hands, as if the very earth resisted his creation and lay limp and diffuse, refusing to be formed out of chaos into that which was human. Again and again Rabbi Low was forced to fashion the torso and limbs, the fingers and toes, the apertures, the head and the countenance, and each time they were reabsorbed into the welter of shapeless clay. How, he thought despairingly, could life be infused into such a lump of earth, how could humanity be breathed into such clods? As he labored in the uncertain torchlight the memory of how Adam was created shook him. In the first hour Adam's handful of dust was collected and in the second his shape took form. In the third hour his head settled on his trunk. In the fourth his limbs knit together and in the fifth the apertures of his body opened. In the sixth hour he received his soul and in the seventh Adam stood upright, on his own feet.

Even as Rabbi Low's fingers strove to master the recalcitrant clay, even as Isaac walked counterclockwise seven times around the slowly emerging form, and Jacob walked clockwise his seven times around, even as together the two of them sang,

Why art thou cast down, O my soul?
And why moanest thou within me?
Hope thou in God; for yet shall I praise Him
For the salvation of His countenance,

Rabbi Low remembered with a start of apprehension that in the eighth hour Eve had come to Adam, in the ninth they had been wafted to paradise, in the tenth hour they had heard God's command, and in the eleventh and twelfth they had sinned and been driven from Eden, forever barred from return by the angel and his flaming sword.

In a trance, Rabbi Low worked feverishly. If even the Lord had taken seven hours, how could he shape creation in half that time? But what the Lord had decreed He could perform. The Lord would guide his hands. Again and again he fashioned the unwilling clay until at last his fingers began to burrow and mold of their own volition and the clay cohered. The outline was as of a tree trunk felled, as if an outcropping so monumental had swelled from the earth that something in nature was trapped and imprisoned in it. Rabbi Low felt a tremor of fear in his fingers, or was that the first beat of life in the golem? Dissonant and clangorous thoughts resounded in his mind like foreign tongues. An anguish in the clay pulsed to his fingers, speaking without speech, "Do not rip me from this womb of clay!"

The great gray corpse, its face toward the rumbling heavens, lay beneath him, and as Rabbi Low continued to knead, he knew the clay's wild plaint, "Did I request you to be my maker? Did I enjoin you to tear me from the bowels of the earth? Leave me embedded in the unfeeling clay, in the silent, peaceful dark."

The plaint stirred tears in the Rabbi's eyes but his hands, powerful with a strength and will beyond them, now kneaded and worked and would not desist. "Help me, O Lord!" his spirit cried.

"Help me!" the clay beneath his hands petitioned.

Thunder reverberated, rain sprayed and hailstones pelted them. The wind howled in pain. The clay pleaded, "Hear me, I beg you!" Then threatened, "If you bring me to life, my rage shall devour the living, my strength shall lay waste the earth."

"*They that sow in tears,*" Rabbi Low sobbed under his breath, "*shall reap in joy.* The Lord has commanded me to bring you forth."

"I know the Lord's decree."

"Then obey it."

"Thou, then, obey it, for if thou shouldst obey it, then might I lie here in my ark of earth, quietly rocked by the centuries, undisturbed by eons."

"We must both obey what has been ordained. You must arise from the clay to do my bidding as I am bent to shape it. You must be our strength."

"A clenched fist, a hulk, a golem!"

"A golem, yes, but one who works the Lord's will."

"A lump of clay. Not fully formed. Incomplete."

"Israel's defender, a Gideon, a Saul, a David."

"A violent hand."

"The Lord's anointed for His holy task."

"To kill."

"To save."

"I beseech thee."

"To save."

"Rabbi!" Isaac's voice called him from his trance.

"Do you hear, Isaac?" Rabbi Low asked. Isaac shook his head. "Jacob?"

"We heard nothing, Rabbi, except the thunder and the wind crying like a lost soul."

They had heard nothing. The clay had spoken only to him, the speech of the earth. Lightning burned, beneath his hands the dead clay quaked, simmered, and turned red as fire, as if pottery were being baked in a kiln. Blazing coppery, then bronze-bright, it was finally glowing scarlet before a burst of rain splashed it blue, gray, and pale as flesh when the fiery clay was extinguished. But the spark of life had been kindled. Hair leaped out of the shaped skull, sprouting like black grass, nails unsheathed like claws.

"Rabbi!" Isaac and Jacob screamed, then fled.

Rabbi Low heard a fading echo, like the rustling of animals in underbrush, the wind rushing water through the trees, and the cry "Rabbi!" reverberating over and over again like an idiot's lament.

From his cloak he drew the parchment inscribed with the most holy name of God, the *Shem*, placed it in the mouth that had now fallen open, put it under the lolling clay tongue, and pronounced the wonder-working name aloud. He stood and bowed north and south, east and west, then once more bent to the mound of clay. With his forefinger he drew the Hebrew word *Emes*, "truth," on the clay forehead, his hand trembling because he had but to smudge or erase the first letter and all would be lost: The word would become *Mes*, "corpse." Thunder boomed, wind raged, and Rabbi Low threw himself on the clay figure and breathed into the clay mouth his own warm breath, the passionate striving of his own spirit, the desperation of his desire to save, declaring,

"And He breathed into his nostrils the breath of life; and man became a living soul."

The long wailing sigh of breath seemed to resound down the centuries, a breath drawn in pain and expelled in longing, then abrupt as a thunderclap he heard the beating of a heart. "Thou sendest forth Thy spirit, they are created!" Rabbi Low exulted.

The Golem opened his eyes, sea green and smoldering with fire, burrowed deep into pale sockets of greenish flesh. The heavy black beard, electric, burst from his face.

"Arise!" Rabbi Low commanded.

The Golem stood, drew himself up to his full height, a giant. His eyes burned fury down and Rabbi Low was struck with terror, regret, remorse—and jubilation.

"I am here," the Golem said, his voice hoarse, untried.

"The Lord has sent you," the Rabbi said, looking fearlessly into the powerful brutish face and raging eyes. *"He hath sent redemption unto His people; He hath commanded his covenant for ever; Holy and awful is His name."*

"I am here," the Golem repeated.

"You are here and you will obey."

"The Lord has sent me, but you have called me forth," the Golem acknowledged, great head nodding.

"You shall be known as Joseph Golem."

"I shall be Joseph Golem."

"You shall live in my house, and through me shall the Lord's will be made known to you. Your task shall be to protect all Jews. What I command, you shall obey. The praise of the Lord shall be in your mouth—and in your hand a two-edged sword."

"You have lifted me from the earth, wrung me from clay. What you propose, I shall obey."

"Speak but little. Remain aloof. Do not stand out. You shall perform great deeds known to but few, but you shall be a great hero to your people," the Rabbi said.

"I shall do."

At the horizon the sky began to lighten, then the silhouettes of Isaac and Jacob loomed above them. The Golem moved awkwardly in their direction, threatening but still uncertain in limbs and gait, and the two of them shrank back. The Rabbi raised his hand and the Golem stopped in his tracks. "These are my son-in-law, Isaac Hayyot, and my student, Jacob Nissan," Rabbi Low said. They nodded in unison, their faces full of astonishment and trepidation; the Golem gave no sign in return.

Isaac took clothing from the sack he carried, the poor, worn habit of a drayman, and handed the clothes to the Rabbi who, in turn, passed them to the Golem. Clumsily, the Golem dressed and the clothes seemed to grow to his girth; soon, but for his size, he looked like an ordinary drayman.

In the distance the first light showed. "We must hurry," Jacob said softly.

The Rabbi glanced at the lifting light and strode swiftly up the bank. They hastened after him, the Golem behind them, and Jacob, in a low voice intended only for the Rabbi, asked, "How will you explain his presence? What will you do with him?"

"He is a stranger come to dwell among us from another realm. I have hired him to be my servant. It is not necessary to say more," the Rabbi replied. "His great duty shall be to protect the ghetto."

Behind him Isaac murmured to the waters of the river the ancient words, "*Thou wilt cast all their sins into the depths of the sea,*" and fervently Rabbi Low spoke a silent Amen. His jubilation had drained away to be replaced by uneasy gloom.

"What do you have there?" he asked Isaac, angry with himself for permitting anxiety to sharpen his tone.

"The yellow hats and armbands. If daylight comes too soon," Isaac said haltingly, then offered a peaked hat and armband to the Golem. The Golem stared contemptuously before rejecting them.

Without another word Jacob extinguished the torches and in the dawn darkness they stole single file along the street, against the sides of the houses, until they came to the Gothic bulwark of the *Altneuschul* and safety.

II

"Who calls?"

Rabbi Low awoke, his sleep-torn cry echoing in his study. Even as he knew it to be his own voice, he feared to reply, "Here am I; for Thou didst call me," though he remembered the Biblical words as well as his own name. Would that some Eli might comfort him with "I called not, my son; lie down again." But I am not Samuel, nor am I the Lord's prophet. No, he reminded himself, enough that you are Judah Low, Rabbi of Prague. He rose from his bed and slowly went to the narrow shuttered window to stare into the shadowed *Judengasse* below. All was quiet. If he held his breath, he was sure he would be able to hear the tremulous nighttime breathing that afflicted the Jews of the Old Town.

Beneath the rabbinical dress, a lean, strong figure moved, impatient, decisive, alert, the still-powerful figure of an old but energetic man. The heavy jutting forehead and great eyebrows were twisted into a contemplative scowl that, combined with the hunch of his shoulders, told of long scholar's hours poring over books. The hands, shapely and with long, strong fingers, seemed never to be still and, even when disciplined, showed powerful feelings under close control. "They envy me my dreams," he muttered to himself, "envy my seeing into the future. And for that"—his smile was self-mocking, ironic—"they call me *Höhe*, exalted."

The Rabbi pushed the shutters open wider and leaned into the night chill with a premonitory shudder. Below, from over his door, the white, stone-faced lion looked fiercely on the *Judengasse*. "Oh my father," he thought, as he did so often when he was troubled, "is this why you named me Judah? *Judah is the lion's whelp; from the prey, my son, art thou saved.*" Once a patriarch's blessing and now he was himself a patriarch, yet the blessing had not helped him. But we are all prey now, he thought, and how shall we escape the lion's paw and the jackal's fangs? He thought of Bezalel, seeing his boy's face, not the man's, transform the leonine stone, make human the bestial, then transformed once more to immobile stone. His patriarchal blessing had no more helped Bezalel than his father's had helped him. Firmly, he put the memory from his mind and instead remembered the comments he had often heard beneath him when Christians passed his house and saw that lion's face. Laughing—they had always laughed—they said, pointing, "A lion on Jew's Street! Ha!" And the guffaws had cut him to the heart. Afraid he had declared himself aloud to the night, he caught himself, yet knew he had not spoken. Softly, he murmured to himself, though not to himself alone, "Forgive me, O Lord, I have made too much of my burden. Blessed be the name of the Lord."

He had disliked the man who the night before had brought him the news, a man with eyes that darted in his head like a cornered animal's, with head thrust forward and shoulders that made his body seem to be fleeing his legs. His voice, too, had been strangely split, an alternating bass whine and soprano assertion. When he introduced himself as Eli Karpeles, "a Jew and a friend," the Rabbi treated him with even greater reserve. Karpeles confessed that he no longer lived as a Jew because he could not bear to feel always under the knife. His voice broke pathetically, yet Rabbi Low felt that he was not without calculation. Under the guidance of the friar Thaddeus, Eli Karpeles had converted and become Ivan Karpic. For ten years he had lived as a Christian; his children had been born and baptized into the church and had grown up believing themselves Catholic. This was the first time in a decade he had spoken to a rabbi. "But," Karpic said, breathing as if he had been chased by demons, "I feel, I feel . . . What does it matter how I feel, or what I am? Jew or Christian, good man or bad man, Rabbi, I have come to warn you that Thaddeus hates us, you, Jews, and he is plotting to charge all the Jews of Prague with murdering a Christian to take his blood for the Passover matzos."

Rabbi Low had shown Karpeles-Karpic out into the night, noting the caution with which the man looked everywhere before he scurried into the shadows, and he was ashamed because he had not been able to bring himself to utter a word of comfort or thanks to the man, but Karpeles-Karpic's visit had only been the last in a series of incidents, which preoccupied him more than the apostate's dilemma.

Blood accusation. Bloodguilt. Ritual murder. Over and over again blown across Europe like a plague, who could know how it had begun, from what deranged mind or tormented spirit it had sprung. The first appearance had been in England, in Norwich, where a boy named William had disappeared. Jews were soon accused of killing the boy, and a Jewish convert named Theobald of Cambridge had thereupon testified that each year Jews sacrificed a Christian child at the Passover. Later, it was discovered that the boy had been found in a cataleptic fit and been buried alive by his stepmother and stepbrother. By then the facts made no difference: The plague had begun.

From that time on, the mania had been a whirlwind blowing across Europe. Gloucester, Bury St. Edmunds, Winchester, Fulda, Vaucluse, Trent, Tyrnau, a west wind full of blood. It had not delayed long in coming to Prague. More than two hundred and fifty years before, John the Landless, King of Bohemia, had burned

Jews for having drunk Christian blood and no professions of innocence could save them. Now Thaddeus had more of that in store.

The dream had, like a fever in his blood, tormented Rabbi Low for weeks, months. He saw himself in the shade of a carob tree whose leaves turned black and fell around him, edges still raging with flame, burning him to the bone. Above, a white sky soared and from it a still small voice leaped like lightning into his flesh: *The time is coming when gladness shall be taken away and there shall be lamentation everywhere.* The waters of the Moldau shall be dried up and the plains of Bohemia and Moravia laid waste. The sword shall be unsheathed and thy people shall be cut down as the wheat falls to the sickle. Everywhere the city shall be plundered and the land made desolate.

He did not have to frame the question. His flesh and blood urged him on, however reluctant he was to go forward. From boyhood, dreams had been God's voice made plain to him, joy and anguish he was free neither to summon nor reject. Dreams came by daylight and by night, sudden and swift, or deceptively slow as the shifting of the seasons. Now, as he saw the path, Rabbi Low shrank from it. *"Then the Lord God formed man of the dust of the earth and breathed into his nostrils the breath of life; and man became a living soul."* A living soul! How had he dared to emulate the Lord's greatness in that which is beyond the making of man's hands? The stern voice within neither attended to his pleas nor countenanced his reluctance. It had commanded that he make a Golem out of clay and with it defend his people. Trembling, Rabbi Low heard his own voice chant, "Thou hast hemmed me in behind and before, and laid Thy hand upon me. Such knowledge is too wonderful for me; too high: I cannot attain unto it. Whither shall I go from Thy spirit? Whither shall I flee from Thy presence?"

At sunrise he awoke again and knew that, however fearful, the task was not beyond him. The *Höhe* Rabbi Low of Prague *had* breathed into a handful of dust and, with God's favor, had made it live. Out of clay had come a Golem with whom he would defend Jews against their adversaries.

Twice that day his wife had quarreled with him about not eating, yet he had not fasted deliberately; he did not want to be distracted by food and now he felt light-headed and cold. He had sent for Isaac and Jacob, and as he awaited their arrival, Pearl came once more to berate him for not having allowed a bite of food to pass his lips and once more he sent her away chagrined. They entered his study soon after evening prayers and Rabbi Low motioned them to be seated. Isaac sat but Jacob, as was his wont, prowled restlessly. Briefly, the Rabbi told them what Karpeles-Karpic had reported.

Jacob nodded. "Passover is never very far away. It is always the season to speak of Christian children with their throats cut and Jewish vampires draining their blood for the Passover matzos and wine."

"The time is ripe for more practical reasons," Isaac added. "The good citizens of Prague owe the Jews of the ghetto a great deal of money. A ritual murder affords a good opportunity to wash out their debts in blood."

"Moneylending is not a business that endears one to one's neighbors," the Rabbi remarked. "Nor have we always dealt wisely in our affairs."

"We have thieves in our midst as do other people," Jacob said hotly. "Shall we all be indicted for each scoundrel among us?"

"We, too, have evil, brutal men," Isaac reflected, "our share of the evil impulse."

"The *yetzer* grows in all men like sunflowers in the field," the Rabbi said. "Even in Jews." His face turned inward, eyes closed, his long fingers tip to tip as if he were trying to hold the recollection of something before them to display it. "When I was a boy, my father told me about a massacre of Jews. The story had come down to him from his father and his grandfather before him. His great-grandfather, I think it was, had actually seen the event and wanted his family never to forget it, to pass it on like the candlesticks and the family names. I have never forgotten and though now I have no sons to pass it on to"—again Bezalel's face, but now the older face of the man, flashed before him—"I have told it to my daughters. Now I shall tell it to you." His eyes opened, scrutinized their faces, and noted Jacob's impatience, even Isaac's, but he did not hasten his story.

"It was the day after the Christian Good Friday and the priests were leading a procession through the streets carrying their host. Some children threw stones at them. Perhaps Jewish children, perhaps not, but it was near the ghetto and no one was sure."

"Have we not been accused of murdering their god for so long that our children stoning his image would seem likely?" Jacob bit out.

The Rabbi ignored him. "It was a sunny, spring day. The grass surged green up the hillsides, the trees had just begun to unfold their leaves, all Prague was filled with the perfume of the season.

"Jesek Ctyrhanny vowed vengeance against the Jews and from the pulpit delivered an oration calling on the people to scourge the Jews. The people obeyed. They came to the *Judenstadt* like wild beasts, howling, shrieking, with pikes and axes and swords, with scythes and sickles, and they killed and raped and burned half the ghetto to the ground. When they were done, three thousand Jews lay dead."

Isaac's hands tugged nervously at his red beard in a gesture of mourning.

"Three thousand. Men, women, and children," the Rabbi said somberly. "As if that were not enough, on the morning following Easter, the royal chamberlain ordered 'legal' punishment of the Jews for having incited to riot. He exacted a heavy fine from the entire Jewish community."

"Five tons of silver, a ton for every stone the children threw," Isaac interrupted.

"Sarah told you," the Rabbi said.

Isaac shook his head. "No, it was before that. Leah told me. April 18, 1389, by *their* calendar," Isaac told Jacob, "a date we should not forget."

"Dates are always soon forgotten," Jacob replied. "Dates of birth and dates of death and dates of marriage. A decade passes, a generation changes, and even the greatest monstrosities become history. They recede into a grandmother's tale to frighten children with."

"Avigedor Karo wrote an elegy for those Jews who died on that day and every Day of Atonement we proclaim it in the synagogue," Rabbi Low reminded him.

"Once a year, dutifully, we recite an elegy. Do we mourn the massacre as our sin or theirs? Is the elegy for those who died or for those remaining alive?"

"You are too young to be so bitter, Jacob," Rabbi Low said. "One must earn one's bitterness through experience."

Jacob's face was dark. "Two hundred years have passed and still we live in fear and trembling. Jesek Ctyrhanny . . . My family has a story too. If ever I have sons, I shall pass it on to them. It was in my grandfather's time, blessed be his memory, when Louis II came to Prague. All the Jewish community went out to meet him carrying the scrolls of the Law under a canopy and singing Psalms as if they were going to greet the Messiah!" His laugh was sardonic and strangled. "When those good, peaceful Jews who were his subjects asked the king to touch their Torah, he did so. The great Louis II condescended, but he did not touch the Torah with his hand, only with his whip. His whip! He told them from his heart and with his hand what he meant for them, and all those Jews who could read the subtlest innuendo in the most obscure text in gratitude for that royal act offered Louis II a gift of a hundred gold ducats."

"The Lord will protect us," Isaac said, "even against the whip of the king."

"We must protect ourselves," Jacob protested.

"We are only a few thousand souls," Isaac said, carefully choosing each word. "What good would taking up the sword be? Even were we all trained and battle-hardened soldiers, could we stand off all Prague, all Bohemia? We should be slaughtered."

"We would die like men, not like cattle. We must not become victims. We have been victims long enough," Jacob insisted. "Too long."

"A branch may be cut off. A limb may die. But the tree lives, its roots sunk in the soil of the Torah. The tree that bends in the wind and does not break is stronger than the one that does not bend and breaks," Isaac said.

"But when the woodcutter comes, what then?" Jacob asked.

The Rabbi intervened. "The Talmud says, 'Whoever raises his hand against his neighbor, even if he does not strike him, is an evildoer.'"

"But when your neighbor raises his hand against you, what then?"

"We are Jews," the Rabbi emphasized. "We do not exalt the sword or the fist. We need not die like cattle, but we must not live like beasts. We can live like men."

"How, Rabbi?" Jacob asked, the words wrung from him.

Rabbi Low's voice was confident. "We have made a Golem, a creature that God has sent us to protect us."

"And if he should fail?" Jacob asked.

The Rabbi looked closely at both of them, then clapped his hands. The door opened and the Golem bent his head to come through the entrance, then stood erect so that he seemed to fill the room, massive, mysterious, powerful. "Look at him!" the Rabbi said. "He will not fail us."

The giant's solemn face looked at them and they could not meet his eyes.

III

In the days that followed, Rabbi Low kept the Golem close to him. The Golem slept on a couch in the Rabbi's study and the rest of the day would follow him unobtrusively on his rounds, remaining quietly in the background but always present until the Rabbi went to bed. The Rabbi sent him to do chores for the synagogue, particularly to chop wood and to draw water, and some who saw him made rude comments about the "dumb Yossel" who was a lumbering hewer of wood and drawer of water, but the Golem seemed neither to notice nor hear them.

One morning when the Golem saw the Rabbi put on his phylacteries, he asked, "Rabbi, why do you put those straps on your head and arm?"

The Rabbi explained the injunction that the Law was to be

studied and obeyed every single day, then showed the Golem how the black leather cubes and thongs were worn, pointing out that they were meant to connect the arm, heart, and head in the performance of good deeds.

"May I put them on too?" the Golem inquired.

Rabbi Low hesitated before saying yes, then brought another set of phylacteries and taught the Golem how to don them. But the *Shel Rosh* barely sat on the Golem's forehead and the *Shel Yad* was so short that the Golem could not make more than a single turn high on his biceps with it, much less wind it down his forearm to shape the holy letter *Shin* on his hand. Rabbi Low took the Golem's interest for an omen, a portent that the Golem would make his strong right arm do that which his head and heart were properly advised, and soon he had a set of phylacteries made that fit the Golem and gave them to him with a glad heart.

In the synagogue the Golem sat off by himself and talked to no one. His great height, his strangely pale flesh, green eyes, and coal black beard attracted attention, and many asked who he was and where he had come from. Isaac Hayyot and Jacob Nissan assuaged the general curiosity by telling people that the man was named Joseph Golem, a poor wayfarer whom the Rabbi had encountered and brought home to help with the synagogue's chores. Though the Golem spoke to none of the congregation, he came to every service and sat, head bowed, eyes glaring, his great fingers twining and restless, until one evening, when prayers were ended and he walked alone with the Rabbi from the *Altneuschul*, he asked if he too might learn to pray. The Rabbi hesitated before agreeing, but the Golem, too, was one of God's children, so he directed Isaac Hayyot to devote a few hours each day to teaching the Golem to read and pray. In the weeks that followed, whenever the Golem had nothing to do, he read, then later studied, and the Rabbi wondered why that should disconcert him. Was not study also a form of prayer?

It was then that Rabbi Low set the Golem's regular tasks, sending him throughout the city by day and night in the guise of a Christian drayman to discover those who plotted evil against the Jews, for daily more reports threatening harm to the ghetto increased his sense of impending disaster. Rabbi Low therefore directed the Golem to loiter wherever Jew-baiters congregated in the taverns, at the public baths, before the apothecary shops, near the slaughterhouse, outside the churches, Thaddeus' church in particular, to look and to listen. From midnight to dawn especially, when they might expect the worst mischief, the Golem walked the tangle of narrow lanes and streets to patrol the wall that was the ghetto boundary and to guard the ghetto gates. And because he knew the Golem was on guard, the Rabbi slept a little more securely.

One morning when the Rabbi came late to his study, the Golem was gone. The Rabbi found him in the kitchen being served by his ward, Kaethe Hoch. As she fetched the food from stove to table, the Golem's eyes followed her as if the girl herself were a delicacy to be eaten. The sense of uneasiness grew in Rabbi Low and he told himself that a golem lived only to fulfill the will of his creator, an incomplete creation deprived of the light of God within him. A golem was supposed to have neither wisdom nor judgment, nor was he endowed with a will of his own or sexual feelings. Yet Joseph Golem had already evinced both a remarkable desire and capacity to learn and pray—Isaac said that he had never taught or studied with a more apt pupil, that already the Golem knew more than most of his students—and the Golem's glances at Kaethe left no doubt that powerful emotions surged within his frame. Though the Golem did the Lord's bidding in the nights, guarding the walls and the gates of the ghetto, and in the days chopping wood and drawing water uncomplainingly, performing any chore he was given, Rabbi Low knew that the *yetzer* lurked in all living beings. The Golem's silence, his study and prayer, even the flawless way in which he donned the phylacteries, were unnerving. And the Golem's sly glances at Kaethe gave the Rabbi further misgivings because he was always uneasy about Kaethe. How many times as a child when the other children had thrown the words *illegitimate* and *bastard* at her like stones—*nadler! momzer!*—had she come running to him, her face dirtied, scratched, and tearstained, to be comforted, yet even as a child she seemed always inconsolable. But that was all so long ago, why did he recall it now? The Hochs had lain in the earth more than ten years, even Meisel no longer mentioned them, yet he remembered the day of their death, the day he and his wife had taken the little girl Kaethe into their house, as if it were yesterday. That was his age telling: He could remember a decade, three decades ago with silver clarity; but he could recall the day before yesterday only in a rusted iron blur.

The Golem sat in a corner of the tavern drinking mead and listening. No one paid him any attention, and as he watched the men drink and grow drunken, quarrel loudly, then fight with their fists, staves, dirks, he wondered what sort of creatures men were. That they did not talk to him seemed natural. No one did except the Rabbi, Isaac, and Kaethe Hoch, and sometimes the Rabbi's wife and Jacob, but except for Kaethe, none spoke to him naturally. His size and strange appearance seemed to intimidate all.

Two men at a nearby table swore loudly that they would make a fire so brave that it could be seen in Vyšehrad. The priest with them looked nervously around, hushed them, then gave careful instructions about how the synagogue might be burned to the ground. "The *Altneuschul*," he said, "is a house of horrors and infidels. Who destroys it works for Christ's salvation and his own."

"Amen!" the two men responded, crossed themselves, and clanked their tankards together to their enterprise.

The Golem took the news to Rabbi Low. In the dark of the night the Golem waited in the shadows of the houses across the *Judengasse* from the *Altneuschul*, and when the two came to crouch at the base of the old synagogue, he stood patiently as they tried to start the fire with straw and twigs they had brought. Finally, when the small flames began to lick the walls, lighting the great Gothic gables and weathered roof of the synagogue, the Golem fell on them, so silently that they never knew what had struck their heads together in a great single blow and left them unconscious on the cobblestones. Cruelly, the Golem used their bodies to damp the fires they had set, then tied them up, threw them over his shoulders as if they were sacks of turnips, and set them down before the magistrate's office.

In the morning he watched when the bailiffs found them, half out of their senses, scorched and blistered and burned, their wrists and ankles swollen and discolored from the cords that bound them, the tools of their arson laid out around them so that the bailiffs could not help but surmise what they had done and why they had been left there. The Golem did not show himself or speak; he waited only until the bailiffs had dragged the men inside, shouting that they had not really meant to burn down the synagogue, then left to tell the Rabbi that matters had gone well.

The Golem was carrying a load of wood past when he heard the group of students discussing what Brother Thaddeus had organized for them that very night. At the Jewish cemetery they would deface and break tombstones, mock the ancestors of those outcasts who were now penned in the Jew Town and required to wear yellow discs on their breasts or yellow armbands when they left the *Judengasse*. To disturb the ancient sleep of their Jew forebears would surely be a lark!

The graveyard had a special place in the Golem's affections. To escape the prying eyes that always stared so strangely at him, to leave behind the loneliness he felt among men, driven by some obscure urge to stretch his body impetuously upon the earth and to feel himself received by it, befriended, restored by it, the Golem often went to the "garden of the dead" to rest and find quiet for his turbulent spirit. That these foolish men would defile it angered him. On many afternoons he would sit in the shade of the powerful, spreading trees, his back braced against the cold sandstone monuments, and sometimes in the mornings he would fling himself down on the wintry-hard but hospitable earth to stare up at the gnarled and naked branches of the trees, listening for the peeping of the birds, the secret scurry of squirrels. There were also the evenings and nights when stealthily he followed Kaethe Hoch there and unobserved watched her as she sat and combed the long blond hair she uncoiled from her braids.

The Golem reported the students' scheme and the Rabbi suggested a plan that pleased the Golem. For the first time, Rabbi Low heard the Golem laugh, a harsh, unfeeling croaking. "Yes," the Golem agreed, when the Rabbi finished explaining, "that will be a good way."

Long before midnight, among the weather-beaten tombstones, the Golem secreted himself close to the cemetery gate. Around

him he had wound two long sheets the Rabbi had given him and
fitted over his head one of the ancient battle helmets called
heaumes that he had found in the loft of the *Altneuschul*. Patiently
hidden in the shadows, he waited until a little after midnight when
two dozen of Thaddeus' seminarians arrived carrying hoes and
scythes and long wooden staves, one of them flaunting an ax.
Having caroused all evening in the taverns and now full of wine
and beer and drunken confidence, they made no effort at stealth
or silence, but sang and joked and were merry, passing a goatskin
of wine one to the other while three or four of them tried clumsily to pry open the gate. With a snap the lock and chain broke,
the gate squeaked open on its rusted hinges and the students
cheered and danced past it, leaping and turning and prancing into
the graveyard, kicking tombstones awry, pushing others over,
smashing a few with blows of hoe and ax. Uproariously they
chortled:

> Jew tombstones we shatter
> To make graves give birth;
> Jew corpses don't matter,
> We'll plant new ones in earth,
> For having killed our Savior,
> For having killed our Savior,
> And blasphemed His worth.

Bellowing, the Golem rose to his full height from where he was
concealed. The students, transfixed by terror, stood just as they
were, one on the verge of overturning a slab, another about to
ax a headstone, still another, open-mouthed, holding the wineskin
askew so that wine dripped across a pale, worn grave marker like
living blood. The students stood wide-eyed and uncertain until
one moaned, "A ghost!" The others took up the cry. "A Taborite
warrior!" "Žižka's comrades are guarding the Jewish cemetery!"
They dropped what they were carrying and began to run, all
except one, Voytek, a great peasant churl of a lad who, ax in
hand, stood his ground drunkenly declaring, "I can kill any Hus-
site swine!" How many times had he cloven a hog's skull in two
with just such an ax, and now, recklessly, he lunged at the Golem,
ax raised high to strike. A blow in the chest knocked him down.

The ax was wrenched from him and swung. Sobered suddenly by pain, Voytek got to his knees and raised his hand in front of his dazed eyes to see that the little finger of his right hand was gone, chopped cleanly off, and lay at his feet. With a cry of outrage, of permanent loss, Voytek bent, retrieved his finger, then fled wailing after his fellows.

The Golem was asleep in Rabbi Low's study, unmoving on the couch, when Isaac walked in. "Good morning," the Rabbi greeted him, looking up from the book he was studying. "What brings you so early?"

"I want to talk to you about him," Isaac whispered, jerking his head in the Golem's direction, "but not here."

"He sleeps," the Rabbi said.

"He might wake," Isaac replied. "He might even be able to hear in his sleep."

The Rabbi suggested a morning walk. In the streets they strolled arm in arm for a considerable time, not speaking, watching the wintry sun gild the houses but not warm them. "Now, Isaac," the Rabbi at last inquired, "what troubles you?"

"The Golem troubles me. And he should trouble you."

"Is he not an apt pupil?"

"On the contrary, he learns marvelously quickly and well. In these past months he has learned so swiftly that even I would think him already a scholar—except that he is fascinated by hatred and evil, by violence and force."

"Is this not a necessary fascination?"

"Is man then all *yetzer*, all evil impulse, Rabbi? Is man not also fashioned in the image of God? Is there no act of goodness in him, no love of righteousness, no affection for other human beings?"

"You know that the chosen destiny of our people, our covenant with the Almighty, has been to uphold righteousness and holiness. But the Golem is as if he were newborn. In spite of his great size, in spite of his new learning—and I have no doubt that you have taught him well—he is yet a child in these matters."

"Rabbi, he is *not* a newborn. He has learned many things that I did not teach him. It is not of covenant and righteousness that the Golem wishes to learn. Everywhere he seeks out murder, war, brutality. Cain murdering Abel. Moses doing the Egyptian task-master to death. Jael driving the tent peg into Sisera's temple. Tamar being forced. Jezebel thrown from the windows and fed to the dogs."

Disquieted, Rabbi Low remembered the Golem's reports of how he had burned Thaddeus' villains in their own fires, how with a single stroke he had cut off Voytek's finger. Were those the acts of a defending angel carried out only for the protection of Jews? Did I, Rabbi Low asked himself, in my zeal to protect my people, misinterpret the dream the Almighty sent me? Was my own fear of Thaddeus and his accusations of bloodguilt a poison that flawed this creature at birth? In my joy that we had a defender, was there also vengefulness and spite, hatred and malice? Would the Lord have strengthened my spirit and my hands to mold the Golem's clay into a living creature had I sinned so grievously? Or has the Lord punished us by allowing me to create a scourge, not a redeemer?

"Rabbi." Isaac interrupted his thoughts. "Ever since I saw him quake into life out of the clay pit, my dreams will not let me sleep. I cannot look into his eyes. I shudder when we happen to touch. I am terrified when he is angered." Isaac's eyes were bright and hard. "And I am not afraid only for myself."

Had it been Jacob, the Rabbi would not have been so disturbed. Jacob did not want the Golem to be their David against Goliath; he wanted all the Jews to fight the Philistines, but that would not cause him to be so frightened of the Golem. But Isaac did not want Jews to shed blood. The Lord had warned them, *You shall not walk in the customs of the nations,* and Jews had obeyed. For more than fourteen hundred years, since Bar Kochba had fought the Roman legions, they had put down the sword, but did that mean that Jews were therefore to die by it? There was no virtue to being eternally a victim. *With the peril of our lives we win our bread, alas! Because of the sword of the wilderness!* If the Golem picked up the sword in their behalf, in their wilder-ness, they would not have to do so themselves. They might still walk in the Lord's way, not in the customs of the nations; they might remain alive *and* Jews.

"Send him back," Isaac urged. "You made him, Rabbi; un-make him."

"It was not I who made the Golem, but the Almighty," Rabbi

Low responded. "You know what he was destined for. Is the danger past? Are the Jews of Prague safe?"

Stubbornly, Isaac insisted, "If they would be safe, Jews must not fight. Nor can anyone fight in their behalf. They must not fight at all; they must rely only on the Lord. Send the Golem back."

Inside him the Rabbi heard his own heart rage: "Until when, O Lord, will you permit the destruction of your people? Shall there be no consolation for Zion, no mercy on Jerusalem?" Yet coolly his mind heard his raging heart and was contrite. The Almighty would not abandon them this time. He had obeyed God's commandment, for otherwise the Lord would not have permitted the breath of life to fill a handful of riverbank clay, and the Holy One had sent him no command to destroy His creation. "No," Rabbi Low said firmly, "the time is not yet."

As Isaac turned away, his voice and body trembling, he said, "The Golem will bring disaster on us all."

Three weeks before Chanukah a Christian butcher named Ivo Havlicek decided to revenge himself upon the Jews of Prague in general and upon Mordecai Meisel in particular. Meisel, the leading financier of Prague's Jewish community and of the entire kingdom of Bohemia, had made Havlicek a loan that the butcher refused to repay, both out of greed and out of resentment at the interest rates he had been charged. Because Meisel was now suing him for those five thousand gulden, Havlicek plotted to involve him in a "ritual murder," for then Meisel would either be executed or forced to flee Prague. In either case, Havlicek would in one stroke be free of burdensome debt and debtor, as well as of a weight on his heart. His plan was simple. He had heard of a child who had died and been buried the day before. With that corpse he hoped to compromise Mordecai Meisel. That night he went to the cemetery and dug up the child's body. In his own slaughterhouse, he slit its throat with his butchering knife, wrapped it in a Jewish prayer shawl, then hid the body in the carcass of a slaughtered hog.

Before dawn, Havlicek loaded two dozen hog carcasses into his wagon, as well as vegetables and other produce, carefully laying aside that carcass which contained the child's corpse and on which he put a mark. In his morning rounds delivering meat to his customers in the Old Town and vegetables to Jews in the ghetto, he had to pass Meisel's house. He had bribed one of Meisel's servants to leave the cellar window of the banker's house open. It would be only a minute's work to drop the child's body into the financier's house through the open cellar window. A hint here and there would soon alert the bailiffs, and then when they went to investigate the haughty Jew's house they would find the child's body in the cellar. Havlicek expected no trouble because there seemed no risk involved, for he went well before most people were awake and it was still dark enough before daybreak so that none would be likely to remember his cart making its routine rounds.

Just as Havlicek drove his wagon down the street on which Meisel lived, the Golem was returning to Rabbi Low's house from his all-night vigil in the ghetto. Havlicek's furtive glances aroused his suspicions. Peering up and down the street, Havlicek then bent to test Meisel's window. It was open. Havlicek walked back to his wagon, took the marked carcass, and lifted it in his arms. As he bent to the window with it, he was flung forward on his face. Afraid to shout for help lest he arouse the entire neighborhood, Havlicek fought back. A powerful and heavily muscled man, used to fighting in brawls, and winning, and now frantic with fright, he battled with all his strength and fury. With a single twist the Golem wrenched Havlicek's right arm, then buffeted him until he lay bleeding on the cobblestones. After he had tied Havlicek up and thrown him into the wagon, the Golem carefully examined the carcass that lay against the wall of Meisel's house. He saw the child's body wrapped in the prayer shawl, and as he set the corpse into the cart he gave Havlicek a volley of blows for good measure. Then the Golem drove the wagon to the magistrate's office.

Awakened by the Golem's pounding on the door, two bailiffs came sleepily outside to find the child's corpse, the stunned butcher, and the wagon. When they saw how the child had been wrapped, they surmised what Havlicek had been up to and accused him of having murdered the child. Dazed by the beating the Golem had given him and terrified that he might be convicted of murder, Havlicek blurted that he had not killed the child. The bailiffs belabored him until he confessed what he had done; then they put him into the jail and sent for a physician to bind his wounds and to set his painfully dangling arm back into its socket, an injury whose exquisite torment they had made full use of in questioning him.

The Golem waited until he saw the doctor arrive before returning to tell Rabbi Low what he had accomplished, but he carefully refrained from reporting either how he had torn Havlicek's arm from its socket or how the bailiffs had further employed it. Rabbi Low blessed him for having saved the ghetto, but still the Rabbi's heart was not set at rest.

IV

Not long afterward Mordecai Marcus Meisel came to visit Rabbi Low. Tall, slender, elegantly groomed, the financier seemed much younger than his more than seventy years. His sedate courtliness was not without a hint of power and prestige, and his hauteur was that of a count. The two men had known each other for decades and were friends, but a tension always flickered between them that plagued them, a tension that both had tried to dissipate and could not, a tension born of differing personalities and contending outlooks strongly and tenaciously held. They had over the years at last learned to deal with the tension by alternating careful public consideration with incautious private candor; privately, from time to time, when the occasion most required, they permitted themselves the liberty of speaking to each other in as prickly a fashion as they felt. Because both were men of strongly held opinions, firm character, and impulse toward decisive action, the occasion often required. Since they thought of themselves not only as individuals, but as leaders and defenders of their people, their clashes were more frequent than they might otherwise have been.

In Rabbi Low's study they exchanged greetings with the elaborate courtesy they sometimes reserved for each other. Kaethe Hoch brought wine, and until she left the room, they sat in silence. Both were discreet men and knew that what they said to each required no witnesses or echoes. Besides, Rabbi Low had noted in the past how on edge Kaethe seemed every time that Mordecai Meisel came to visit, how she lingered, hanging on the financier's every word, and he did not like that. "Rabbi," Meisel began at last, "I have not been able to thank you personally for what Joseph Golem did in my behalf until now, but I was, and I am, most grateful."

"The Almighty sharpened his eyes," the Rabbi murmured.

"Surely, but his eyes were there to see."

The Rabbi sipped his wine without comment.

"Who is this Joseph?" Meisel continued. "People tell me he is a strange man, that though he has lived among us for many months now, he keeps to himself, speaks little, and walks softly. You found him, they say, a wayfarer, and brought him home as your servant."

"It is true that he lives in my house. He even sleeps on that couch." With a gesture of his wineglass, the Rabbi indicated the place. "He does chores for the synagogue."

"A hewer of wood and drawer of water?" Meisel smiled.

The Rabbi shook his head. "No. Joseph Golem is more than that, much more."

"Your meaning?"

"He is more valuable. He shall be more valuable still."

"As always, Rabbi, you are cryptic. People fear him. Why is that?"

"The stranger evokes fear of the unknown in men's hearts, fear of the unknown that is in their own."

Meisel's smiled thinned. "Mystery! Perhaps it is only because he is so big and looks so fierce."

"Much in life is mysterious. The mystery of the stranger both fascinates and repels."

"So the Christians seem to feel about the Jewish strangers in their midst. But some special fear seems connected with this man, as if he were some sign, some wonder, as if—I don't know quite what. People fear something dreadful is about to happen these days, and perhaps it is only that which makes them irritable with newcomers. They gather in knots and talk in low voices, looking over their shoulders as if they were already being pursued. They go about their business halfheartedly, their minds and hearts elsewhere. They hold their children too close to them, clutch the little ones by hand, and keep the women and children off the streets as much as they can. Their terror is real as the smell that sometimes comes from the Moldau when the wind shifts, a smell of vinegar and ashes, of death and dying. Only their laments echoing in the synagogue rafters seem real and wholehearted. Rumors of ritual murder are rife, of charges to be brought against us, of pogroms, expulsions, of heaven alone knows what else."

"Persecution, Marcus, is the water in which Jews swim; it is the medium we learn to breathe in or we die."

"Shall I speak to the Emperor?"

"That cannot harm."

"But cannot help?" Meisel's eyebrow rose.

Rabbi Low set his wineglass down with care. "We are caught between the Emperor's needs and the *burggraf* and town council's demands, between the gentry and the tradesmen's guilds, between Catholic intransigence and the Protestant impulse for change. Each may choose to help us, for his own use—but only against the other."

"We *are* of use."

"But who uses whom?"

"We use each other, which is the best that can be arranged on earth."

"For what?"

"We give our treasure in exchange for our blood," Meisel replied decisively.

"Treasure can be restored; blood cannot."

"A rebuke, Judah?"

"Should I rebuke Mordecai Marcus Meisel? Does he not rebuke himself more wisely and well than could anyone else?"

"Your spirit is, as always, generous." Meisel took a small snuff-box, beautifully lacquered, from his pocket and sniffed a pinch.

His sneeze was restrained yet full of pleasure. "I know you do not share my confidence that money and influence can buy safety, or perhaps can even buy anything; but what else can?"

"Money and influences have their uses, Marcus. But when great conflicts are brewing, their issue is small. A man can be saved, perhaps a family, but not a community, not a people."

"In great conflict, in profound upheaval, only force remains," Meisel said in a flat voice, "and it does not always accomplish what it set out to accomplish.

"Twice in my lifetime all our people were driven from this city," Meisel continued, "in 1542 and in 1561. Money did not help, nor influence. But would force have? I don't think so. You were in Posen, Judah, and I am glad you did not have to witness such things, but I and all my family were then expelled from Prague. The first time I was only a boy, a little past *bar-mitzvah* age, and I made up my mind that I should never forget what it was like. Because a child sees such things so clearly, his eyes undimmed by years and experience, I saw madness I did not forget.

"The second time I was a grown man, in my early thirties, and I saw it with different eyes. By then I understood that the problems were so much more tangled than I had imagined at fourteen. I could explain and make excuses—but I never quite succeeded in persuading myself that the plain, simple sense of evil madness I saw at first was not far better than the more 'reasonable' view I managed to acquire in time. Later, I believed, perhaps I had to believe, that even that evil madness could be dealt with, partially, with money and influence; but then, as a boy, I was certain it was amenable to nothing."

"The *yetzer*," the Rabbi commented.

Meisel nodded. "Now I am an old man and not, I think, a bitter one, but I see no end to man's hatred for man, no end to the second Cain who would always murder his brother Abel."

"The *yetzer*, the propensity for evil, lies deep-rooted in us. Murder, suffering, injustice come into the world with man. They will leave the world only when the Messiah comes."

"And while we wait for him?" Meisel asked.

Rabbi Low set his wineglass aside, his eyes on the ceiling of the room. "You remember, Marcus, what the Midrash says of the first night after man was created? Adam and Eve were left in the

Garden. In terror that the serpent would attack them in the darkness, they dreaded that they might never again see the light of day."

Meisel nodded. "I remember, Judah. The Lord set two flints before Adam and the man struck them together to make fire."

"Then Adam pronounced mankind's thanks: *Blessed art Thou, Lord our God, King of the Universe, who creates the light of fire.*"

"Thus have I tried to create light all my life," Meisel said, his smile restored, "though my flints were usually ducats and thalers."

"Jews know God set those flints in the Garden to comfort man, to light and lighten our way. We did not have to steal our fire from the Gods as the Greeks had Prometheus do," the Rabbi said.

"My ducats and thalers do not light or lighten enough, Judah?"

"Who would dare gainsay Mordecai Marcus Meisel's accomplishments? Is there anyone in all Prague, in all Bohemia, in all the empire, who does not know the sparks he has struck from his coins? Clothing for the poor, dowries for destitute brides, charity for widows and orphans, ransom for prisoners of the Turks, synagogues and houses of study and hospitals, even the paving of the very streets of the ghetto."

"You flatter me by reciting my accomplishments, only to remind me of how little consequence they are." Meisel's eyes closed and his head fell on his chest. His fingers continued to fret the snuffbox, then grew purposeful and restored the box to his pocket. "I shall speak to the Emperor," he said at last. "We are his *property*, serfs of the crown. He must protect us."

"*O God!*" the Rabbi intoned. "*Other lords besides Thee have ruled over us, the raging waters have almost consumed us; while Thou made Thyself as one holding His peace and hiding His face, the enemy came and smote mothers and children.*"

"Where have I heard that lament?"

"A Joseph of Chartres wrote it perhaps five hundred years ago."

"And things have not changed?"

"Things have not changed."

Meisel stood and began to pace. "Things have changed. Our lives are better, easier now. They will be better, easier tomorrow. And much of the improvement arises from our wealth, from the influence we can bring to bear."

"I do not share your confidence, Marcus, but speak to the *burggraf*, the Cardinal, even the Emperor. Especially to the Cardinal because Thaddeus, more than anyone else, foments violence against our people."

"Thaddeus feeds fires already burning, flames fed by commerce. They accuse us of usury and enslavement when they mean that they dislike paying their debts. They force us into usury by enjoining us from trade, refusing us entrance to their guilds, prohibiting us from owning land—and then they condemn us for being usurers. They allow us to deal only in secondhand goods, then despise us for being peddlers. They will accuse us of treason, of secret relations with the Turks, with anyone, so they can expel us and confiscate our properties."

"We both of us take both sides, Marcus. Is that the influence of commerce? But you know that it is more than that. Much more. Evil. Fear. Envy. Meanness. That men should concern themselves with feeding and clothing and housing themselves is necessary and good. Natural. That men fear hunger, not being able to provide for themselves, is understandable. But such fears can be set at rest with small sustenance."

"Thaddeus dangles our properties before their hungry mouths like bait before fish," Meisel said sharply.

Rabbi Low nodded. "Of course. Perhaps they even fear and hate those riches that you say buy our safety, our *leibzoll*. But Christians fear us because they think we are different, perhaps even morally superior. That is why they must profane us with charges of godlessness and blasphemy for not accepting their gods and their ways, for refusing to convert. And they will accuse us of infanticide and ritual murder because, in spite of all that common sense would seem to dictate, in spite of fire and sword, we continue to cultivate our difference. Who would do that? Only madmen. So they lock us away in airless ghettos and mark us with their perverted yellow discs so that, if only for an instant, they can assert and protect their superiority."

"We are only men, as they are, Judah."

"Yet different also. For more than fifteen hundred years we have refused their kingdom and their power, their coercion and oppression, their wars and their destruction," Rabbi Low declared.

"And have been their victims in all of them." Meisel shook his head. "We have not taken up the sword only so we would not be cut down by it."

"*Sword, wherefore turnest thou in all directions, consuming all around thee? Thou diminishest and makest an end of the best among us,*" Rabbi Low said.

Meisel stopped pacing and stood looking out of the window into the courtyard. "In Frankfurt, in the ghetto, it was like this. Jews standing in knots talking, arguing, pleading, their eyes round with fear, their hands fluttering like birds eager to be aloft and away, their feet restless to run. A pogrom was coming. Everyone knew it, Jew and Gentile alike. Yet none seemed to know how to stop it. Jews did not have the power; Christians did not have the desire. Both seemed to be slaves."

"The shame, Marcus, is not in being a slave, but in remaining a slave."

Meisel shrugged impatiently. "They have driven us out before. They can do it again."

"They may, but we shall have a defender."

"Only one? *A* defender?"

"He will be the Lord's hand."

"We have almost ten thousand souls in the ghetto, Judah."

"Do you doubt that the Lord can win with one as with many?" Rabbi Low asked.

"Not unless that one is Mordecai Meisel," Meisel said, suddenly laughing. "Or Judah Low."

"It is no laughing matter."

"Seriously, then, Jacob Nissan talked of fighting."

"He should not have done so without speaking to me first."

"He said he had, but you would not countenance such a thing."

"I would not."

"Do you forbid it?"

"I advise, I reason, I implore; I do not command. You yourself have said that force would not, could not have kept them from the two expulsions your family experienced. There are too many Christians, too few of us and too scattered. And we are Jews; their ways are not ours."

"We too have waged war—and well."

"Long ago, Marcus, before we became what we are now."

"And what are we now?"

Rabbi Low also stood. "Jews, Marcus. We do not sully ourselves with the sword. We do not violate humanity, others' and our own, with war. And, as a practical matter, as a handful of Jews in the sea of peoples around us, we would only provoke slaughter."

They stared at each other, neither giving ground, until Meisel said, "Very well then, Judah, there is no other recourse. I shall go to the Emperor Rudolf to pay—and to plead our cause. And you will go to the *Altneuschul* to pray and plead our cause with the Almighty."

"Each our separate ways," the Rabbi replied, "to do what we can."

"Even if it is not enough?"

"It is never enough. Man is not enough. Your fears are real. Your hopes must be as real. Your faith even more real. We are old men, Marcus, and we know, we have seen, miracles occur. Only they are harder to see and take longer than we think. The Lord's arm does not wax short."

Meisel wrapped himself in his cloak.

"Be of good cheer," Rabbi Low said. "We must show faces of cheer and hope. We especially."

"Peace, Judah."

"Peace, Marcus. Go your way. Each of us must do his daily round. Always the hardest task of men. Each day to work for righteousness and holiness—and never to despair."

"That *is* a hard task."

"But having done it for so long, we both know that it can be done."

The door closed behind Meisel, and Rabbi Low sank back into his chair. He closed his eyes, covered them to blot out the light, and prayed fervently:

> In the day of my trouble I seek the Lord;
> With my hand uplifted, mine eye streameth in the night
> without ceasing;
> My soul refuseth to be comforted. . . .
>
> I am troubled, and cannot speak.
> I have pondered the days of old,

The years of ancient times.
In the night I will call to remembrance my song;

Will the Lord cast off for ever?
And will He be favorable no more?

Whatever Mordecai Meisel's influence and wealth, Rabbi Low
doubted that they would be sufficient to the task. He remembered
his own father's constant admonition, the reminder of Rabban
Gamaliel to all and sundry: "Be ye guarded in your relations with
ruling power; for they who exercise it draw no man near to them
except for their own interests. Appearing as friends when it is
to their own advantage, they stand not by a man in his need."
But Marcus knew the *Ethics of the Fathers* as well as he did—
and he was not a man easily duped.

V

The *Altneuschul* was filled for the evening prayers. In the opening of the service, Rabbi Low chanted, "With His wisdom He makes the gates of heaven, and with His understanding He makes the cycles of time and He sours the seasons." No sooner had he made the error than he knew he had said *umachmitz es hazmanim*, "He sours the seasons," when he should have said *umachlif es hazmanim*, "He changes the seasons," and he was profoundly alarmed. Surely the error signified something important and calamitous; the Lord had twisted his tongue that He might communicate with him, but Rabbi Low did not know what the error meant. Though greatly troubled, he did not want to frighten the people, so he permitted evening services to be completed, but his heart pounded as if he had run for a great distance and his teeth felt as if they had ground themselves into dust in his mouth. Even the words of the *Alenu*, which ordinarily made his spirit soar, did not comfort him, and when he spoke them his tongue cleaved to the roof of his mouth:

> It is for us to praise the Lord of all,
> To acclaim the greatness of the God of creation,
> Who has not made us as worldly nations,
> Nor set us up as earthly peoples,
> Not making our portion as theirs,
> Nor our destiny as that of their multitudes.

When services were over, Rabbi Low returned to his house and in his study concentrated until, in a waking dream, he saw a mountaintop of snow hurled wildly on wheatfields with golden shocks already gathered and sunny people tying the shocks. As the clumps of snow fell, shocks and stubble alike were transformed into a sickly white mold, the people's skin was flaked and leprous, and their empty eyesockets wept streams of white maggots. As they perished, he heard their parched lips moaning, "This matzo is not the manna of our people."

No sooner had he opened his eyes than the Rabbi called the Golem and sent him to the kitchen for one of the Passover matzos. Because the bakery was small, they usually began to prepare the holiday matzos very early and to store them for the Passover, so that many had already been baked. The Golem returned to the study with a single matzo. The Rabbi took it from him and placed it on the table between them. He looked at it for a long time before silently indicating that the Golem was to taste it.

The Golem refused. "The bread is leavened with death," he said somberly.

"Truly bread of affliction. You must learn which our people may eat so that they will not be afflicted."

"So that they may be my death?" the Golem asked. "Am I to die for them?"

"If you must die, then you shall die for them. That is your calling. But you shall not die of this unleavened bread. Your time is not yet come. Nor is your calling ended."

"My calling is always to pain."

"Your calling is to what is necessary to be endured. To live is to endure again and again."

"And that which cannot be endured?"

"For what cannot be endured the Almighty in His infinite mercy has provided the Angel of Death."

Antagonists, they stared at each other across the table, neither flinching.

"Taste!" the Rabbi commanded.

"In the Garden the serpent also promised, '*Ye shall not surely die.*'"

"Your eyes shall open mine to good and evil in this threatened bread," the Rabbi said. "And you shall *not* die."

The Golem winced. "*My* pain will be multiplied, not yours. I shall go on in my travail, twisting and turning in agony."

"There is agony in the command as there is in obeying it." The Rabbi severed a corner of the matzo and gave it to the Golem to eat. For a long time the Golem held it in his palm, gazing at it, unable to lift it to his mouth. Finally, with a despairing gesture, he bit it and ground it between his teeth until suddenly he began to slaver at the mouth, his lips white with foam. Clutching his stomach with one hand, his throat with the other, he fell on his knees, looking piteously up at the Rabbi, then slid to the floor on his face before convulsively heaving over on his back, eyeballs leprous white. From between his lips a broken bird's croaking emitted, "This matzo is not the manna of my people." Then the Rabbi knew that the matzos had been poisoned.

Swiftly, thankfully, Rabbi Low knelt beside the Golem and pressed his fingers against the Golem's temples until the thrashing body was stilled into sleep. For an instant, he remembered how it had been when they called him to Kolín for Bezalel, when no laying on of hands, when no remedy, no physician could help. Those hands that could so often cure, that could, with the Almighty's blessing, even create life, had held no power to save his own son.

Rabbi Low sent for Abraham Chayim, the *Altneuschul* sexton, and dispatched him to all the ghetto synagogues and houses of study to announce in the name of Judah ben Bezalel Low, Rabbi of Prague, that the matzos baked for Passover were to be regarded as ritually unclean. "No one," he charged the sexton to declare, "is to eat a single matzo. It is a matter of life and death. No one is even to touch the matzos until I have found them ritually clean." Abraham Chayim nodded sagely, in the way old men do when, too excited by news, they have not fully comprehended it, so the Rabbi repeated his instructions once more before the sexton hastened away to announce the edict.

The Rabbi sat over the sleeping Golem, looking at him. Had the Golem changed? There seemed to be a finer grain in the coarseness of his features, some sensitivity that had not been there before. Even the great blunt fingers had grown more tapered and graceful. Had Joseph become less Golem and more human, or was it that he was now more familiar so that his strangeness had been lessened by time and usage?

In the morning, when the Golem awoke, Rabbi Low stood over him. "Are you well?" he asked anxiously.

"I am well," the Golem replied.

"You did not die."

"No. But I have endured an agony."

"That is what all men feel in life."

"Then I have felt like a man, for I remember the pain," the Golem said. "You have taught me suffering."

"That is far more important than learning to read," the Rabbi remarked.

"The matzos *were* poisoned?"

The Rabbi nodded. "Now we must find out how—and why."

In the bakery, the Rabbi questioned each of the men who prepared the dough and baked it, but none could offer any reason why the matzos should be poisoned. Because the Rabbi offered no explanation, the bakers were puzzled and offended, as if he were questioning their skill and honor, until one baker chanced to recall that because they had been so busy, they had summoned two non-Jewish baker's apprentices to help them. The apprentices had not been allowed to handle the kneading or baking, but they had been permitted to inscribe the lines on the matzos with the toothed wheel. Called "the redbeards" because both had spade-shaped, rusty red beards, the apprentices were well-known to the bakers and to the Jewish community and had often worked among

The prefect had not spoken to the redbeards once. Now he rose, them. Rabbi Low nodded and, as soon as they left the bakery, instructed the Golem to search out the redbeards.

By afternoon the Golem had found the small house in which the men lived. They were not at home, but the Golem climbed through a window to search the house. After much rummaging, he found a small chamois bag of powder in the toe of an old, worn boot. The powder had the same smell as the poisoned matzos. The Golem found a hole in the boot sole, held the mouth of the chamois bag over the hole, and sprinkled a trail of the powder from the boot halfway across the room before hiding the boot once more; then he returned to Rabbi Low, reported what he had found and done, and the two of them went to the office of the prefect of Prague.

The prefect, gray-haired, gray-eyed, slender and slippery as a fish, listened to the Rabbi's story, then objected, "I know the redbeards. Honest, hardworking fellows. True, they take a cup more than they should now and again. But they have worked among you Jews for a long time. Why should they suddenly decide to poison people from whom they earn their livelihood?'

"I do not know," the Rabbi acknowledged.

"Has there been trouble between your people and the red-beards?"

The Rabbi shook his head. "There has been no quarrel."

Finally the prefect agreed to investigate, but he was obviously skeptical. The two apprentices had not yet returned home but the prefect and two of his bailiffs soon found the track of the powder, the boot, and the chamois bag. The prefect shook some of the powder into a wooden bowl of milk and set it before the redbeards' cat, a brown, tigerish-shaped tom. In moments the cat began to froth at the mouth and moan, then, yelping, ran madly in circles until it collapsed in a paroxysm and died. The prefect was at last convinced.

In less than two hours the bailiffs had brought the redbeards to the prefect's office. When the baker's apprentices were accused of trying to poison the ghetto's matzos, they sat morose and obstinate, their arms folded, their lips thin lines, unspeaking. The bailiffs cajoled the redbeards with promises of release and short terms, then threatened them with imprisonment for so long and under such harsh conditions that they would forget their names and birthplaces, but the two remained silent.

ponderously brought the dead tomcat in by the tail, and threw it at their feet. "See your cat?" he asked. "That is what we shall do to you. No trial. No warm food. No cold cell. No bread and water. We fed your tom some of the powder we found in your boot." From the chamois pouch he sprinkled some powder into two mugs of water. "Now we feed you some. Drink," the prefect bid them. "If you are innocent, if your powder is harmless, you'll be all right. If not, you'll be dead as that cat."

The redbeards' hands shook so badly that the water slopped over the brims of their mugs.

"Drink!" the prefect ordered.

They refused.

"Drink!" he roared.

By now they were so frightened that they could not have raised the pewter mugs to their lips even had they wanted to. At a sign from the prefect, the bailiffs began to force the cups to their lips.

"No," one cried, as the water slopped over his chin. He flung the cup to the floor before the bailiff could stop him and cried, "I won't drink. I don't want to die."

After that the redbeards talked, one completing the half-finished sentence of the other, their words jumbled or unintelligible, pacing each other in confessing. For years they had worked in the houses of Jews, and in Jewish businesses in the ghetto. They had resented not being allowed to handle the actual flour or bread they baked for Jews, or the wine they assisted in fermenting, though they were permitted to make beer: It was insulting and made no sense to them. Also, though the Jewish women were very flirtatious, they would only tease and then act greatly affronted when one or the other of the redbeards was provoked to some physical overture.

A few weeks before, the friar Thaddeus had sent for them. They had often done chores for him in the past and knew him well. He told them that before the Passover it was likely the Jews would need them for work. Thaddeus asked a favor for which all Christians would be thankful. He gave them a small vial of fluid and told them that when Berger, the wine merchant, should call them to work, they were to pour a few drops of the fluid into each wine barrel; but Berger had not permitted them to come near the barrels.

Later Thaddeus advised them to get work in baking the matzos for the Jewish community and so they had. This time the friar gave them a chamois pouch of white powder to empty into the flour to be used in baking the ghetto's matzos. When the redbeards had been hired to help prepare the Passover matzos, they had thrown some of the powder into the flour, but by now, because they knew what Thaddeus meant them to accomplish, they had not thrown in all the powder.

"Why?" the prefect inquired.

"Because," they said in unison, "we felt sorry for the Jews. Many had helped us and given us work. We did not want to cause their deaths."

For the first time during the interrogation, the Rabbi spoke. "Why, then, did you do it at all?" he asked.

The redbeards shrugged. "I don't know," one of them replied.

When they had told all their story and put their marks on the confession, the bailiffs took them to the jail.

"Are you satisfied?" the prefect asked the Rabbi.

"Would you be?" Rabbi Low countered.

Reluctantly, the prefect shook his head. "Shall I speak to Thaddeus then?"

"Is that not your duty?"

"Not a pleasant one."

"Is duty ever pleasant?"

The prefect shrugged, then bid them farewell, cautioning the Rabbi to inform those Jews who had poisoned matzos to deliver them up to the authorities for evidence at the redbeards' trial. This the Rabbi promised to do. In the next few days the Golem assembled enough evidence to fill a wheelbarrow, then trundled it down to the prefect's office. The remainder of the poisoned matzos were collected in a cart, which the Golem drove out into the forest, where he buried the matzos.

Weeks later the prefect sent for Rabbi Low. "I talked to Brother Thaddeus," he explained apologetically. "He denies everything. Yes, he is acquainted with the redbeards. They are heavy drinkers, unreliable lads, with imaginations easily inflamed by drink. He knows nothing of an outlandish plot such as they describe, nor did he have any part in it. Why should he want to poison the Jews of the ghetto? Is not the Jews' denial of Christ poison enough?"

"He denies everything," the Rabbi said.

"Everything."

"So you will be unable to convict him?"

"Convict him!" the prefect exclaimed. "We can't even accuse him. The redbeards' confession is the only evidence, and who would take their word against that of a holy brother of the Church?"

"No one," the Rabbi admitted softly.

"No one," the prefect repeated firmly, not meeting the Rabbi's eyes.

New matzos were baked and carefully supervised, and the men of the ghetto came to help the bakers, standing at the tables to knead and roll and mark the dough with the rodel. They sang as they worked because they knew that they had been saved.

The redbeards were tried and, with the evidence of the poisoned matzos and the testimony of the bakers, the Golem, and the Rabbi, they were sentenced to five years in prison.

VI

Day by slow spring day Passover approached and all Prague was filled with the perfume of the newly flowering lilacs, white and purple, along the banks of the Moldau. Even in the narrow, crooked lanes of the ghetto, breezes stirred the heavy scent of the blossoms, but now, when Jews usually looked forward to the joys of the Passover, there was only gloom and trepidation. Nerves grew taut and rumors were whispered until all were so unnerved that tension could be felt like a presence in the streets. During the days Rabbi Low managed a serene demeanor to reassure his fellow Jews, but at night he was unable to cast off the burden of his anxieties. Dreams of impending doom quickened him awake every dawn, leaving him shaken; he struggled to curb his misgivings, to rein in his fears lest their clamor drown out the small voice he awaited that would make clear God's will.

Of Mordecai Meisel Rabbi Low heard only that he was traveling to attend to his far-flung interests. The financier had known kings and emperors, Habsburg, Bohemian, Polish, Hungarian, yet he had staked his life and fortune, and perhaps the lives and fortunes of all in the ghetto, on keeping the Emperor Rudolf's goodwill. Was lending large sums of money enough to buy the Emperor's benevolence? Certainly the privileges Rudolf had bestowed on Meisel had been lavish, but they were princely favors the prince could overnight revoke.

Daily Rabbi Low sent the Golem roaming the city to spy out each hostile group and nightly kept him patrolling the ghetto to keep it safe from marauders. The Golem slept but little; the Rabbi slept little more. Sullen and withdrawn, the Golem exuded anger, yet neither of them spoke of it.

News of another accusation of ritual murder against the Jews came from a completely unexpected source. In the early evening of a day when dusk hung in the air like pollen, a messenger from the Cardinal of Prague, Johann Silvester, came to see Rabbi Low. A great-bellied florid man with a rusty mustache and beard, dressed in brilliant scarlet, his presence seemed to fill the Rabbi's study with ebullience and laughter. Too alive, too merry, too colorful to belong in the drab, despondent ghetto, he made the Rabbi realize how long it had been since he had heard the sounds of mirth and gaiety. "The Cardinal sends you his respects," the man, whose name was Ladislav Pokorny, announced. "Though you have not met before, he would like you to meet him this evening, if you are able. And I," he made a deep bow, "Count Ladislav Pokorny, shall take you to him."

Just then the Golem entered the room. "I was weary and would sleep," he announced.

"You *are* a big one," Count Pokorny said, admiring and envious at once. "I don't think I have ever seen a man quite your size before, not even among the Swedes."

Before the Rabbi could introduce them, the Golem had seized Pokorny by his doublet and effortlessly lifted him off the floor. Pokorny looked calmly into the Golem's face, and added, "Nor anyone quite so strong."

"Put him down!" the Rabbi commanded.

Disdainfully, the Golem let Pokorny down, and when the

Count had rearranged himself, he bowed to the Golem. "If you are ever in need of work," he said, "come see me. I guarantee you a place in the Emperor Rudolf's guard."

Pokorny turned to the Rabbi. "If you are ready, it is best that we leave now. Night has fallen and the darkness will conceal us. The Cardinal prefers that as few people as possible know that you and he have met."

Rabbi Low donned his cloak and they went out. They had walked half down the *Judengasse* before he was aware that the Golem was following. "Go home," Rabbi Low ordered, but the Golem stood waiting for them to resume their journey.

"Let him come with us," Pokorny suggested. "He is concerned for your safety. A stout fellow. If we meet any of Thaddeus' ruffians, he will prove of use and give a good account of himself."

The route they took was long and devious and did not lead to the Cardinal's palace, but instead to a great house in the Malá Strana. There Pokorny led them through a garden fragrant with evening dew, through a side door into the gray stone house, then down a long, unadorned corridor into a salon where the Cardinal waited. A short, powerful man with a halo of white hair on an otherwise bald head, the Cardinal wore a fur-trimmed purple gown whose fur matched his hair. "Good evening, Rabbi Low," the Cardinal greeted him, rising from his chair. "Please come in. Pokorny, thank you for bringing the Rabbi here. Were you observed?"

"I do not think so, Your Eminence," Pokorny replied.

"See that Rabbi Low's man is taken care of while the Rabbi and I have our talk."

Pokorny bowed and took the Golem's arm, but the Golem stood fast. "Go," the Rabbi commanded. "I shall call you when I am ready to return home."

Only then did the Golem permit Pokorny to escort him out.

Once they were seated, the Cardinal's smile faded and the blunt powerful bones behind his flesh seemed newly emphasized. "Time is short, so we must limit the formalities, Rabbi. This meeting is unofficial. I must ask that you do not report it to your people, or, for that matter, to mine. Should it become public, I would deny that the meeting took place. You understand?"

"I understood even before you spoke—by the way we were conducted here," Rabbi Low replied.

The Cardinal nodded. "I would not have taken the risks of this meeting, or disturbed you from your accustomed rounds, had I not deemed it urgent. A new charge of ritual murder has been lodged against your people, one that I am not able to set aside."

"Because you know it to be true?" the Rabbi asked.

"Are we discussing truth or reality?"

"Must the two necessarily be distinct and separate, Cardinal?"

"In the next world, no," the Cardinal declared, "in this one, almost always."

"I see."

The Cardinal eyed him shrewdly, appraising him. "I hope you do, Rabbi, for although I have no sympathy or liking for Brother Thaddeus, or for his rabble, my powers to deal with him are limited. He has the ears of powerful people in the Church and in the monarchy, and like most fanatics Thaddeus is not a man who is subject to reason."

"We have not been spared our share of fanatics either."

"Thank God!" the Cardinal exclaimed, and they laughed together. After a pause the Cardinal asked, "Do you know Dinah Meridi?"

"The surgeon's daughter?"

"The same."

"Dr. Meridi has for a long time separated himself from the Jewish community. I have not seen him for many years. Nor have I seen his daughter since she was a child. I believe he has for some time been a widower and brought the girl up himself. I also know that Dr. Meridi no longer considers himself part of our congregation. He did not ask us to perform the burial services for his wife, nor did he bury her in the Jewish cemetery."

"Thaddeus is zealous in the service of the Church, Rabbi. He would reclaim for it all lost souls, particularly those of your people, toward whom he feels a special mission," the Cardinal said. "Dinah Meridi has become one of his converts."

"We are grieved, but we do not force people to remain Jews."

"It is not the most comfortable of stations."

"That is true, Cardinal, but comfort is not always virtue. Many of us find it not comfortable, but necessary."

"The necessary rarely is comfortable, Rabbi, like this talk we are having." He carefully picked a tiny thread from the sleeve of his robe. "Dinah Meridi's conversion poses special problems beyond the loss of one of your flock. She has given sworn testimony to Thaddeus that a Christian servant girl of the noted financier Mordecai Marcus Meisel has disappeared. Dinah Meridi further attested that this Christian woman was murdered so that her blood might be used in making the ghetto's Passover bread."

"Bloodguilt once again, Cardinal? Three hundred years ago the Emperor Frederick II of Germany convoked a meeting of eminent scholars, among them Jewish converts, to investigate such charges," Rabbi Low said wearily. "The conclave reported that Jews do not thirst for human blood or use it in their ceremonies. On the contrary, Jewish ordinances prohibit Jews from defiling themselves with blood."

"Frederick II may have exonerated your people. The facts themselves might. But the accusations—and their dire consequences—continue, do they not?" the Cardinal inquired tactfully.

"So it would seem. They have for three hundred years. Yet, there is no reason," Rabbi Low observed.

"But there is, Rabbi. To them. To us. You are strangers in our midst—and different. You do not work with us, drink with us, pray with us, or intermarry with us. You hold yourself separate and aloof. You are isolated in the *Judenstadt* as if you carried a plague. And you *do* carry a plague. *Apostasy.* The denial of Christ Jesus. The rejection of the Mother Church. You are the adversary, the accursed, the enemy," the Cardinal said without heat.

"Your religious ceremonies are strange and mysterious to our people, so they compare them to the ones they know, their own. Your Passover bread can be likened to and confused with the wafer taken in the Eucharist. A Christian partakes of the consecration of the bread and wine into the blood and body of Christ, so he assumes that your unleavened bread and wine are what he knows. Since you are Jews and deprived of the one true faith, you need *real* blood, miracle-working Christian blood, for your Passover bread and wine so that they will contain the necessary wonder-working ingredient that can cleanse man of his sins and wash them away."

"I see then that it is not difficult for your people to believe when an apostate tells them with certainty that Jewish belief calls for Christian blood," the Rabbi said.

The Cardinal threw his short arms wide, his rings glistening in the yellow light.

"Let me tell you what the Meridi girl testified when she was brought before me."

"Thaddeus brought her before you?" the Rabbi asked.

"It is customary for me to pass on those who wish to convert to our Church," the Cardinal replied blandly. "The sincerity of conversion must be established beyond doubt, the motives must be impeccable."

"Are they, usually?"

"Rarely," the Cardinal said, and he smiled. "Humanity is very frail. Most men's motives will not usually stand the closest of scrutinies.

"She was very zealous. Most converts seem to be. As if they need not only to impress us with their zeal but, in a quite different sense, as if their zeal is the energy they require to carry them over the border to us from the place where once they lived. I asked the Meridi girl why she wanted to change her faith and she replied that she was filled with loathing for the fanatical rites of the Jews. An unusual reply. Most converts speak of having found 'the true faith,' a better one. They do not often deprecate what they have cast off, they only compliment what they would put on. But Dinah Meridi was different. What she found especially loathsome, she said, was the yearly custom of murdering a Christian whose blood was then drained for ritual use in the Passover.

"I questioned her closely. I asked if she herself had witnessed such ritual slaughter, or was simply repeating tales she remembered from childhood.

"She was very specific, very matter-of-fact. Perhaps a little too much of both. She told me that shortly before Passover, every year, a man brought a vial of blood to her father's house. The man was always one of the Rabbi's servants. Her father received the vial and in exchange always gave the man some money for the synagogue. The blood was then handed over to her mother, never the servants, for baking the unleavened bread and mixing into the wine for the Passover service. Though she had for a long time felt alien to her people and their faith, that particularly bloodthirsty custom revolted her, moved her to forsake both her father and the religion of her fathers."

"The Rabbi who was supposed to have sent that blood was, I take it, myself?" Rabbi Low inquired.

The Cardinal nodded. "Of course." Impatiently his beringed fingers drummed the table. "I did not leave it at that. I asked her how she could be sure that what she had seen was a vial of Christian blood. Might it not simply have been wine, or the blood of some animal, or even some unguent that merely resembled blood sent by some solicitous neighbor or friend for a special holiday recipe. But no, she was certain it was blood. So I asked what had happened this year. No murder had been reported, no assault, no Christian was missing."

"She had an explanation?"

"She did. This year the circumstances were altered because she could no longer take part in such a barbarian ritual. She heard Mordecai Meisel's servant tell her father that their Christian woman was gone and soon, with God's help, they would have another."

"Which Dinah Meridi took to mean that we Jews had murdered Meisel's maidservant for Passover," Rabbi Low commented sarcastically.

"However absurd it sounds to you, Rabbi, and I must confess, to me too, you must take the matter seriously. This year, she said, the blood was delivered by a mute, accompanied by another servant who reported the servant girl missing. It is well known that Meisel has two such servants. Rumors that the Jews have killed a Christian girl for their ritual are already common in the city. In the taverns there is talk of vengeance. The only way I have been able to keep matters in control is to promise Thaddeus a public trial."

"A public trial! Of whom? For what?"

"Of Mordecai Meisel, for murder."

"Putting the most prominent Jew in Prague on trial for ritual murder is more likely to produce violence than anything the tavern frequenters can concoct. Have you investigated the Meridi girl's testimony? Is Meisel's maidservant really missing? Does Dr. Meridi confirm his daughter's testimony? What do Meisel's servants say?"

Affronted, the Cardinal leaned back in his chair, fingers prayer-fully interlaced across his chest. "You do me an injustice, Rabbi. Mordecai Meisel is in Posen on business and has been traveling for some weeks. I was told that he had also been to see Emperor Rudolf."

"You know that he is a close advisor to the Emperor."

"I know, Rabbi. It helps less than you imagine. The town councilors and the *burggraf* are not so reluctant to be a thorn in the Emperor's side as you might think."

"All would like to milk the Jewish cow," Rabbi Low said bitterly.

The Cardinal inclined his head, looking down at the rings on his fingers, then continued as if he had not heard the remark. "Meisel returns tomorrow. In the meantime I directed one of the bailiffs to talk to Meisel's wife, who said that the girl, a Jitka Myslikova by name, has disappeared. The girl had several times before simply gone off for a time, sometimes days, some-times weeks, so they were not alarmed. In fact, they were not very happy with the girl. She was lazy and probably guilty of petty thievery. A ring and some other jewelry were missing. They even hoped the girl would not return, so that when she did not appear for work, they were not very concerned. They assumed she had, as before, gone back to one of the villages where she had relatives and sometimes stayed."

"The relatives' names?"

"Dame Meisel did not remember, was not even sure she ever knew. Also, Dr. Meridi is in England and his daughter says she has no address for him there. She does not know where he is go-ing or if he is to return to Prague. I have the impression that the doctor and his daughter quarreled bitterly about her decision to convert, that although he himself was no longer a believing and practicing Jew, he could not countenance her apostasy and therefore left for England."

"And the two servants?"

"We are holding them. The one who speaks says that he never has even seen a vial of blood, much less delivered it to Dr. Meridi. The mute can neither speak nor read and write, and he is so terri-fied that, when questions are put to him, he has convulsions."

Rabbi Low sat staring hypnotically at the rubies in the Cardinal's rings until the Cardinal rose unhurriedly from his seat. "We have not been so remiss as it might seem to you, but some things have been and are beyond our power."

Rabbi Low stood also. "Justice seems always to be beyond our power."

"Rabbi, I believe this whole bloodguilt accusation to be no more than the sick fantasy of a hysterical girl and the overzealousness of a fanatical friar, but unless you can find Jitka Myslikova . . ." He left the sentence unfinished.

At the door Rabbi Low turned and said, "Thank you, Cardinal. I am deeply in your debt, as are all my people. We shall bend every effort to find the woman."

"No thanks are due me. I do what I can, Rabbi, though, unhappily, it is all too often not enough."

Pokorny and the Golem waited in the corridor, but once the Cardinal had closed his door and Pokorny had led them out of the house and beyond the garden gate, Rabbi Low assured him that they could find their way back alone. It was better for all concerned, he said, if Pokorny was not seen with them. Pokorny's misgivings were plain, but he assented and stood at the garden gate following them with his eyes. When once the Rabbi looked back, Pokorny waved cheerily and then was gone.

VII

When Mordecai Meisel returned from Posen, he was met by two bailiffs from the city magistrate's office. Before he had stepped down from his carriage, they had served him a warrant and put him under arrest. For the prominent financier to be led through the streets of the ghetto in shackles was enough not only to shake Meisel's hauteur, but to jar the confidence of all the Jewish community of Prague. Rabbi Low hastened to the city magistrate to request that he be permitted to see Reb Meisel, but, as had been the case previously when he asked to see Meisel's two servants, the magistrate refused, declaring that for the time being his orders were to permit no one but Meisel's wife to visit him in prison. Though Rabbi Low believed that he might himself be arrested for supposedly having supplied the vial of blood to the Meridis, he was not afraid for himself, or even for Mordecai Meisel: What he feared most was that Meisel would be tried as a representative of the Jewish community so that, in fact, all the Jews would be on trial.

Late that night, when he was certain that Meisel would not be released from prison, Rabbi Low hurried home, conscious of the immediate tasks, as if they were three separate burns on his flesh: to find Jitka Myslikova; to discover Dr. Meridi's whereabouts; to attempt to postpone the trial to give them more time to accomplish the first two tasks.

The sleeping Golem lurched restlessly on the couch as Rabbi Low gently shook him awake. "Arise, Joseph," he said, "you must go on a long journey."

The Golem sat up, his eyes clouded with dreams, his great fists opening and closing as if they had lost irretrievably what they had, in sleep, within their grasp. "I am ready," he muttered. "Send me."

"Thank you, Joseph." Rabbi Low extended his hand to bless him, but the Golem shrank from his touch.

"Command me. Compel me. Send me. Do not speak kindly to me, Rabbi, do not be gentle."

The Rabbi was moved. "Why not, Joseph? Are you not one of God's creatures?"

"No, I am a golem."

"Is that not worthy of gentleness?"

"If you touch what is man in me, it hurts. If it hurts, it makes me more human. I cannot bear the pain of either."

"Can you not reconcile yourself to the great destiny that is yours?"

Stubbornly, the Golem shook his head.

The Rabbi stepped back a pace, his voice and mien severe. "You know what happened to Mordecai Meisel? You know what will happen if he is convicted of a ritual murder?"

"I know."

"You must find the Meisel maidservant. Would you recognize her?"

The Golem nodded. "I have seen her in the marketplace."

The Rabbi told him the names and locations of the four villages where Jitka Myslikova had relatives. "Go, seek her out.

I have made inquiries and she may be in one of those places. She has gone there before. When you find her, tell her nothing of what has occurred. Only give her this letter and bring her back to Prague as rapidly as you can."

The letter read:

> The ring that was lost has been found. I hope you will forgive us for having accused you unjustly and forget our disagreements. Know that we need you here and look forward to your return. Please come back to Prague with the man who gives you this letter. In his care we send you twenty-five gulden for traveling expenses.
>
> *Frumett Meisel*

When the Golem was dressed in peasant clothes, the Rabbi warned, "The trial is only four weeks off, so you must hurry. If the woman is not alive, you must find out how she died and bring back evidence of her death and burial. If she is alive, return with her like the wind."

The Golem dipped his head in acknowledgment.

At the door he set off at a trot and as he faded into the darkness, the Rabbi raised his hands after him and blessed him anyway.

For three days the Golem trudged along the dusty roads, taking only a few hours to sleep in the fragrant spring fields before pushing on. On the fourth day, he made his way into the first village and went to the local tavern to see if there he could learn of Jitka Myslikova's whereabouts.

Sitting by himself, he ate bread and cheese and drank the local wine. Under his breath, he made the blessings, wondering, "Why should I bless the fruit of the vine that God made for man's comfort if it brings no comfort to me? Why should I bless the fruit of the earth when I am torn from its womb?" But as he ate, feeling all the while isolated from the company of men, he listened to the peasants talk of weather and crops and cattle, of girls who had disappeared and some who had reappeared, of old feuds and new grudges. "In this, at least, Jacob Nissan is right," the Golem thought. "I am as strange to other men as Jews are. As they are outcasts, so am I an outcast. If for nothing else, I am a Jew because of that."

When finally the Golem asked the tavern owner about Jitka Myslikova's relatives, he was told that they were all dead, had been for more than two years. Yes, the tavern owner acknowledged, he remembered Jitka. Who could forget her? Quite a girl she was, full of life and mischief, always ready for a good time, but wasn't that the way with all those redheaded Moravian girls with freckles? The tavern keeper laughed, and the Golem tried to laugh with him but could not.

In Prague Rabbi Low lay sleepless through the nights, anxious lest the Golem fail to find Meisel's maidservant before Thaddeus succeeded in rousing the rabble or the magistrates sent Mordecai Meisel to the gallows, or both. Beside him, Pearl stirred and said finally, "Judah, you can do nothing now."

"No, not even close my eyes," he replied.

"Sleep," she said. "Let your spirit rest."

But his spirit would not rest. It kept taking him back to that clay pit on the bank of the Moldau, back to Worms where as a boy he had sat on the bank of another river and watched the broad Rhine flow toward the sea. Then he wondered if his life would flow like that, great, green, and powerful, a placid river flowing home to the sea, useful—its waters making the land fertile, its current bearing commerce, its flood seasoning the climate —and beautiful. Passover was not far away; the first Seder night was his day of birth, a man now more than fourscore years who would soon come to rest in the earth, yet whose life stream had not flowed serenely. If this Passover the Angel of Death did not pass over the doors of his people, if the ghetto should be gutted, would it all have been worthwhile? Was this not what he had studied and learned for, suffered his disappointments for, borne his burdens for? Had he not lived his life to protect his people and their faith? If he failed now . . . Golem, his spirit groaned, bring that girl back.

Pearl touched him. After the years, her touch was still a spark, no longer a spark that ignited a flame, but one that still animated and nettled. "You have been a good wife, a pearl among women," he told her. It was an old joke between them, and Pearl squeezed his arm to say that she was still grateful for its utterance.

"Low the Bachelor," she teased.

"How long ago that seems."

"How long ago it was," she said, "and how long a time it was to wait."

"Even your father admitted that, blessed be his memory."

"Well," Pearl said smartly, sitting up in bed, "for a fifteen-year-old betrothed, it could not have been so hard to wait. You were only a boy drunk with his studies, who wanted to be the rabbinical star of greatest magnitude in the heavens of Jewish learning."

"Star but not a pearl."

"But you sought the star first, the pearl later. It was longer for me than for you, Judah," Pearl said tenderly. "A girl of fifteen is a woman, a boy only a stripling."

She lay back and they were quiet until she asked, "Do you think the Golem will bring the girl back in time?"

"If the Lord is with him, he will."

"Judah." Pearl's voice was distant. "I do not like Joseph Golem. When this is done, send him away."

"I have."

"Send him away for good." Beneath the bedclothes her shudder was clear. "He makes me afraid as I have not been since childhood, since my father wrote that you were free to break our troth because his business had failed."

"But I did *not* break our troth. There was no need to fear then, there is none now. The Golem is the Lord's emissary, His right hand."

"You treat him like a son, and yet, yet, I do not like the way you treat him. I do not like what you become when he is about. It is as if, suddenly, you were David, Josiah, Bar Giora, a commander of armies sending soldiers to their deaths."

"Have you ever known me to send a man to his death?"

"Not even Bezalel?" she asked.

She had still not forgiven him.

"I could do no more than I did."

"You think to recapture your youth with another son, with this . . . this vessel of clay?"

"There can be no other to replace Bezalel in my heart. This

Joseph Golem is but a poor creature, lonely and bereft. His path is full of stones. If I am father and mother to him, he is not yet a son to me."

"Daily," Pearl said hesitantly, her face turned toward the wall, "he grows stranger. You cannot hear him walk. He slips up behind you like a ghost and gives you a start. His face changes. He is always so, so . . . I don't know, Judah. Even when he studies, his eyes seem to singe the pages. He speaks wisely when he is spoken to, softly and politely as one should speak to a *rebbetzin*, yet the wisdom seems green and raw on his tongue, the politeness like honey beneath which is only vinegar. Do I speak a woman's foolishness?"

Pearl was a shrewd and perceptive woman, and doubtless she sensed something strange in the Golem's nature. She had seen, as he had, that daily the Golem changed, the face, the gait, the movement of hands. When he was not walking in the ghetto, the Golem studied, with Isaac Hayyot, or by himself, prayed, and observed others, humorlessly, relentlessly, driven. "I cannot say," he replied.

She was offended. "I do not like either the intimacy or the distance you betray with this creature. He makes me afraid, but I am more afraid of the way you treat him."

"How do I treat him?"

"As if he were a *korban*, a bullock you were hastening to place on the altar of the Lord."

"Is an *Akédah* not sometimes the duty of the Rabbi of Prague?" he asked, thinking not of the Golem but of Bezalel.

"You have already made your sacrifice, at Kolín. You are not the Patriarch Abraham, nor was Bezalel Isaac, nor what you did to him an *Akédah*. And the Almighty did not stay your hand."

Outraged, he made no rejoinder. Stay his hand indeed! As if what had befallen Bezalel was something *he* had done, as if he had deliberately courted an *Akédah* for his son and carried it out. No man, not the Rabbi of Prague or anyone else, could guard a son's life forever, or even for very long. A child grew to be a man. He went his own way. People, the community, the world did terrible things to him. A father could do only so much, no more. He had done all he could, perhaps more than he should have.

"Do not do to the Golem what you did to Bezalel!" Vehemently, Pearl gestured to the heavens. "The Almighty does not require human sacrifice; He forbids it. Do not contend with the Lord, Judah. Do not let your pride in being the *Höhe* Rabbi Low lead you astray. You are not the Messiah. You are an eighty-one-year-old man. Let some other now be a hero, responsible for saving the ghetto."

You are not the Messiah! Did he not already know that? How much she sounded like Job's wife. Were he to answer her, which he would not do, because it could lead to no good, he would speak only Job's own words—but in reverse: "What, shall we receive evil at the hand of the Lord, and shall we not receive good?" But he said nothing. Everything had been said before, when Bezalel had gone to Kolín, and many times afterward when he died, when a part of them had died with him.

Finally, Pearl slept, but though he closed his eyes, he could not fall asleep. The accusations Pearl had made so many times beset him. Had he, out of ambition and pride, forced Bezalel against his nature to follow in the footsteps of the *Höhe* Rabbi Low and so led him to his death? He lay there, stiff, the muscles of his calves painfully knotted, unable to relinquish the recollections of his son that lay heavy and undigested on his heart until on his eyelids he saw imprinted the throat of heaven, cut, the skies raining blood and hailing clots on the huddled houses of the *Judenstadt.*

When Jacob and Isaac came to offer their help, Rabbi Low was newly aware of how little he had seen them since the Golem was created. Once they had been in and out of his house daily, like sons, and that Isaac was, in fact, only his son-in-law seemed accidental. They had helped to fill the place in his life left vacant by Bezalel's death, yet now Jacob began, "Once you relied on us and on our judgment. You even seemed to take pleasure in our presence, but now we are scarcely told of events of great moment."

Isaac's bent head bespoke the same disappointment, but he said only, "How can we help concerning Reb Meisel?"

"There is little we can do. I have written to England to see if Dr. Meridi can be found, but even if we should find him, and he should agree, the time is too short until the trial for him to return to Prague."

"Could we not have his deposition sent?" Isaac asked.

"I have instructed some of our friends in England to obtain a deposition from him if they can find him."

"Is there no possibility of postponing the trial?"

The Rabbi shook his head. "The magistrates have refused Frumett Meisel's request and mine to postpone the trial for two months more."

"What of Meisel's maidservant?" Jacob inquired.

"I have sent Joseph Golem to search for her."

"Would it not have been wiser to send me?" Jacob asked. "Am I not, still, a bit more clever than he?"

"Also a bit more conspicuous."

"Who could be more conspicuous than that great menacing hulk?" Jacob remarked.

"Joseph Golem looks more like a peasant than you do, Jacob," Isaac intervened, "though huge and strange."

"He's strange all right. How do you know that he will return or bring the girl back?"

As they argued about whether the Golem was shrewd enough to find the girl, experienced enough to persuade her to return, or loyal enough to want to return, the Rabbi was conscious again of what an odd contrast they made. Not only did they seem to him different people, but almost different nations. Dark, short, and muscular, Jacob was passionate, impatient, and quick to anger. Isaac was tall, fair-skinned, and red-haired, slow-moving, patient, gentle.

"Jacob," Rabbi Low said, trying to end their dispute, "there is enough for you, for us all to do here. The ghetto grows increasingly melancholy and nervous. We must keep our people cheerful and full of hope."

"The situation is neither cheerful nor full of hope," Jacob snorted.

"All the more reason to try, then," Isaac said.

Jacob turned on him once again. "You are always defending him—because he is your wife's father."

"No, Jacob, not because he is my father-in-law, but because he is the father of the ghetto, the *Höhe* Rabbi Low."

"I thank you both, but do not quarrel. There is as yet no inheritance to wrangle over." As he spoke, he knew there was an inheritance, far more important than an estate, the inheritance bequeathed to them through the centuries, of how Jews were to live and die. "Jacob is not so cheerful and full of hope as you are, Isaac," Rabbi Low continued, anxious to ward off further discussion, "because he is still single. We must marry him off to give him more hope and cheer."

Isaac grinned, always eager to make peace. "You remember the story of the dancing bear?" he asked Jacob. "A man and his son were walking in the street and the father was weary of hearing his son complain over and over again how much he suffered in marriage. Nearby, a musician played a flute for his dancing bear, whose ankles were chained but who danced nonetheless. The father pointed to the bear and, rebuking his son, said, 'See, even a bear in chains can dance and be merry.' The son turned away, furious, and said, 'Marry the bear, Father, and give him a wife. See if he dances then.' "

Jacob smiled, then laughed briefly, angrily, as if he had been amused, deflected from his purpose—as he had—against his will. Then, somberly, he asked the Rabbi, "And what happens if our dancing bear does not return with his woman?"

VIII

In the second and third villages on the Rabbi's list, the Golem was able to search out Jitka Myslikova's relatives, but they would not tell him much about the girl, except that she was not staying with them; nor would they suggest where he might find her. None mentioned the fourth village, the most remote from Prague, where they all had relatives. None would even guess if the girl was still alive. Farmers, herdsmen, lumberers, tanners, hunters, and trappers, they all seemed to dislike the girl. They made cruel remarks about her that showed they did not care a fig about what happened to her, nor would they be concerned about anything she did. No matter what the Golem said, they assumed that the magistrate's office or the prefect of Prague had sent him to pursue her. In all these things they made themselves unmistakably clear: "Gone up to the city. . . . Never could sit still. . . . Pins and needles in her behind. . . . Too smart for her own good. . . . Worked for some rich Jew up in Prague. . . . Just like her mother, good for nothing. . . ."

The picture of the girl he pieced together was somber. Though Jitka Myslikova was still in her early twenties, she had already had a child that some said had been strangled, others said had been given to unnamed relatives to bring up. She had an unquenchable taste for bright things, scarves, jewelry, beads, and had been known on more than one occasion to appropriate someone else's property. From her childhood, after her father had been killed in a tavern brawl, and her mother had put her out as a servant girl, she had been a wanderer. Jitka Myslikova, he realized, sounded as much an outcast among her own as he was, and the Golem felt sorry for her.

With each new encounter the Golem found men more distasteful: dishonest, mean, shifty, violent, stubborn, selfish, and stupid, yet still he felt driven to seek their company and felt himself deprived of their approval and companionship. His appearance alarmed people—he looked strange and was a stranger to them—but unlike the beggars and dwarfs, clowns and cripples, ancient crones and madmen he met in his wanderings, who were taunted and beaten, kicked, spat on, and stoned, his height and powerful frame prevented men from molesting him or mocking him to his face. Because he spoke but little and listened much he soon learned that what men valued most was riches, then a proud lineage or title, and finally force and power to impose their wills on others: rich men, nobles, and warriors were their heroes and those they envied—and hated. And he also learned that what men valued least, he coveted most: the daily round of their work, however dull and laborious; their wives and children, however clamorous; the good-fellowship of their fellow villagers, however raucous and unruly.

In the last village on the list the Golem found Jitka Myslikova. He arrived there late at night, hungry and wearied by his long day's journey. A pouring spring rain had fallen all that day and soaked him through. In the entire village, only a single light guttered feebly in the tavern and there he pounded the door until the innkeeper, half-asleep and in his nightshirt, came complaining to see who it was. After the first and instinctive recoil at his size and strangeness, the reflex endeavor to slam the door in his face that the Golem had learned to thwart by keeping his shoe in the door, the tavern keeper relented, gave him half a loaf of bread, some cold turnips, and milk for supper, then let him sleep on the warm kitchen floor near the stove.

The red-haired, freckle-faced girl who woke him in the morning with her imperious toe he recognized instantly as Jitka Myslikova. "Up, you lout!" she bawled. "The sky is getting light and the fire is almost out. Go and chop some wood and"—she stooped and pulled his hair—"if you chop enough and quickly, I shall give you a good, hot breakfast before my uncle awakens."

The Golem stood and stretched and Jitka watched wide-eyed. "How did you grow so tall?" she asked. "You look like an oak growing and spreading its branches."

"It is the way I was made," the Golem answered.

"I like the way you are made," she said.

"Thank you," he replied, warmed. No one had ever paid him such a compliment before.

When he had chopped and stacked enough wood, and carried some into the kitchen to keep the fire going for the day, Jitka brought him a basin of water and a clean threadbare cloth. Out of the corner of her eye she watched him as he stripped down to the waist and washed; afterward she took his food to a small table in the kitchen and sat with him while he ate his breakfast.

"What's your name?" she asked.

"Joseph. Joseph Golem."

"I am Jitka Myslikova."

"I know," the Golem acknowledged. "I have come from Prague especially to see you."

Instantly she was wary. "Who sent you?" she asked suspiciously.

"Your mistress," he replied and handed her the note.

She did not unfold it, but sat staring alternately at his face and the note. Finally, shamefaced, she confessed that she could not read. The Golem took it back and read it to her.

Jitka's face was wreathed in smiles. Her milky teeth glittered, her blue eyes shone, her coarse reddened hands were thrust out. The Golem thought she wanted the note and returned it to her, but she burst into laughter, stood up and danced a little jig around his chair, her hands cupped like a beggar's bowl before her. "Fool!" she chortled. "Not the words, the money. The twenty-five gulden!"

"The money is for your return to Prague."

"Go yourself! I'm not going anywhere. Give me the gulden."

"I was told to give you the money for the journey."

Jitka snapped her fingers and clicked her heels like a gypsy, pulled a long lock of hair across her face and beneath her nose like an immense red mustache, and with her other hand extended, sang, "Cross my palm with silver and I'll tell your fortune." Then she straightened up, danced closer to his chair, caressed his cheek, stroked his arm, ran her fingers through his beard and hair, chanting, "Give me the gulden. I'll buy us some wine and we'll sing and dance and get drunk, and make love."

"Don't you want to go back to Prague?" the Golem asked.

"Why should I? Clean and cook and make beds for those high and mighty Jews. Bah! I'd rather stay here and hand out wine and beer in Uncle Karel's tavern."

"You clean and cook and make beds here too, and wait on tables. Didn't Reb Meisel treat you well?"

"Sure, he was all right, but his wife was always watching me, always saying, 'Jitka, polish those candlesticks! Jitka, who told you to wear my earrings? Jitka, the neighbors saw you drinking in the taverns with the students.' What did she expect, that old cow?"

"You should go back to Prague."

"Why?"

"Are you not happy that your mistress discovered the ring was misplaced, that you did not steal it?"

"I didn't steal it." She guffawed. "But I *did* borrow it."

He looked at her fingers, but they were bare.

"You'll see. I'll wear it for you later."

"Won't you come back to Prague with me?"

"You stay here instead."

Jitka Myslikova was headstrong and stubborn, so he decided not to press his case further just then.

As soon as her uncle came down that morning, Jitka took him into the tavern, and for half an hour there was loud argument that the Golem could not understand. When Jitka came back into the kitchen, she said only that Uncle Karel had agreed that the Golem could stay if he would chop wood and draw water and do the heavy chores. He would have a small room in the eaves under the roof, next to hers—she winked—as much as he could eat, and a few gulden a month.

That was not much, the Golem knew, but it was more than he needed, as much as he wanted, and he thought that after a few days he might be able to persuade her to return to Prague with him.

In the mornings he did the chores and in the afternoons Jitka would pack some food for them and a skin of wine, and she would lead him across the fields into the low, pine-covered hills to a blue-green lake near an abandoned shepherd's hut. Wild game came there to drink, and Jitka showed him hare and partridge, wood grouse and deer, and even a blundering small black bear. She taught him to fish and to recognize the animals' tracks, and as they lay there together in the leaf-dappled sunlight, hearing the wild echoing cries of the wood grouse, and admiring the brilliant scarlet crests that topped their blue-black feathers and white breasts, he felt human. There, away from everyone except Jitka, he was not a Golem but a man, and he was happy.

"Why do you never laugh?" Jitka asked one day after they had bathed in the cold waters of the lake and were lying together in a patch of tepid sunshine that warmed them and the odorous balsam and pine needles beneath them.

"There is not much to laugh about," he replied.

"You are big and healthy and strong," she said, propping herself on one elbow. "You look a bit strange, as if you were from another world, but I like that."

"Others do not."

"Who cares?"

"I do. I am without family, without friends, altogether alone. People shun me, or fear me."

"What do you want family for? A sack of stones on your back. And friends? If you have friends, you don't need enemies. Another sack of clawing cats."

"You can say that because you have relatives and friends."

Jitka burst into laughter. "Relatives! Friends! Why, not one of them would lift a finger if I was drowning. Might even push my head under to hurry things along. Work in the tavern? Why not? Borrow money? Sure. Pay back? Never. A quick poke? Sure, but sneaky, and don't tell the wife. Clean. Cook. Look after the kids. Milk the cows. Feed the pigs. Help in the fields. Anytime. But give somebody a bit of land of her own, or a cow or a pig? Never."

"It cannot all be like that. Though people spurn me and make me wretched, I would be among them. I would help them."

"Help them? I'd rather do them in. Every time. Use them and spit them out like peach pits when you're finished chewing. I hate the people who lord it over me and are mean to me. If they make me miserable, I try to make them miserable too. A little more than they make me. I steal a ring, or I take a ham hock, or a goosedown pillow, or I drink a bottle of their oldest wine, or just pour it out, anything that they'll miss and hate to lose."

"Is that why you took the ring from the Meisels?"

"Lady Frumett! You'd think she was King Wenceslaus' wife!"

"Do you want to do me in too?" the Golem inquired.

"Why should I? You never did me harm. You're nice to me." Jitka snuggled contentedly against his chest.

Living as he was, a hewer of wood and drawer of water, the Golem was still happy because Jitka was with him. Yet Mordecai Meisel's trial drew daily nearer and he grew increasingly uneasy. In the afternoons, after they swam in the waters of the lake, they would nap in the abandoned shepherd's hut; but that day, while Jitka slept, he lay next to her and could not fall asleep. He was haunted by what might happen to the Jews of the ghetto should he fail to bring Jitka Myslikova back before Meisel was tried and condemned by the court. The smell of balsam and fir were aromatic in his nostrils. In the clearing outside, the grouse stalked, their ruffs preened, their wings beating the air, the tattoo of their mating calls like distant drums. The sunlight danced through the leaves and shaped the form of Rabbi Low out of light and dark; the sounds of water and grouse combined into the Rabbi's voice, mournful and entreating, "If she is alive, return with her like the wind." The voice rose in pitch and intensity, calling, "Israel's defender, a Gideon, a Saul, a David." Suddenly, the green earth, the cheerful chirrup of birds, the dark wings of the grouse, which had been so beautiful, were bleak. The afternoon enchantment had flown. Now, not even Jitka's apple-round breast pressed against the resinous earth, snubbed against fluted brown balsam, seemed lovely.

Could he not leave the Rabbi's strictures unheeded? Why did he have to conjure him up, his face and figure, his voice and stern command, in this sun-splashed glade? Why should he feel compelled to return to his lonely life in Prague, to follow his destiny of hateful violence? What did he owe his creator except the dubious debt of having been brought forth an outcast for whom there was neither family nor friends, neither past nor normal future? Yet, outcast and spurned though he was, Rabbi Low was his father on earth, his family, and the Jews his people. He could disown neither, nor flee his responsibilities for them, not even when for the first time in his brief life he had found a small, quiet happiness with Jitka Myslikova, however uncertain that happiness might be.

The groans that welled out of him woke her. Gropingly, even before her eyes were open, she reached for him, saying, "Joseph, what is it?"

"I must return to Prague."

"Why?"

"Because I am commanded."

"Commanded?" She sat up.

"It is ordained." The Golem sat up beside her. "You must return with me."

Jitka bridled. "I *do not must* anything."

Tell her nothing of what has occurred, the Rabbi had cautioned. Only give her the letter and bring her back to Prague as swiftly as you can. He had shown her the letter and tried to persuade her, but he had failed, and in two days' time the trial began.

The Golem said no more until they were dressed and walking down the thickly wooded slopes of the hills toward the village. As they plunged into the fields, he disobeyed the Rabbi's injunction and told Jitka what Thaddeus and Dinah Meridi were trying to do, and how, if she did not return to Prague with him, Mordecai Meisel would die and so, likely, would many Jews in the ghetto.

Until he finished explaining, Jitka did not speak. Then, quizzically appraising him, she asked, "Are you a Jew?"

The Golem considered the question before he nodded. "Yes," he replied, "I *am* a Jew."

They spoke no more until they were back at the tavern when, just before they parted to do their separate chores, Jitka remarked, "In two days, you said?"

"Yes. In two days, the trial begins."

She woke him gently, but the moonlight through the window was so bright in his eyes that he could not at first see who it was and so, seizing her roughly, he pinned her arms to her sides. "You're hurting me," she complained in a whisper. "Let me go."

"Jitka!" he exclaimed and set her free.

She stood there rubbing her arms where he had held her. "I'll be black and blue for days," she lamented.

"I'm sorry."

"So am I. Get dressed. I borrowed a wagon. If we hurry, we can make it in two days."

"Make what?"

"Prague, you fool! The trial!"

IX

Daily, reports were brought to Rabbi Low that Thaddeus' seminarians were going through the city and into the surrounding countryside to stir the people up against the Jews. They told the old tales of ritual murder until the simmering hatred seemed about to boil over. They repeated stories of how the Emperor Rudolf was in the clutches of the Jew banker Meisel and promised that no sooner was Meisel convicted and hanged, they would kill the Jews, burn the ghetto, and drive the Jew usurers out of Prague as Christ had driven the moneylenders from the Temple. Jews were spat on and stoned, some children and old people beaten, and two Jewish girls raped in the narrow streets off Alchemists' Lane.

The Cardinal sent a message to Rabbi Low through Pokorny, warning of the impending storm, urging in the strongest terms that Jitka Myslikova or Dr. Meridi be found, but Rabbi Low had to confess that he knew no more now than he had before. Though the day of the trial drew ever nearer, there was no sign of either the Golem or Jitka Myslikova, and from England came only word that Dr. Meridi could not be found.

Rabbi Low continued to request permission to see Meisel in prison, but under the orders of the *burggraf* and the town council, the magistrate remained adamant about not giving anyone access to the financier except his wife. Through her Rabbi Low sent messages to her husband, and Frumett Meisel informed him that Meisel had already dispatched emissaries to the Emperor to intercede on his behalf, but the Emperor had not yet replied or given any sign. What those things portended, neither husband nor wife was willing to speculate about, but they would not relinquish the hope that the Emperor would intervene to save them. They believed the Emperor to be somewhere in Germany so that their messages had not yet reached him; otherwise the Emperor's silence and Meisel's protracted imprisonment did not make sense to them. Rabbi Low had less confidence in the Emperor's concern and goodwill, but he said nothing to discourage them.

Two days before the day of the trial, the Rabbi had almost given way to despair. Had the Golem failed in his task? Had the Lord forsaken them? Rabbi Low gave orders that for the entire Jewish community the next day was to be a day of fasting and mourning. Business was to cease; Jews were to remain in their homes or at prayer in the synagogues. On the morning of the trial itself, the people were also to assemble in all synagogues to beseech the Almighty's mercy and to call for His help.

When the fast was done, Pearl brought him a cup of hot broth and a tiny jar of rose jelly she kept for occasions when she thought his spirits were flagging. She sensed his chill in the dank, evening air almost before he felt it and wrapped a warm shawl around his shoulders. Then she left him to his thoughts. Eyes closed, the Rabbi sat back in his chair, the cup of broth warming his fingers, then gradually turning cold. More than an hour passed, the silence broken only by domestic stirrings in the house or the occasional voice heard dimly from the courtyard or the *Judengasse*.

It was necessary to do something—and now. But what? Should

he have told his people to flee? That would have been interpreted as a confession of guilt and sealed Meisel's fate. Nor would it have saved his people. Ritual murder was a crime for which they would all have been held accountable. Besides, where could they have fled? Who would have hidden them, offered them succor and haven? Should he have called for the Jews to arm themselves, as Jacob had demanded, yes demanded in the synagogue that afternoon, prepared to fight what violence was unleashed against them? They would not take up arms, he had ordained; they would not lose themselves to save themselves. *Not by might, nor by power, but by My spirit, says the Lord.* Who kills Cain shall suffer vengeance sevenfold. Who kills Cain becomes Cain. In slaying a single man, all the generations after him are slain.

Concentrating with all his strength, the Rabbi tried to conjure up the image of the Golem and was unable. So great was the effort that his mind knotted as sometimes the muscles in his calves did when he strained. Was his creation accursed? Had he created a Golem not in the image of God, but in the image of the Adversary? Had the Golem abandoned him as the Lord had?

Outside of the windows, the dusk had thickened into night and in the semidarkness of the room Kaethe came and lit his lamp, its flame faltering in the draft from the open door. For a passing instant he hoped she might speak to him, hoped that a human voice would distract him from the voices within, but she glided noiselessly out without a word. Used as she was to the solitary habits of his study and contemplation, he knew she did not wish to disturb him. Besides, what did a young girl have to say to an old man in the twilight of his life? He fought down his rage, that old blood-blinding anger that all his life had risen when he was faced with despair and saw no course of action to take against the events that conspired against them, the same fury he had learned to conquer but that each time he had to conquer anew.

He drowsed and a dream caught him up that yet left him the knowledge that he was dreaming. He walked the streets of the Old City and the cobblestones turned to burning desert sands beneath his feet while wild winds tore up cobbles and dashed them against his flesh until his bones were stripped clean and charred. Across the glowing cobblestoned street that was blazing desert sand and flaming ocean waves a wagon that was both caravan and quinquereme rode. In it, standing tall, was the Golem, his face taxed with strain, the Tetragrammaton gleaming on his forehead like scars, a whip in his raised arm lashing the cobbles, sands, and burning seas into a furor. In the heavens a voice of scarlet soared and trumpeted like a ram's horn: *I have set thee a watchman unto the house of Israel; therefore, when thou shalt hear the word at My mouth, warn them from Me.*

Somewhere a shutter slammed and woke him, and in the silence he heard the muffled drip of rain on the roof tiles. An anxious calm descended on him like the fog on the windows. His hands behind his back, he walked around and around the wavering circle of light from the lamp until he felt the hand of the Lord upon him in the evening. The Lord had opened his spirit so that it was no longer dumb or cast down.

In the morning service, when they came to the special prayer for the ten martyrs he had decreed for that day, the synagogue rang with the voices of the whole congregation, bass and baritone, alto and soprano, men, women, and children blending into a single-minded petition to the Almighty. They stood as one man and prayed, *"Behold the ten martyrs massacred by the dominion. Their blood has been shed and their strength failed. When I remember this I cry out bitterly for the flower of Israel, pure in heart and holy they died a dreadful death."*

Next to the cloaked majesty of the Holy Ark Rabbi Low stood looking out over his people and listening to their recitation of each martyr's death. Rabbi Simeon bared his neck for the sword, Rabbi Akiba was flayed with an iron comb, his soul expiring with "The Lord is One" on his lips. Rabbi Hananiah wrapped in the scrolls of the Law and set aflame. Rabbi Elazar, the last of the martyrs, who as he began to recite the *Kiddush* on the eve of the Sabbath was pierced by the sword that did not allow him to finish the prayer alive, but who gave up his life with the words "which God created." Stoning, flaying, burning, beheading, stabbing, strangling, they had endured all and stood fast in the name of the Lord and for the protection of their people. Now it was his turn, the *Höhe* Rabbi Low of Prague, who would die with his hopes for the Golem "which God had created" still in his breast, unless the Lord or His creation could at the very last moment shape a miracle.

When services were over, the Rabbi announced from the altar that women and children were to return directly to their homes and to stay there. Jacob Nissan and his defenders, the group of more than two hundred youths he had organized without the Rabbi's permission, would remain behind to protect them and the ghetto. The others would accompany the Rabbi to the trial.

Before he was able to leave, Jacob drew him aside. "Rabbi, neither the servant girl nor Dr. Meridi has returned. Surely they will convict Meisel today and will turn on all of you. Afterward it will be the turn of the women and children in the ghetto. *Do not go!* Let us all stay here together and protect our own as best we can."

"And leave Mordecai Meisel to his death?"

"We cannot help him."

"The Talmud says, Jacob, that if murderers should fall upon a community and insist that it deliver up one of its members as a victim or the murderers would slay all, then the whole group should die rather than deliver up one of their number to be murdered."

"But," Jacob argued, "the Law says that if the murderers specify the man by name, as in the case of Sheba ben Bichri, then the people may deliver him up and so save their lives."

"Our Sages have always been uncomfortable with that law, Jacob."

"But it remains the law, Rabbi. I know. You taught me well."

"Not, I fear, well enough," the Rabbi replied, and left him.

Slanting gray drizzle burnished the streets and roofs. Church steeples thrust into the drab sky like swords. Pealing church bells declared the importance of the day. One concession the *burggraf* had extended: He had given permission to Rabbi Low and the congregation to walk with the bailiffs when they marched Mordecai Meisel from the prison to the courthouse. They had only moments to wait before the bailiffs brought Meisel out between them. Though shackled and pale from his confinement, Meisel was neatly groomed, clean, and newly clothed. His head held high, his wife walking a pace behind him, her fingers lightly attached to his cloak, the financier had lost none of his hauteur.

"*Shalom*, Judah," Meisel said.

"Courage, Marcus," the Rabbi said, embracing him.

"Have you found Meridi or the girl?"

Rabbi Low shook his head, then asked, "Have you heard from the Emperor?"

Frumett's downcast eyes were answer enough.

Before the courthouse a great crowd was gathered, restive, sullen. The bailiffs shouted, "Make way! Make way!" but they could not get through. Hooting and jeering greeted their efforts and the line of the throng held firm against the bailiffs and the Jews. A great roar of "Christ-killers!" boomed from the mob and beat down on them like clubs. Pokorny and his company of horse came around the sides of the courthouse then, lances at the ready, forcing the crowd to give way. Guards with halberds pushed down the courthouse steps, and between them order was restored just as the black-clad phalanx of Thaddeus and his seminarians arrived. A ragged cheer rose from the crowd. "Thaddeus! Brother Thaddeus!" The crowd eddied around Thaddeus' group, but the hussars and guards drove them back. The courthouse tocsin rang, announcing that the trial was about to begin and the multitude's attention was diverted; meekly, they began to file into the courthouse.

The crown attorney read the indictment against Meisel, accusing him of ritual murder, and his two servants of being accomplices. The presiding judge asked each of the defendants to stand and, shackled between two bailiffs, they stood. The prosecutor then called on them to plead to the charge: "Is it true that you are guilty of the murder of Jitka Myslikova for her Christian blood and that you distributed her blood to the Jews in the city for use in the Passover wine and bread?"

The charge was read once each for Meisel, Hugo Den, Meisel's factotum, and Petr Singer, Meisel's deaf-mute footman. In a calm, even voice Meisel denied the charge. Hugo Den spoke his "no" so loudly it rang in the rafters, but the deaf-mute did not understand what was being asked of him, so the presiding judge beckoned him to the bench. There he showed the bottles of blood held in evidence and tried by signs and gestures to make clear what he meant, which was to ask the mute if he had ever carried such flasks for Meisel. The mute nodded and grinned, then put his finger in his mouth.

Instantly, Thaddeus, seated next to the crown attorney, was on his feet proclaiming that the mute had just confessed his guilt. Putting his finger in his mouth, Thaddeus said, was the mute's way of indicating that the blood had actually been used for food and drink. A flurry of applause greeted his speech.

Meisel's attorney objected, maintaining that the mute was thirsty and thought the bottles contained something he might drink to quench his thirst. Meisel's attorney then produced a knife and after suitable flourishes before the judges, crown attorney, and spectators, brandished it and put the point to the mute's throat. At the same time, he gestured to Meisel and the bottles of blood as if to ask if Meisel and the blood were connected to cutting someone's throat. The mute began to tremble so agitatedly that he fell to his knees until the bailiffs yanked him rudely to his feet. Eyes rolling fearfully in his head, face white as chalk, his whole body was contorted into a gesture that pleaded that he knew nothing of murder, nothing of blood.

Once more Thaddeus harangued the court and spectators, insisting that what Petr Singer was thinking was that the defense attorney had asked whether Mordecai Meisel should be executed. Those fearful signs the mute had made explained his terror of the just sentence that should follow.

Angry argument between the defense lawyer and Thaddeus flared, growing increasingly heated, until the presiding judge called both of them to order.

For an hour or more then, the crown attorney called Christian scholars to attest that Jews had always committed ritual slaughter as a necessary part of their celebration of the Passover. Each was greeted with louder acclaim from the spectators. The last such learned witness was Thaddeus himself, who reviewed the history of ritual murders in a baritone voice that could be heard in every part of the courtroom. "The Christian youth Simon of Trent was murdered by Jews," Thaddeus declared. "The Jews confessed then that they required fresh Christian blood because in that year of 1475 the Jews were celebrating a Jubilee year."

Rabbi Low, who had deliberately sat silent through the foregoing testimony, rose to his feet, bowed to the presiding magistrates, and said softly: "Jews have not celebrated the Jubilee since the Babylonians under Nebuchadnezzar destroyed the Temple in Jerusalem more than two thousand years ago." He resumed his seat to the audible hissing of the spectators.

Thaddeus continued, telling of the ritual murders said to have taken place in neighboring Hungary in 1494, at Tyrnau, where the Jews had also confessed their guilt.

Once more Rabbi Low stood up. "The women and children who confessed at Tyrnau were tortured," he said coldly. "Those poor creatures confessed that Jewish men menstruated and therefore practiced drinking Christian blood as a remedy." The audience tittered, then broke into coarse laughter. The Rabbi, unsmiling, sat down.

In Bösing, also in Hungary, Thaddeus testified, thirty Jews had bled a nine-year-old boy to death, hoping to use his blood for ritual purposes.

Again the Rabbi got to his feet. "The boy was later found alive and unhurt in Vienna. By then, however, those thirty Jews had been burned. Of course they confessed. As I said, torture can make most people say almost anything in order to end their torment. The boy mentioned was abducted by Count Wolf of Bazin, the man who had accused the Jews of the crime in the first place. In fact, the Count had deliberately created the charge, fabricated the occasion to rid himself of the Jews to whom he owed considerable monies."

The clamor from the spectators had now reached epic proportions, and someone threw a fruit that landed near the Rabbi. Rabbi Low turned to face the people, staring at them, until row by row they grew silent.

The crown attorney at last brought forth his chief witness, the convert Dinah Meridi. Escorted into the room by two of the magistrate's bailiffs, she was kept away from the side of the court where the Jewish defendants sat. Dark-haired and dark-skinned, she stood tense and withdrawn, but her eyes burned with an intensity that had the flare of madness. Her every movement had so little harmony that her limbs seemed momentarily about to depart in different directions. A silent shriek emanated from her that Rabbi Low heard at once. So plain was this cry to him that he half started from his seat to go to comfort her before he saw the burning-eyed malevolence and the curled-nostril disdain she turned on the Jews in the court, the special rancor and antipathy she fixed on Meisel and himself.

In a low, penetrating voice, every gesture charged with passionate conviction, she repeated almost word for word the testimony she had earlier given the Cardinal. In the telling, however, the depths of spleen and ardors of abhorrence sent a current of feeling through the entire court far more extreme and violent than the words Rabbi Low remembered from the written testimony.

"Can you identify the men who brought the blood to your father's house?" the crown counsel asked.

"My father's house," Dinah Meridi repeated, as if considering what the three words truly meant. "I would know them anywhere." Her finger pointed at the defendants and she said, "The men were Hugo Den and Petr Singer." Then, contemptuously, "Mordecai Meisel's servants." As she indicated the mute, he smiled and bowed to her, happy to be recognized, until the bailiffs guarding him yanked his shackles to make him subside.

"Who sent the blood?" the lawyer asked.

Again the imperious finger pointed and Dinah Meridi fixed Meisel with her hot stare, which the financier returned coldly, unyieldingly. "In the past, when the flasks of blood were sent from the Rabbi, my father would give monies to the synagogue."

"You mean then the blood came from Rabbi Low?"

Dinah Meridi did not look at the Rabbi, but kept her eyes focused on the crown counsel. "I do not know. I think it was his brother-in-law, the Rabbi who preceded him."

The silence in the courtroom became a hum.

"This year, did you learn whose blood was to be used?"

Her dark head nodded, bobbing like a crow's, quick, affirmative but separate from the rest of her tensely held self. "The blood was from Meisel's servant girl, Jitka Myslikova."

"Are you certain?"

Again Dinah Meridi explained what she had overheard Hugo Den tell her father.

The defense attorney insisted either that the crown counsel produce Dr. Meridi to corroborate his daughter's testimony, or that the judges disregard her charges.

The prosecutor offered the information that Dr. Meridi had gone to England for his health.

The spectators guffawed.

The presiding magistrate asked if anyone knew where Dr. Meridi was, or if he had given a written deposition. His daughter and the two attorneys shook their heads simultaneously. "My father feared for his life," Dinah Meridi said, "if he remained in Prague to testify against the Jews. He too was disgusted with the barbarous practices of the Jews, but he was afraid to speak out. He even warned me to be silent because of the power and influence of Mordecai Meisel."

"Then why did you speak out?" the crown counsel inquired.

"Because *those* people"—Dinah Meridi pointed generally to the Jews who sat among the spectators—"are an accursed tribe. They who seek salvation from the blood of others fill me with horror. They will call me renegade, apostate, traitor, because I have left their fold for the true faith—but I do not care."

The applause from the audience was prolonged. When silence was restored, all eyes sought those of Rabbi Low. Shoulders bowed, head down, he sat for a time without moving. Even when he spoke, he remained seated, and his words were so gentle that the people were taken by surprise. "Every tree loses some of its fruit," he said, "and even some of its branches. It is not always bad fruit or rotten branches. Often it is only the weaker fruit and frailer branches of the tree that give way. Sometimes it is because of the way the storms blow that tear them from the tree out of which they grew. To find oneself cut off from one's own people, from the religion of one's fathers is for most people one of life's most painful torments. But there *are* those who find attachment to their people so painful and heavy a burden that they must lay it down. To be a Jew is a heavy burden to carry willingly, an impossible burden to carry with a hating heart. And to be a Jew is an honor, a great privilege one cannot enjoy without bearing the burdens as well."

Dinah Meridi would countenance no such gentle rejoinder. She shouted her reply. "The Jewish stench reeks in the nostrils. It rises up to and offends the heavens. The odor of Jewish blasphemy and godlessness, of the blood of ritual murder on Jewish hands makes them pariahs among men. Cast them out!" For only the fraction of a second, she hesitated, then, raising her arms, she cried out in a voice of stone, "Kill them! Kill the Jews!"

The breathing in the courtroom rose and fell hoarsely. All eyes were fastened on the slim dark girl who stood in the witness stand, her arms akimbo, fingers bunched into tiny fists, eyes aflame. The judges shifted uncomfortably on their benches. The crown attorney stood and cleared his throat, but was unable to speak. Hugo Den lunged toward Dinah Meridi, but like a hound on a leash was hauled back by his bailiffs. Petr Singer drew his knees up to his chin and began to rock himself to and fro as if his deaf ears heard some distant lullaby. The moment seemed unending, until from the open window were wafted the clatter of horses' hoofs and wagon wheels, a hussar's challenge, and the Golem's booming response, "Let us pass, let us through quickly. This is Jitka Myslikova, the missing girl. She is not dead. She is here alive. No blood has been shed."

The tense silence was drawn out until the courtroom doors burst open and Pokorny led the girl and the Golem in, then a long sigh, like the receding wave from a beach, quavered through the court.

The Golem led Jitka Myslikova toward the Rabbi, but the bailiffs intervened and took the girl to the crown counsel who, in turn, escorted her to the magistrates' bench. Judges, counsel, and Jitka held a whispered conference, and were joined by the defense attorney. Pokorny remained at the Golem's side, patted him on the back, nodded to the Rabbi, then went to the back of the courtroom.

The Rabbi put his hand on the Golem's arm and softly, fervently intoned, *"Blessed art Thou, O Lord our God, King of the universe, who bestows favor on the undeserving, and who has bestowed on us His good favor."* The Golem withdrew his arm and went to the rear of the court to stand next to Pokorny.

Dinah Meridi, her face a melancholy mask, her arms sunk to her sides, stood rigid in the witness stand until Thaddeus led her from it. He spoke into her ear, but, mechanically, she shook her head. The faces of the Meisels turned toward the Rabbi, hers joyous, his still alert and unbending. The babble in the courtroom rose and fell, until the presiding magistrate stood up and signaled for silence. "The trial of these men is finished," he announced. "Clear the court."

The spectators, hesitating, stood but did not move toward the exits.

"Mordecai Meisel, Hugo Den, and Petr Singer are hereby declared innocent of the charges of murder lodged against them."

From the black-clad seminarians, the cry went up, fierce, thwarted, "Kill the Jews! Will you let the Jew banker go free? Kill him! Kill him! Kill the Jews!"

Pokorny's dismounted hussars and the court halberdiers swiftly surrounded the seminarians and began to shove them through the crowd, propelling them more rapidly than they were willing to move with blows from the hafts of their weapons. The crowd, whose indecision had teetered on the edge of violence, was now docile. As hussars and halberdiers slowly cleared the court, the throng moved as they directed.

The presiding magistrate commanded the bailiffs to remove the prisoners' shackles and to set them free. He ordered Dinah Meridi to be held in custody. The bailiffs shackled her while Thaddeus, protesting, went along when they took her from the court. Mordecai and Frumett Meisel and Rabbi Low walked to the bench to thank the magistrates, and there Frumett embraced Jitka Myslikova. "You came back," Frumett exulted. "Thank God, you came back. And thank you."

"Thank Joseph Golem," Jitka replied, disengaging herself from her former mistress's embrace. "He persuaded me." Shamefacedly, then boldly, she reached into her bodice and drew out a ring. "Here"—she held it out to Frumett—"I took it by mistake."

Meisel intervened. "Please keep it, Jitka," the financier insisted, "and this one too." From his finger he drew a second ring and pressed it into her palm. "We are greatly in your debt."

"What will happen to Dinah Meridi?" Rabbi Low asked.

The presiding magistrate's face was set. "She will be tried and sentenced for criminal calumny."

"And Friar Thaddeus?" the Rabbi persisted.

The presiding judge looked over his shoulder to where Pokorny now stood.

"The Cardinal will see to him," Pokorny promised.

The presiding magistrate gave a brief speech asking them not to worsen circumstances by taking too firm a stand about their rights. Sometimes it was wiser to overlook things, especially when the temper of the mob was so inflamed. "The people are a balky horse," Pokorny added. "Better to keep them saddled and reined in, not give them a chance to run wild."

Meisel nodded without delay, but the Rabbi was longer in giving his acquiescence and finally did so with obvious reluctance.

It was clear that neither magistrates nor the Emperor, whose absence had been noteworthy, nor the Cardinal, whose representative Pokorny was, were interested in having the trial end as a vindication of Meisel and a victory of sorts for the Jews. So when the presiding judge called on Pokorny to escort them all out of the courtroom by a rear entrance, the Rabbi refused. "My people await me," he said firmly. "I led them here today and I must now lead them back."

The presiding judge and Pokorny exchanged glances before the magistrate said, "Yes, perhaps it is better so. That way you can insure that there are no outbreaks between the people and the Jews."

"I shall do everything I can to prevent the shedding of blood," the Rabbi promised.

The Golem, who had stood silent, eyes fixed on Jitka Myslikova, now bent and spoke into the Rabbi's ear. "And the girl?" the Rabbi asked.

"She must remain in custody for a time. We must question her and take her deposition. She will be released in a few days, a week at most. All in good time."

Meisel inquired if Jitka might stay at his house, where she would be more comfortable than in jail. He would guarantee her presence at the court's convenience, but the judges denied the request. Though Rabbi Low regretted that the girl might have to spend some days of discomfort, he was relieved because Thaddeus might make such an arrangement seem to be a matter of the court's collusion with the Jewish community, a consequence to be carefully avoided.

Later, when the Rabbi questioned the Golem about why he had taken so very long to return with the girl, arriving only at the very last minute, the Golem shrugged. "I could not persuade her at first," he explained. "She would not come. But when she made her mind up, she wanted to make a great show of it, arriving like Žižka and his Taborites to take the Vítkov, at the last moment."

"And you permitted it, while we waited with failing hearts?" the Rabbi asked harshly.

"What would you have had me do?" the Golem asked. "Kill her?"

X

———◆•◆◆◆•◆———

When Dinah Meridi's sentence was announced—the magistrates had meted out a term of six years' imprisonment—Rabbi Low asked to see her. The magistrates granted his request, but Dinah Meridi did not care to receive him. Rabbi Low went to visit her nonetheless, because three days after Mordecai Meisel, Hugo Den, and Petr Singer had been released, he had received a letter from her father. The letter had been delivered by a Jewish merchant recently in England who was traveling through Prague on his way home to Cracow. The merchant had been given the letter not by Dr. Meridi himself, but by a third person whose name he did not know, for delivery to Rabbi Judah ben Bezalel Low in Prague. The letter, in fluent literary Hebrew, had been most pain-

ful for the Rabbi to read and he took it with him to give to Dr.
Meridi's daughter.

When the bailiffs ushered him into her cell, the Rabbi was ap-
palled to see that Dinah Meridi wore what looked like a nun's
habit. All her beautiful hair had been shorn and her head shaven.
She did not acknowledge his presence until he mentioned that
he had received a letter from her father. "Read it!" she demanded,
unwilling to accept the letter from his outstretched hand to read
it herself.

Slowly, Rabbi Low read it aloud to her.

"To the honored Rabbi Judah ben Bezalel Low, famous scholar,
teacher and leader, great in the Law and in good deeds:

"Your various emissaries have not been able to reach me though
I am living in London and have heard, in a roundabout way, that
you were trying to find me. I knew why. I could not be part of
my daughter Dinah's conspiracy with the friar Thaddeus, but I
could not find it in my heart to expose her to obloquy, perhaps
even to death, by revealing that she bore false witness, so I fled
from Prague. What kind of man, you will ask, would expose all
the Jews of the ghetto to the peril that such charges of ritual
murder were bound to arouse in the breasts of the Jew-haters of
Prague? What kind of man would permit an entire community to
be punished, expelled, perhaps killed, rather than expose and condemn his own daughter? A father. A foolish father and a weak
and irresolute man.

"For the fault of it, Rabbi Low, is mine, both for her apostasy
and her treason. Thaddeus was the instrument but I the cause.
The friar and I became acquainted by chance when I was, one
night, called hurriedly to treat one of his fellow friars who was
gravely ill. By my skill as a physician and likely you would say
with the help of God, I was able to save the friar's life. Afterward
it became Thaddeus' obsession to convert me to Christianity, and
I became a fortress besieged.

"Thaddeus came to my house often, to talk of the Christian
faith. He saw that I was estranged from my people, that I did
not live within the ghetto walls, and the two of us wrestled for
my soul. We argued about the merits of Judaism and Christianity
as if I were a true defender of our faith when, even then, no god
but blind chance seemed to me true of human life, and history

only a series of blind, malevolent, or stupid accidents. To defend myself, although I was not sure why I should want to, I went back to study the Scriptures, the Talmud, and the history of our people as I had not studied them since I was a boy. The more immersed I became, the stauncher my defense of the Jews became. I knew that, in one sense, I had never left the fold, and in another, that I could never leave it. If I could not see the lineaments of the Lord in what had been done to our people over thousands of years, I could see even less justice or love of man in the viciousness Christianity had engendered in human beings.

"My daughter was then still a child. Though her age and body are now that of a woman, she is perhaps still a child, with all the naïveté and harshness of children. And with all their simple, irrevocable certainty about life. When Thaddeus and I talked, Dinah sat quietly and listened, drank in what we spoke, and was made drunk. One day she came to ask my permission for her to be baptized. She had already spoken of this to Thaddeus and he was filled with joy that he should be privileged to lead my daughter into the arms of salvation. I was thunderstruck. I was astonished to find that I resented fiercely what he had done. I felt that he had violated my hospitality, that he had stolen my daughter from me in my own home. But I said nothing.

"I did not, as perhaps I should have, attempt to dissuade Dinah from her course, but I had long ago concluded that to remain a Jew in a Christian world was to seek to be murdered or maimed, to be an eternal victim. It was not a role I had enjoyed in my own life, nor was it one I could regret having my child cast off. If her life might be made happier and more pleasant, why not? Yet, then as now, I asked myself why had I not also sought to be baptized, why had not conversion and apostasy been that easy logical step for me that they seemed for Dinah—and I found no answer.

"It was some time after Thaddeus launched her long course of instruction that Dinah told me that the friar had informed her that she would have to prove the sincerity of her conversion by trial. She had earlier been approved by the Cardinal himself so that I had foreseen no such contingency. Thaddeus now wanted her to condemn totally the community she was leaving. He had concocted a plot that would accuse Mordecai Meisel of bloodguilt and that would implicate you, Rabbi, and the entire Jewish community. Because Dinah was a Jewess and a convert, she would be the essential and knowing witness; she would be believed.

"I did, however, try to dissuade Dinah from such an evil scheme. If I had separated myself from my coreligionists, I had not done so because I hated them but because I could not bear their burdens, because I sought a freer life outside the walls of the ghetto, because I was interested in worlds other than religion. I bore them no more ill will than I bore myself, though that was considerable; and I bore them a great deal less ill will than I bore the Christians who had plundered, burned, and killed them over the centuries.

"But my daughter would not listen. She was afire with the love of Christ and his Church. She raved about the *Jewish stench*! To me, her father, a physician *and* a Jew! The sight of a peaked hat or yellow disc made her spit or cast a stone at him who was forced to wear it. Her hatred knew no bounds; it was greater even than Thaddeus'. Not only would she testify, but she insisted that I publicly corroborate her testimony. I was unable. I could not betray my daughter, but I could not bear false witness against my own people, whatever abyss separated us. I spoke to Dinah again. We quarreled. I raged, commanded, pleaded, but she set her face and heart against me like stone.

"Finally, one night, dagger in hand, I stole to her bedchamber prepared to kill her. She lay there asleep, so pale and quiet, scarcely breathing, so terribly young, looking so much like her late lamented mother I so loved, that I could not raise my hand. I stopped and kissed her lips and that very night I stole from the house, from Prague, from the Continent, to come here to England where I am only a physician, no longer a father, no longer a Jew, perhaps no longer even a human being. I am beyond help now, honored Rabbi, but please, if you can, help my daughter.

Bedrich Meridi."

Not once while he read the letter did Dinah Meridi raise her eyes. When he was done, she stood trembling, hands joined prayerfully together over her bosom, her eyes pressed tightly closed, her lips moving so that he could only barely hear her murmur, ". . . *our trespasses as we forgive those who trespass against us.*" Then Dinah Meridi walked to him, reached out, and took the letter from his hands. For an instant she looked at the handwriting, then tore the letter to shreds and let the fragments fall around her. "My father lies in his beard," she said and turned her back on him.

Before Rabbi Low had gone to the trial magistrates to ask to see Dinah Meridi in prison, the Golem had requested him to inquire about Jitka Myslikova. The magistrates explained that Jitka was still in custody because her testimony was not yet completed, but in a few days she would be free to go. When the Rabbi reported that to the Golem, the Golem's face fell and he stalked sullenly away.

A few nights after he had gone to see Dinah Meridi, Rabbi Low was invited to attend Mordecai Meisel at his house. There, Petr Singer opened the door to him, took his cloak, and bowing, his hands and body miming his thanks with every sinew, led him into the Meisel salon. Meisel, leaning on a cane, was waiting and limped forward to embrace him with one arm. "Judah, I should have come to you, but I am not yet recovered from the ministrations of the Emperor's magistrate." The open warmth and sincerity of the embrace and the irony were unexpected and they touched the Rabbi. "I am deeply grateful to you and to your Joseph Golem."

"For the Lord will not cast off forever. For though He cause grief, yet will He have compassion according to the multitude of His mercies," the Rabbi declared.

When they were seated and after Meisel, with a gesture, had sent Petr Singer for wine, the financier smiled his fine, ironic, and intelligent smile. "Yesterday I heard from the Emperor. At last. One of his equerries brought me his personal greetings. The Emperor was devastated that he had not learned of my difficulties previously. The Emperor was full of profound regrets that he had not been able to come to my assistance. The Emperor is deeply pleased that no harm has come to his most treasured friend, Mordecai Meisel, and will be pleased to entertain his presence at the Castle as soon as he is able to return to Prague."

"Where has the Emperor been?" Rabbi Low inquired.

Meisel laughed. "Vyšehrad." Vyšehrad was no more than a half hour's gallop from the prison and the courtroom.

They talked about the Passover, made preparations for a special celebration of the festival this year because the Lord had truly guarded His people and this time the Angel of Death *had* passed over the houses of the Jews. It was clear that the financier was very tired and still not fully himself, so Rabbi Low soon rose to go. Leaning heavily on his cane and limping, Meisel accompanied him to the door, and there, just as the Rabbi was about to take his leave, he asked, "That girl, Jitka Myslikova, what happened to her?"

Meisel shook his head. "She's run away with a Hungarian ostler who came to Prague to sell some horses and was returning to Buda."

"So swiftly?"

"He was tall and blue-eyed, with fair blond hair that fell to his shoulders, and a blond mustache thick as a bramble. Frumett gave Jitka a chest of new clothes and I gave her a dowry."

"Was she going to marry the fellow?"

"She didn't say. But she told Frumett that the ostler had a horse farm in the Puszta, a small one, but it would be hers, all her own, if they married. With the dowry, she thought he would be willing."

"So be it. It is better that she is gone."

"Yes, Judah, but good that she returned."

Again, Meisel embraced him and then the Rabbi went home. Directly, he climbed to his study where the Golem lay on the couch, his great arms behind his head, staring up at the ceiling. Until the Rabbi had lit and trimmed the lamp, the Golem did not stir; then, in a frayed voice, he said, "She is gone."

"Yes, to Buda, with a Hungarian ostler."

"She will not return?" The question was put without hope.

"Reb Meisel said that the ostler had a small horse farm in the Hungarian plains and that Jitka Myslikova was going there with him, to marry him."

"Is this my reward for bringing her back? for saving Meisel and the ghetto?" the Golem asked, sitting up.

"A good deed is its own reward, Joseph. In this life there is no more reward than that." Seeing the pain on the Golem's face, the Rabbi added consolingly, "Is it not better that she leave now than later?"

"Must she have left at all?"

"She wanted a place she could call her own. A man she could call her own."

"And I am not such a man and do not have such a place for her," the Golem added, his head in his hands.

"You are more important, Joseph," the Rabbi replied, "with a more important place."

A moan escaped the Golem's lips and he sat there rocking his head in his hands as if it was too much, too heavy for him to carry on his shoulders.

XI

———— ◆·◆◆·◆ ————

When Rabbi Low awakened him to put on his phylacteries and to say the morning prayer, the Golem not only rebuffed him but refused to get out of bed altogether. "What ails you?" the Rabbi asked.

"My spirit weeps," the Golem groaned, his face distorted by sorrow.

"For what does your spirit weep?" the Rabbi asked, knowing that it was Jitka Myslikova the Golem mourned.

"I have neither father nor mother, brother nor sister. I have no wife or child, no comrades in work, not even any neighbors. I am a creature totally alone."

"The Lord is your Father, and I am your brother, and your comrade."

The Golem turned his face to the wall.

"Get up!" Rabbi Low ordered.

"No," came the muffled reply.

"Arise, I command you!"

Reluctantly, the Golem rose and dressed, but he would not wash or say his prayers or eat. In his plain face the hatred was strong.

"You are a stranger here and must remain a stranger," Rabbi Low chided. "Yours is not the ordinary man's destiny, of work and family, friends and study. You are called on for things of greater moment. Such a duty requires you to deny yourself the ordinary satisfactions."

"Deny myself? *You* deny me."

"The Lord has marked your road."

"I did not choose to be such a creature as I am."

"None of us choose to be the creatures we are. We are and we become. We are chosen and then choose to accept what we are."

"Or refuse to accept."

"None can refuse to accept. In the refusal is also the acceptance."

"Let me go."

"I cannot."

"Please."

"It is *my* duty to command as it is *yours* to obey. Neither commandment nor obedience is without anguish."

"Set me free, Rabbi."

"The Almighty has set you free and forged your chains. Only He can strike them off."

"I shall free myself. If I must be a murderer in defense of your Jews, then I can be a murderer in my own defense. I will be free. I will kill you first, my jailer, my enemy. I hate you! I hate the sight of your face and the sound of your voice that taunt and pursue me wherever I turn. Go! Obey! Journey! Seek out! Protect! Fight! Destroy! I shall take your head between my hands and crush it like an egg. I shall smite you into the earth from which you drew me forth." He sprang toward the Rabbi, but the Rabbi did not flinch. Trembling, the Golem stood over him, his great fists raised high, then he turned aside and hurled himself against the walls, striking them with his shoulders, his fists, his head, until the house shook.

Rabbi Low went to him at last and touched his arm. "You are blessed to do deeds of greatness. From your hands shall come our redemption. Neither greatness nor redemption is achieved without pain. Sit still in your anguish and it shall pass away in the joy of your mission. You shall be our suffering servant."

"I do not want the deeds of greatness you commend. Let the Jews' hands redeem themselves from the oppressor. Why should I be their bludgeon, their ax, their hired assassin? Better wife and child, friends, hard work, and peaceful sleep."

"Passover is close and our time of trial is near. Your trial shall not be long in coming."

"Rabbi, I do not want to be tried as a hero. I want to try myself with ordinary life."

"You are not an ordinary man."

"No, I am not, but you might make me one."

"You are Joseph Golem."

"Yes, I am a Golem, bastard progeny of the Almighty, the exalted Rabbi of Prague, and a Moldau riverbank."

"You speak now in the bitterness of your soul, but you shall yet sing in the ecstasy of your fulfillment."

"*How shall I sing the Lord's song in a strange land? In a land where I am a stranger?*"

"You have learned well, but you remember what follows in the Psalm?" Rabbi Low chanted:

> If I forget thee, O Jerusalem,
> Let my right hand forget her cunning.
> Let my tongue cleave to the roof of my mouth,
> If I remember thee not;
> If I set not Jerusalem
> Above my chiefest joy.

The Golem hung his head. "I shall do," he said finally. "And I shall obey." Without another word he lumbered from the room.

But Rabbi Low could not put out of his mind the abject misery that had informed him. Truly, he had thought to bring forth the Golem for an exalted task, but he had brought him into grief as well. He had disinterred the Golem from an Eden of clay and now he himself stood like the Lord's flaming sword that turned every way to keep the Golem from returning to that Eden, or going forward into the lesser paradise of common life.

In the courtyard Rabbi Low heard the thump of the ax, and when he looked out of the window he saw the Golem attacking only the thickest logs, setting them upright like men, then splitting them down the middle with great blows of his ax. So, the Rabbi reflected sadly, was anger resolved into heating the synagogue. What shall a man do to live? the Sages asked; and replying to their own question, declared: He shall deaden himself.

It was Isaac who brought the news that Joseph Golem was in love with Kaethe Hoch. Shyly, Isaac explained that in passing the cemetery he had seen the two of them sitting in the "garden of death" under the newly minting green-leafed trees. "They sat like children," he told the Rabbi hesitantly. Kaethe Hoch had shamelessly loosed her hair like a curtain of gold, Joseph caressing it as if it were the covering of the Holy Ark. She was feeding him, peeling and cutting small bits of some fruit or bread, which she brought to his mouth from the edge of her paring knife. Starlings flew above them in a canopy of chatter, as if celebrating their marriage with song. The girl's flowerlike face had turned up to Joseph's and the sap of his life seemed to spring green in his strange eyes as his great fingers touched her cheeks and shaped her mouth. "They did not speak," Isaac explained, "only eyed each other with loneliness and longing."

How well Pearl had chosen for his daughter, Rabbi Low thought, how tender, courteous, and compassionate Isaac was: a good husband, father, and son-in-law, a good man, and a good Jew. That he himself could afford no such compassion for the Golem's longing pained him; but that was what being the *Höhe* Rabbi Low meant. The Golem had already lost one companion in Jitka Myslikova; he must now lose another in Kaethe Hoch. With Passover descending on them, all else was indulgence.

It would, he knew, be worse when he saw to it that Kaethe was affianced. Kaethe was now of marriageable age so it was his duty to see her properly married. His wife would complain perhaps, for she was as fond of the girl as if she were their own daughter and would miss her in the household; but for Kaethe's sake Pearl would search out a proper husband.

He broached arranging the marriage to Pearl and instantly she was wary. "You think it is time for her?" Pearl asked.

"Isaac has seen her with Joseph Golem," the Rabbi said.

"The Golem has led her astray?"

"I do not think so, but perhaps it is time for her to marry."

"Kaethe is so very young, only fifteen."

"You have often told me that a girl of fifteen is already a woman."

"So I have." Pearl turned to her tasks, carefully rolling the dough for bread and kneading it.

"You will see to it?" he asked, so she would know it was not merely suggestion.

Pearl's reply was muffled by the concentration she was demonstrating over the bread. "I will see to it."

His wife's grudging acquiescence was a rebuff he recognized, but could overlook because he knew that she would carry out his wishes.

No more than a fortnight later Pearl came to his study at the end of the day. It was dusk, the lamps had not yet been lit, and the Golem was in the courtyard, the steady thwack of his ax rhythmic on wood. It was a time of day the Rabbi found congenial, when the Almighty seemed intent on conveying the fallibility of human vision and judgment, when light and dark were so melded that the shape of a tree or a building could not be clearly discerned, when human faces were as shadowy and dubious as human motives. Only the evening prayer could rescue him from that twilight, only that and the Almighty's impending clarity of moon and stars to remind him that day was day and night night, as clearly severed as good and evil that they might be defined and judged. When Pearl coughed to remind him that she was in the room, he was sharper with her than usual, angry and grateful for having lifted him out of the twilight's equivocation.

"Kaethe's betrothal can be arranged if we are willing to provide the dowry," she said. "The man is a good man and a scholar, but poor."

"As which scholar is not?" the Rabbi asked rhetorically. "Does he know Kaethe?"

"He has seen her many times and she him."

"Have they spoken?"

"As man and woman?" Pearl shook her head.

"Will they be suited?"

"Who can tell?" Pearl looked at him skeptically. "Were we suited? A match may be made in heaven, but it must be lived on earth."

"What does that mean?"

"Can an eighteen-year-old boy be suited for a fifteen-year-old girl except by the evil impulse?"

"The impulse of a man for a woman, or a boy for a girl, need not be the *yetzer*. It may be the best of impulses."

"So you have assured me, many times."

"And meant it."

"Doubtless."

"Is the boy only eighteen?"

"Twenty-two, and you have yourself long wished a bride for him."

"Jacob Nissan!"

"The very same."

Jacob did indeed need a wife. Or his hotheaded passions would lead him into bloody contention with the world, as his actions during Mordecai Meisel's trial had shown. Jacob should devote himself entirely to study and a sensible wife would help bind his passions with children and responsibilities. He had long been conscious of the need to find Jacob a wife, but the boy was poor and none of the ghetto's well-to-do Jews had come forward with a suitable daughter and dowry. Now, with one stroke, he could provide a dowry and a good husband for his ward, and at the same time provide a wife for his best student. Everyone would be content, everyone, that is, except Joseph Golem.

"I shall consider it," Rabbi Low promised. Pearl's face fell, so that he felt impelled to add, "The match seems like a good one." More than that he could not utter.

As he and Jacob sat studying the passage on the creation of Eve, Rabbi Low read the words with a shade more fervor than usual: *"And the Lord God said: 'It is not good that man should be alone; I will make a helpmeet for him.'"* Why, he wondered, had the Lord caused a deep sleep to fall upon Adam while He had taken one of Adam's ribs to shape woman? And why a rib and not some other organ? *"This is now bone of my bones, and flesh of my flesh; she shall be called Woman because she was taken out of Man. Therefore shall a man leave his father and mother and cleave unto his wife, and they shall be one flesh."*

"The Sages also say," Jacob reminded him, youthfully disparaging and shy, "that the Hebrew words for *helpmeet, ezer kenegdo,* also mean *opponent.*"

"Sometimes, Jacob, the greatest helpmeet is an opponent, in marriage or without. *He who finds a wife, finds a great good and receives the favor of the Lord.*"

"I am not unwilling to receive the Lord's favor, Rabbi," Jacob said, "or even a woman's, but I am a poor student, as you know, and without prospects."

"Poor and student is by no means a hopeless state. I have been a poor student myself."

"The tales of Low the poor bachelor and student are told and retold among the people."

"They still tell those stories?"

"Of course! How you were betrothed at fifteen and waited for your bride almost as long as the Patriarch Jacob waited for his Rachel, until you were twenty-eight. How your bride waited while you went to Lublin to study. How Reb Schmelke, your father-in-law, released you from your troth when his money and your wife's dowry were lost in misfortune. How Elijah the Prophet himself, in the person of an officer of hussars, left a dowry of gold ducats so that at last you could marry. . . ." The faintest tinge of irony colored his voice.

"Men tell tales swiftly, but how long and arduous is the road to truth," Rabbi Low remarked. How could any of those years be explained to a twenty-two-year-old? His had been another time, so very long ago that Jacob would not even believe what it was like if he described it to him. His Uncle Jeremiah's dark, vibrant voice echoed in his memory speaking Eve's plea to Adam after the two of them had been driven from the Garden. "Why do you not slay me?" Eve asked. "Then God will permit you to return to paradise from which you were driven only because of me." And he recalled Adam's voice, concealed in his Uncle Jeremiah's, answering, "How can I raise my hand against my own flesh?" Those words from a lifetime ago, spoken to him first in study, by an uncle so long dead, and the recollections of his life shook him like a chill. The long journey of a marriage, helpmeets and opponents bound together as one flesh, comrades and prisoners, goads and solace, could not be described to one who had not yet himself even disputed a part of that passage. "Jacob," Rabbi Low announced, "it is time for you to marry, past time. I am willing to give you my ward, Kaethe Hoch, in marriage. I shall provide the dowry and wedding feast so that nothing will be lacking."

"Kaethe Hoch?" Jacob seemed stunned.

"Yes."

"I have watched her over the years," Jacob murmured, dreaminess stealing over his face, unfocusing his eyes, "a little girl when first I came to your house to study. Then, like a flower of the field, bursting into the bloom of a comely woman."

"Remember the *yetzer*," the Rabbi cautioned.

Jacob's face was suddenly tormented, frightened. "Your Golem will hate me even more than he hates me now," Jacob blurted.

"You have nothing to fear from him."

"I am not afraid. Not *of* him, but *for* him."

"Then I shall make the arrangements," Rabbi Low concluded, but with an inflection that left the sentence half a question.

"You are very generous," Jacob said finally, then bowed his head, which the Rabbi took to mean that he signified his agreement.

Speaking to Kaethe was more difficult, even embarrassing, though he knew that Pearl had already broached the subject of marriage to her. Kaethe came to his study the next day after the midday meal, her hair glowing as if it had caught the afternoon sun, her eyes alight. "Kaethe," Rabbi Low began, "we have thought for a long time about your betrothal. Because we are so fond of you, as of our own daughters, we have not wanted to lose your presence in the house and have therefore delayed unduly. But in a few weeks you will be sixteen and the time of marriage can no longer be delayed."

Fair face flushed, lips quivering, and eyes downcast, Kaethe said, "I thought I might be left over, an old maid, because my parents left no dowry."

"We shall provide your dowry," Rabbi Low promised, "and be happy to do it. Doubtless, Reb Meisel will want to add a portion. He knew your parents well and has liked you from childhood."

"Why then did he not keep me himself?" she asked.

After all these years that still troubled her, the Rabbi thought. People did not easily forget. When she was a child, Pearl had often answered the same question, reassured her, but here it was, once again, still unanswered to her satisfaction. "Because his wife was ill, his first wife, Eva, may she rest in peace," the Rabbi replied. "Because he already had two nephews to look after, and because he traveled so much he did not think he would make a good guardian for you."

Kaethe's face was torn with doubt.

"You must not let that upset you, child," the Rabbi said, "or we will think that we did not fulfill our obligations to you."

"Oh, no, Rabbi. I mean yes." She was dutiful, but he saw that, like an ache, it would continue to pain her for life. "I am glad you have chosen him for me, Rabbi," Kaethe said softly. "I know he is strange in his ways and in appearance, but he has been kind to me, and gentle, and I like him. I think he will be good to me. And I to him. Though he is only a woodcutter, we shall be content."

"Jacob Nissan is not strange in appearance, nor in his ways," the Rabbi declared. "And he is not a woodcutter."

"Jacob Nissan!" Kaethe cried the name out in pain. "I thought you meant Joseph Golem."

"Did my wife say that?"

The girl shook her head. "Only, I thought . . ." Her voice disappeared. Head bent, tears streaming down her cheeks, lips trembling with unspoken words, she sat there silent.

Rabbi Low went to her and stroked her hair. "Jacob is a student and a fine man. One day he will be a rabbi and a scholar of renown. You will be very proud to be his wife." Her shoulders shook with sobbing and little repeated gasps: "Jacob Nissan . . . Jacob Nissan," and then, hands over her ears, she ran from the room.

Talking to the Golem proved to be most difficult of all. Rabbi Low was almost certain that Kaethe had already spoken to him by the way the Golem lumbered into his study and stood towering over him, green eyes like jade, black beard bristling, great hands shaking. Suddenly the Golem was Isaac on Mount Moriah and the Rabbi himself the Patriarch Abraham, Isaac fearful, knowing he was to be the sacrifice yet not knowing how, Abraham uncertain but committed. God had provided no burnt offering, for the Golem was both Isaac and the ram waiting in the thicket. He would lock horns with Thaddeus' seminarians, his head would know the axes and staves of the guildsmen and peasants, his flesh would be snared by pikemen and halberdiers: he would be the sacrifice, the ghetto's *korban*.

The Almighty had forbidden human sacrifice, the *Akédah* symbol of that divine mandate. Yet what was the Golem but a human sacrifice? Only, instead of taking the knife into his own hands, as Abraham had done, he had put it into the Golem's. Had he misunderstood the Lord's command as some said the Patriarch Abraham had? Where was his pity for the Golem's agony and ordeal? All the congregation of Israel seemed to chorus in his head, *"Be mindful of the time when our father Abraham bound his son Isaac on the altar, suppressing his compassion that he might do Thy will wholeheartedly."*

Was it easier to suppress his compassion because he thought the Golem an incomplete man, not truly a human being; or simply because he had forced himself to concentrate on the Golem only as an instrument of salvation? In the months since that dark midnight on the banks of the Moldau, the clay from which the Golem had been formed seemed to have grown daily more sensate, thoughtful, and pained. How then could he deny the Golem's humanity? In the iron grip of the Lord's vision, his truth was a command to create the Golem to protect His people. Was that his *Akédah*? Though God did not covet human sacrifice, men sometimes did; and men sometimes had to be martyred to rescue His people Israel, slain to sanctify His holy name. The Golem had been created for such a just sacrifice. No matter how his own spirit was violated by the fact that for a hundred generations and more, human bones had been buried beneath the threshold of every house built, human flesh imbedded in the cornerstones of every temple, human skulls under the gateposts of every city, it had been and still was the way of the world. *This* world they lived in, not the world to come. He must suppress his compassion so that he might do the Lord's bidding. *What must a man do to live? He must deaden himself.*

"You called me?" the Golem asked at last.

"The Passover draws near and with it the time of your triumph," Rabbi Low said. "There can be no distraction, no over-sight now. You must be engrossed in the Lord's work, preoc-cupied only with saving His people."

"But not my own salvation?" the Golem asked. "I brought Jitka Myslikova back and saved Mordecai Meisel and his men. Yet you did not help me keep her. And now you have taken Kaethe from me."

"Kaethe Hoch *must* marry Jacob Nissan."

The Golem snapped his fingers and it was as if a great branch had cracked from a tree. "You have ordained it and so it must be. Are you the Almighty?"

"How many times must I say that you are fated for a destiny greater than that of other men?"

"Your speaking it a hundred, or a hundred times a hundred, makes my burden no lighter to bear."

"The Lord leads the willing; He drags the unwilling in His wake."

"And my vaunted free will? That will which the Lord has boasted of giving man?"

"The will is destiny imbedded in the flesh. *Everything is in the hands of God, except the fear of God.*"

"And if it is my will to marry Kaethe?" the Golem challenged.

Only when the Golem had repeated his challenge, saying, "I *shall* marry her," did the Rabbi speak the searing words. "Joseph, you can have no children. It would be a grave sin to inflict such a future on Kaethe."

"I can . . . have . . . no . . . children." The words were torn from between the Golem's teeth.

"It is the Lord's command."

"The Lord's command is *Be fruitful and multiply*."

"Not for you."

"Not for me! Three words that make my life without hope of redemption, yet not a single word of comfort, of pity from your lips. My father! How unfeeling you are!"

"The Lord's yoke is heavy, for all men, though not for all men alike."

"Even for a Golem who may have neither wife nor children to comfort his soul?" His face was bewildered, his clasping and unclasping hands bereft.

"The Lord shall comfort your soul with the rescue of your people and His."

"No love to warm my spirit, to assuage my anguish that all my generations go down to the grave with me? Not even tender Kaethe, who loves *me*, not Jacob Nissan."

"Kaethe is to be his bride."

"*For love is as strong as death, Jealousy is as cruel as the grave; The flashes thereof are flashes of fire, A very flame of the Lord,*" the Golem said. Two single tears descended slowly from his green eyes on to his bearded cheeks.

Rabbi Low was moved, but unflinchingly he spoke the words he knew were the only possible response: "*If a man would give all the substance of his house for love, He would be utterly condemned.*" It was the same sentence he had imposed on himself all his life, imposed on Bezalel, but Bezalel had refused the sentence, flouted it, and so lost forever his opportunity to serve.

"Oh, my teacher, how you have taught me now! My creator! Cursed be the day that ripped me from the earth's womb! In the bitterness of my spirit, from the depths of my hatred, I curse you and your task. I curse your people and their accursed fate. I curse God!"

"Silence! Let your tongue not blaspheme!"

"Yours is the blasphemy, not mine. Even beasts and birds have mates and whelps, but I, I . . . I shall do . . . what *I* want! Engine of destruction you have made me. Monster misshapen you have created me. Despoiled of God's image and bereaved of man's solace, I shall wreak havoc on this world. From out of this hell you have made within me, I shall make a hell without. Everywhere I shall sow ruin and plant destruction. Whenever I see man, like a wild beast, I shall destroy him. From this day forward it shall be war between me and men, between me and you, between me and God!"

He raised his hands to the heavens, pleading, rebellious. "Strike me down with a bolt! Almighty, melt me once more into the clay I was when I lay at peace with myself in the darkness!" Then, with a look of fierce loathing, the Golem fled.

XII

The time had come to confer once more with the Cardinal, for, with the Golem's disappearance, Rabbi Low now sought the prelate's protection. The Cardinal, he knew, would be little disposed to provide such help and Pokorny's hussars would be even less disposed to stand between their own people and the ghetto's Jews. More often than not in the past, the soldiers had made common cause with the rabble and joined in the pillage, plunder, and killing.

"Convince them," Meisel advised, "that we are necessary to their commerce, to their prosperity, to their very survival. They will be persuaded by their pocketbooks and their bellies, not by their Christian consciences. Moral exhortation is useless. The *yetzer tov* is a rivulet, the *yetzer hara* a waterfall. Remind them

that when Ferdinand and Isabella drove our brethren out of
Spain, the fortunes of Castile went over the Pyrenees, across the
Straits and the Mediterranean, never to return. Remind them—"

"As you reminded Emperor Rudolf, Marcus?" the Rabbi asked.
"As you convinced him that you were essential to his good
fortune?"

Meisel did not give ground. "The Emperor was at Vyšehrad.
On every other occasion he has come to my aid, defended my
house, my very life."

"He need fail you—us—only once, as he did at Vyšehrad, and
all is lost."

"Has not the Lord Himself failed us?" Meisel asked.

Perhaps the Golem's flight signaled that the Lord had indeed
turned His countenance away. Yet as Rabbi of Prague he would
have to defend Jewish innocence because the Jews *were* innocent, but to proclaim that innocence meant proclaiming the guilt
of the Christians; for if the Jews had committed no crime, then
Christians for a thousand years, from Constantine onward, had
committed the most monstrous crimes of murder and mayhem,
torture and ostracism, hatred and intolerance against them. Did
he dare accuse Christians of what was clear for all clear-eyed
men to see?

Addressing his letter to the Cardinal, Rabbi Low recalled the
ruff of white hair, the ironic flourishes of beringed fingers,
the quiet cynicism of the worldly, pursed mouth, aware that
the tolerant skeptic was often as great a threat as the firebrand
fanatic. The Cardinal would act only in what he deemed to be
his interest, or that of his Church; he would swim with the tide,
taking advantage of every eddy and current. That was part of
what had made Johann Silvester a Cardinal, and wasn't it after
all a form of wisdom not to fight the tide—of ignorance, violence,
hatred, evil—if one would not be inundated? If Jews were assassins of God, and therefore beyond the pale, how could any moral
appeal in their behalf carry any weight?

The Rabbi's believing fingers wrote even as his questioning
mind doubted. "I demand justice for my persecuted people. It
is a sin against God, against humanity, against the very teachings
of Jesus, to persecute those who were Jesus' brethren, whose lan-

guage he spoke, whose land he trod, to whom he hoped to bring redemption." Rabbi Low requested the Cardinal to give him the opportunity to hold a disputation with the priesthood on those matters which were inflaming the populace and which, if not checked in time, were sure to end in violence and bloodshed. Since Friar Thaddeus was most vehement in the charges against his people, charges of ritual slaughter and blasphemy that were most likely to result in discord, the Rabbi suggested that Thaddeus be his opponent in the disputation. Such public airing of their differences he knew was instinct with danger to his people and to public order, but with Passover and Easter close upon them, and with the tension between the ghetto and the rest of the community already on the brink of violence, such a disputation might be risked in the hope that public discussion would dispel some of the tensions.

Closeted in Meisel's sumptuous salon, Rabbi Low showed the letter to the financier before dispatching it. Meisel was pacing, having only recently recovered sufficiently to dispense with the aid of his cane. "Even if the Cardinal agrees, what useful purpose can it serve?" Meisel asked. "There is no possibility of overcoming the ill will that Thaddeus has so assiduously cultivated. And you cannot win such a dispute. If you win, you lose. That risk a prudent businessman does not take."

"I am not a businessman," Rabbi Low said bluntly.

"Nor prudent. If you lose, the entire Jewish community loses with you."

"I had hoped other measures . . ."

"Your Joseph Golem?"

Rabbi Low nodded. "But I can think of nothing else now."

"Has he run away?"

"Yes."

"All for a wench. Couldn't you have let him have the girl? Or told me, so that I could have kept Jitka from going off with that popinjay of an ostler? Not that I believe any one man, even your vaunted Golem, could hold off Thaddeus' hordes."

"Kaethe Hoch is my ward. She was not to be traded like a pelt, or used like a towel."

"How lofty!" Meisel muttered. His face changed abruptly as he realized who Kaethe was. "The Hochs' child. My old friends."

The soft radiance suddenly suffusing his features made Rabbi Low wonder if there had truly been something between Marcus Meisel and Malka Hoch. Was Kaethe their natural child and not the offspring of Joachim and Malka Hoch? the *momzer* Marcus had refused to acknowledge? It might even explain why long ago Meisel had suggested that the girl be taken into the Rabbi's house and not into his own.

"If Joachim were alive, I am sure he would have been happy to have his daughter marry Joseph Golem so that the community might be saved," Meisel remarked.

It was not the remark of a father about a daughter, even a daughter denied—yet it could be. Who knew the serpentine mysteries of the *yetzer* and its resentments? And surely it was the comment of a childless man.

"You suggest? The Emperor once again? The Cardinal's hussars? Jacob Nissan's callow youths?" the Rabbi asked sardonically. "Or perhaps you would again like to try to buy off Brother Thaddeus?"

Meisel stopped pacing. "You know?"

"Prague is a great city, but in some ways it remains a village. I had the news six hours after your emissaries made Thaddeus your offer."

"And a good offer it was. Twenty thousand gulden!"

"The friar is a zealot, Marcus. Madmen cannot be bought off that way."

"Nor reasoned out of their madness either."

"I doubt that Thaddeus will be persuaded."

"Then whom are you persuading?"

"All of them," the Rabbi acknowledged.

"If my reliance on gulden and thaler is foolish, Judah, how much more foolish is your reliance on reason and argument."

"And faith?"

The financier looked at his shoes.

"Every day man is sold and every day redeemed, Marcus. Every day miracles are performed for him as they were performed for our forefathers who were freed from Egypt."

"The Lord commands us *not* to await His miracles, Judah."

"That is why I want to send this letter to the Cardinal."

"Judah, you are carried away with your obsession to be a savior."

"If no one else can save, shall I forbear to try? Is it evil to wish to save one's people?"

"It is the *yetzer*, Judah, the pride that apes humility, the arrogance of one who sets himself in the forefront without remembering that those who remain behind him must pay for his affront. You are not the Messiah nor were meant to be."

The Rabbi raised himself from the chair, his deeply lined face sorrowful. "I must go ahead, Marcus."

Meisel's pacing stopped. "I too would save Jews, Judah. I, too, have lain awake in the nights trying to find a way, *the* way. I have talked to the Emperor. I went to the Castle myself. Rudolf has promised that his own soldiers will guard the ghetto. He has given me his word that there will be no desecration of the Passover."

"Do you have confidence in his word?"

Meisel gestured uncertainly.

"Or his troops, even if the Emperor should keep his word?"

Firmly the financier shook his head.

Dozing and jarringly waking that night, Rabbi Low lay on his bed and saw an apparition that was the Golem running wild on the mountainside, uprooting trees and cleaving rocks, howling at the stars. Joseph Golem. Was he now only a predator at the edge of the human flock waiting to seize a lamb and rend it limb from limb? The Golem's flight, Isaac's fears, Jacob's belligerence, and Meisel's calculated opposition all bid him withhold the letter, but his own instincts urged the disputation on him.

In the morning after he had prayed and had no sign, he gave the message to Isaac to be conveyed to the Cardinal.

The Cardinal's reply was not long in coming. Pokorny delivered it himself, smelling of perfume, dressed like a fop, but his dirk and sword loose in their scabbards. The Cardinal welcomed the Rabbi's suggestion. The disputation would probably take place very soon, though a date had not yet been decided upon. All would, of course, be able to speak freely, without fear of reprisal. Thaddeus was more than willing to be the Rabbi's antagonist. "But," Pokorny added, with his usual flourish, "the friar also insisted that, should he win, he must then be allowed a greater latitude in making converts among your people."

"I did not know he had been restrained at all," Rabbi Low remarked.

"He has been restrained," Pokorny replied, laughing, "gently, but not too gently."

"Do you mean that the Cardinal cannot forever restrain him?"

"Even a Prince of the Church can do only so much. For a long time the friar has wanted to burn your holy books too. The Cardinal has laughed away his obsession. If the friar should win this dispute, laughter will not be enough."

"The Cardinal will then reward him for winning."

"Or losing. You must throw a dog a bone." Pokorny laughed again, then was abruptly serious. "Rabbi, I cannot see what you hope to gain from such a contest."

"Is that the Cardinal's view too?"

"The Cardinal is a Prince of the Church," Pokorny said loftily, yet not without mockery, "and his duty is to capture souls for the faith."

"The view is your own then as well?"

Pokorny made a low, formal bow. "If a plain soldier may have a view of his own."

"The plainer the man the plainer his opinion," the Rabbi murmured. "What then would a plain soldier suggest for dealing with Thaddeus?"

His left fist clutching the handle of his sword, the heel of his right palm resting lightly on the haft of his dirk, his eyes so narrowed that their color disappeared in the slits, Pokorny said coldly, "Kill him. One thrust beneath his ribs with a dirk and you have done the friar the great service he covets. You have dispatched him to heaven, to joy everlasting."

"And made him a martyr," the Rabbi added.

Pokorny shrugged. "Martyr. Saint. What does that matter?"

"The making of Christian saints and martyrs has too often been attended by spurting Jewish blood."

"Kill him," Pokorny advised again. "Even if it means a little of your fellow Jews' blood. Unless you do, Thaddeus will be a thorn in your side as long as he lives. He will give you neither peace nor rest until he has driven you out, plundered your possessions, or brought you to the baptismal font." His wintry laugh echoed bleakly in the room. "I forget. You Jews don't know of the therapeutic virtues of killing, do you?"

"*Whoever kills Cain shall himself be killed*," Rabbi Low replied. But the Talmudic injunction also declared that if a man came to kill you, you were permitted to kill him first. Yet once the killing began, there was no end: Killing followed killing to the end of time. Hatred bred revenge and the desire for revenge bred new murder. And so man lost his most valuable possession, his *tzelem Elohim*, his Godly image, that within him which distinguished his humanity. Redemption was not in the hands of those who killed, but in the hands of those who yearned for peace. Yet, he reminded himself, he had put the redemption of the ghetto in the hands of the Golem, given him the right, no, commanded him, to shed the blood of those who came to kill Jews. And he had felt free to do so because the Golem did not have the *tzelem Elohim*, was only a vessel of clay, perhaps now already shattered.

For a long while Pokorny stared at him, unbelieving. Then, as if pronouncing sentence on all of them, he said, "You are a doomed people. You seek death as lovers seek an embrace, as if it could warm your flesh. Sometimes you must kill a man because he carries the plague." He was about to depart, but remembered something and turned back again. "The Cardinal said that the *first* disputation will, of course, be private." A curious lilt at the end of the sentence left the Rabbi guessing whether it was a statement or a question, but before he could inquire further, Pokorny was gone.

Rabbi Low sat staring into space, seeing a sickle-shaped sword reaping a harvest of Jews by a frozen river where all the trees had been peeled and stood like skeletons, deformed, iced. In that endless forest of frozen corpses death had swallowed up all mankind and the earth was left forever barren. The vision burned, fire and ice, without a single green leaf on any tree, until he buried his face in his hands to shut it out.

XIII

For the day of disputation, Rabbi Low decreed that all the Jews of Prague were to fast and to pray in the synagogues, especially to recite the Psalms. Before he set out, the Rabbi himself sang softly the prayerful words to give him courage:

> . . . And he will deliver thee from the snare of the fowler
> And from the noisome pestilence.
> He will cover thee with His pinions,
> And under His wings shalt thou take refuge;
> His truth is a shield and a buckler.
>
> A thousand may fall at thy side,
> And ten thousand at thy right hand;
> It shall not come nigh thee.

Meisel's carriage was waiting. The financier, about to take snuff, forebore when the Rabbi sat next to him. As they drove off and Meisel's footman, Petr Singer, let the curtains down, Rabbi Low caught a glimpse of the Golem standing in a narrow alleyway, but when he parted the curtains to look again, no one was there. They rode until Rabbi Low recognized the gates of the residence into which Pokorny had once before led him and the Golem. When the carriage came to a halt, Meisel said softly, under his breath, "Sometimes it pays to give the appearance of losing to win."

"Marcus, I want to win only peace for our people, nothing more."

"A very great deal to win, Judah. It requires skill, forebearance, and good fortune."

In front of the ornate entranceway Pokorny, blank-faced and formal, greeted them and led them to what evidently was both a dining room and meeting hall. Although they had arrived early, the others were waiting: the Cardinal, the *burggraf*, two members of the town council known to be the most powerful, and two Dominican friars, one of them Thaddeus. Already seated at the long, highly polished table, the Cardinal at the head had the *burggraf* at his right, Thaddeus on his left; at the other end of the table two empty chairs had been left for them.

The formalities were swiftly dispatched, and when they were seated, the Cardinal began immediately. "This is to be an informal discussion among—shall we say?—friendly contestants. If we are able to reach agreement, perhaps we shall have no need of more formal and public disputation. Under the circumstances, and for everyone's benefit, it seemed wiser to have these exploratory talks first.

"We have come together to deal with a very delicate matter. Rabbi Low has requested an opportunity to dispute charges made against the Jews. He believes those charges will result in violence against his people and he knows the charges to be unjust. Such accusations, particularly that of ritual murder, he finds especially abhorrent and he would like, once and for all, to lay them to rest.

"Brother Thaddeus, on the other hand, sees our Christian community threatened by the presence of Jews in its midst. He believes that at best the Jews must be brought to the true faith, at worst driven from Prague and Bohemia. If neither can be accomplished, he would at the very least require the Talmud to be burned because he claims that the book is godless and blasphemes Christ. In spite of the testimony of the Popes and many other scholars, Jew and Christian alike, Brother Thaddeus remains convinced that Jews require Christian blood for the celebration of their Passover, but until he has absolute proof, he will hold this charge in abeyance. Lastly, he would like the Jews' commercial activities curtailed as a threat to the commerce of good Christians." The Cardinal's eyes swept the faces at the table and Rabbi Low watched their answering expressions with misgiving.

"We have asked Rabbi Low to come here, and the Emperor Rudolf himself, his gracious Majesty, has requested that Mordecai Meisel be permitted to accompany him, to which we have"—a condescending wave of beringed fingers—"of course consented." All nodded in Meisel's direction, except the two Dominicans who, hands bestowed beneath the table, sat rigidly unmoving.

"We all know the Emperor's great money magician," the *burggraf* said too heartily.

A thin smile gleamed on Meisel's lips, then was gone, but he said nothing.

"Brother Thaddeus will speak first," the Cardinal announced.

Thaddeus stood and walked away from the table, turning his back to them, his shoulders hunched, his hands prayerful in front of his chest. Among the others' brightly colored garments the monkish black and white habits and the Rabbi's dark gray clothes stood out stark and somber. Rabbi Low had never before been so close to the friar and he was seeing the man's face anew, a countenance he would not have recognized as the same one he had previously seen from a distance. Clean-shaven, his pale-as-parchment skin was drawn tightly over the bones of his face, his lips compressed into a thin mauve line of purpose. Taller and thinner than he seemed at the Meridi trial, Thaddeus had what Rabbi Low recognized as the slight questioning stoop of shoulder and tilt of head that bespoke the scholar; but with it were the quickstep march, the jerky motion of arms and legs that betrayed the barely contained flames of fanaticism. Abruptly, Thaddeus whirled to face them and, pointing an accusing finger, whispered hoarsely, "Why does your Rabbi Simon ben Yochai say, 'The best among the Gentiles deserves to be slain'? Why does your Talmud call for Jews to hate and do injury to Gentiles, to steal and plunder our possessions, even to kill us?"

There was a hush, but Thaddeus did not wait for an answer. He plunged on. "But that is *not* why your people are a bone in the throat to us." His hands clutched his windpipe, then relaxed and opened wide as the smile that accompanied the gesture. "We are not afraid that *you* will kill *us*, or seize our properties, or harm us—in a material way. The harm you threaten is to our faith, to our immortal souls. It is for these that we are locked in combat, mortal enemies."

His smile vanished, his voice grew more raucously resonant. "For sixteen centuries we have tried to show your people the light of salvation, to make them understand that Jesus the Christ came to earth, the Incarnation of God, His one and only begotten Son, have tried to reclaim them and all men for the Lord, to convince the Jews that in Jesus they would find fulfillment of all the hopes of Israel, of all the promise of the Messiah their own prophets had foretold. Matthew himself tells us that Jesus said, *Think not I am come to destroy the law or the prophets: I am come not to destroy but to fulfill.*"

Thaddeus' hands covered his face, slender, wiry hands covered with short ginger-colored hair, the blue veins on their backs prominent. In his Dominican habit, his feet shod in rough herdsman's leather sandals, their thongs biting into his ankles, his whole body quivered in ecstasy of accusation. That is what Amos must have looked like, Rabbi Low thought, when the prophet came up from the herdsmen of Tekoa to preach the Lord's word to the corrupt and mighty of Jerusalem. Without removing his hands from his face, his voice muffled as if with tears, Thaddeus cried out, "Though He came to earth incarnate, the Lord's one and only Son, you killed him. You crucified our Lord! *Depart from me, for you have had intercourse with my murderers,* Saint John Chrysostom says to you for all Christians, for the crime you have committed is without parallel—and without expiation. Because of it every Christian's duty is to shun and hate you.

"Yet Christ is merciful. His Church is merciful. Our outstretched hands have pleaded with you to join us in His brotherhood. Our Church has offered you the baptismal font to cleanse yourselves, called you to conversion to renew yourselves, to seek salvation, the only salvation for the human race, through the death of the crucified Christ, a crucifixion to atone for that original sin with which mankind has been infected through Adam's fall.

"But no call has convinced, no kindness softened your hearts. Though the Lord has driven you into exile over the face of the earth, afflicted you with persecution, you have rejected our comfort, blasphemed our Savior and our Church, and gone your own stiff-necked way, a people accursed, reviled of all men, anathema." His hands fell away from his face, his eyes closed, his lips purpled in anguish. "Your fate has been beautifully published by Pope Innocent III: *The Jews, like Cain, are doomed to wander the earth as fugitives and vagabonds, and their faces shall be covered with shame.*

"Yet"—the friar's arms reached out to beg them, his eyes opened tear-filled to beseech them—"we are charged with the holy task of saving Jewish souls, of recalling them from the errant road they had trod for centuries; and unremittingly we have striven to perform our holy duty. We do so here, now."

As the friar sat down, the other friar crossed himself, as did the *burggraf* and one of the town council members, but the Cardinal seemed unmoved. His fingers drummed silently on the table for a few minutes, tribute to Thaddeus' ardor, before he turned and said, "Rabbi?"

Rabbi Low stood and felt his age drop away like a skin of ancient use. The sense of foreboding was in his throat but his mounting anger drove it out, turning his words to fire in his mouth. "For sixteen centuries," he began, "you have treated us to your Christian love—and we have nearly died of it. For more than a thousand years, in Spain and France, in Germany and England, here in Bohemia itself, you have shouted, 'Death to the Jews!' and burned us at the stake, driven us over cliffs and into rivers, violated our women, seized and forcibly converted our children. *All in the name of Christian love!* You have herded us like animals into our synagogues and set them to the torch while you danced around in religious raptures and sang, *Christ, we adore Thee!*

"All forms of love are sanctioned by the Church in saving souls. For if you torture us, flay us, burn us, behead us, those are after all only temporal pains soon to be submerged in death, and you are struggling for our eternal life. Is this the way you seek to lead us to the baptismal font? Is this the Christian love you seek to demonstrate to us? We have heard often enough of Jesus' command to Peter, *Put away the sword*, but we have seen no sign of it.

"Did Jews ever use crucifixion as a form of punishment? Crucifixion was a contribution *not* of Mosaic law but of Roman law. The Jews have killed our lord, you berate us, and for that murder you condemn us like Cain to eternal wandering and homelessness. If my people did crucify Jesus and Jesus willed his crucifixion, then we have only obeyed his desire and helped him perform the miracle of his crucifixion and resurrection that you hold so dear. What cause is there then for hating and persecuting us for it thereafter? If Jesus' crucifixion was imposed on him against his will, how then can he be god and still too powerless to thwart the will of those who nailed him to the cross? How, too, can he be the Messiah? If he did not have the power even to save his own life, can he be the savior of all mankind? Can man kill God at all? What logic is there, what reason in such dogma?" His hands trembled before him as if palsied and he clasped them together to stop their shaking. "What faith?

"And then, displaying your vaunted Christian charity, you promise to forgive us for a murder we have never committed if only we will be sweetly reasonable and accept Jesus as savior and fall into the arms of your church. Only then will you permit us to be redeemed from our exile, only then will you allow our fate to be transfigured.

"You damn us as stiff-necked and self-willed, obstinate and blind, for not being able to see our salvation in Jesus and the church. Yet where you see salvation, we see only idolatry. To assert that God was born of woman and took human form is blasphemy. Must omnipotent God stoop to be born of woman?"

Thaddeus could bear it no longer. Eyes blazing, face aflame, he leaped to his feet shouting, *"Salus extra ecclesiam non est!"*

No one spoke. The friar and the Rabbi stood facing each other until, with an effort, Thaddeus brought himself under control.

"The Messiah has come," he declared firmly, "that same Messiah prophesied by your own prophets, that Christ Jesus whose Incarnation has redeemed Adam's fall and all men's sins. Yet you will not accept that sacrifice and redemption. Are we not justified in condemning your obstinacy?"

Ignoring Meisel's warning look, repudiating the quavering of his own limbs, Rabbi Low replied, "Are we accursed and nefarious because we do not accept Jesus as the Messiah foretold? If the incarnation of Jesus was the Almighty's way of liberating the world and man from sin, would we not have more tangible signs of that liberation? Are men or the world better since? Do we not still murder and cheat and steal and bear false witness and commit adultery? Have we come to love our neighbors as ourselves? Have we stopped making war and brought God's peace to all the earth?"

The friar stared into each of their faces, then turned his eyes up to the heavens and, wringing his hands, announced, "In the name of the Father and of the Son and of the Holy Ghost, give judgment for me, O God, and decide my cause against an unholy people. . . .

"I believe in one God, Father almighty, Maker of heaven and earth, and of all things visible and invisible. And in one Lord, Jesus Christ, the only-begotten Son of God. Born of the Father before all ages. God of God, light of light, true God of true God. Begotten not made: of one being with the Father; by whom all things were made. Who for us men, and for our salvation came down from heaven." He genuflected. "And was made flesh by the Holy Ghost, of the Virgin Mary: and was made man. He was also crucified for us. . . ." As Thaddeus went on intoning the creed, the others bowed their heads and joined him. Rabbi Low caught the Cardinal's eyes then; cold and hard, they reflected the light now as harshly as did his rings. His pursed lips did not move: He simply waited for the others to finish. ". . . in one, holy, catholic and apostolic Church. I confess one baptism for the remission of sins. And I look for the resurrection of the dead. And the life of the world to come. Amen."

The Amens echoed around the table, then Thaddeus spoke directly in what could only be a warning and a threat. "For Jesus said, *Do not think that I have come to send peace upon the earth; I have come to bring a sword, not peace.* And the Christ advised,

And he that hath no sword, let him sell his garment, and buy one."

The Cardinal let the silence be prolonged until all attention was focused on him, then he began, "*Rabbi* means *teacher*, does it not?"

Rabbi Low nodded.

"To be a teacher means also to be a student, for one can teach only what one studies. I see that you have studied our faith, Rabbi, and tried to know it, but perhaps you have not truly understood what our Church can and must do. Our Church is the Messiah of the Messiah. On our ample shoulders has devolved the duty to lead men on earth, to govern them here, to provide the spiritual needs whereby they ultimately ascend to bliss everlasting, for man does not live by bread alone.

"Yet bread he must have. And with the sweat of his brow earn it as his women must in sorrow bring forth their children, for this world is a vale of tears. In that vale of tears men must have a Shepherd to lead them and the Church is shepherd to the flock.

"*And the flock must be led.* With care and concern and strength, and always with absolute certainty. For what man covets beyond all else is certainty in this uncertain world. Certainty and bread, bread and certainty.

"You and your people, Rabbi, threaten both our bread and our certainty. We must see your people in our midst as a foreign body, a social irritant, as Brother Thaddeus put it, a bone in the throat of our Christian society. To accept too large numbers among us of those who, because they are different, necessarily turn the eyes and hearts of our people from the Church is difficult for us. If it is our Christian duty to hate the Jews for being the assassins of God, Saint Augustine has also cautioned us"—he looked significantly at the two Dominicans, but particularly at Thaddeus—"that the Jews are a witness people and though they must bear on their foreheads the mark of Cain, they must not be slaughtered."

"We are not a proselytizing faith, Cardinal," Rabbi Low said. "We do not seek new adherents; we discourage them. The conditions of our life discourage them."

"True, Rabbi, which is one reason we do not permit those conditions to improve overmuch. But one diverts, converts, and even perverts simply by being there. An example? An alternative? As you endure our persecution and dislike, perhaps even our compassion and our desire to turn you to the true faith and the true Church, so too we find distasteful your pride. You do not marry among us, or join us in our amusements, or eat and drink with us. You hold yourself separate and above us. You are forever turning your other cheek to remind us how brutal and savage we are. You are forever at your books and business when we are carousing or sporting. You are forever working when we are lying abed or staring up at the heavens from a field of rye. You show us your scorn on every occasion, betraying a moral aversion to us and an intellectual superiority over us that we find intolerable."

The Cardinal's glance grazed their faces, before he added, "And you do not work with us. You do not till the soil—"

"Forgive me for interrupting," Mordecai Meisel said.

"Reb Meisel," the Cardinal acknowledged, "I wondered when we should hear from you."

"Theology, Your Eminence, is not my métier, so I have held my tongue in the presence of my betters. We Jews do not, in the event, care much for theology. Ours is a people obsessed by God, but concerned less with the problems of theology than with those of justice and morality, less with the abstractions of the next world than with the concrete difficulties of this one.

"But about work and finance I do know something. You have organized your society to exclude Jews. You have striven to create a social structure neatly divided into those who work, war, and pray, and we have been denied all those functions. You have driven us off the land by tithing us and by prohibiting us from employing Christian laborers, by making ownership of land, or membership in a guild, a matter of taking a Christian oath, and finally you forbid us to own land altogether."

"*In Nomine Patris et Filii et Spiritus Sancti*," the other Dominican murmured.

"You forced us into trade and banking, which you condemn. You stimulated our taste for it by taxing us grievously, by confiscating our properties. You even made us *buy* the right to live, the *leibzoll*, with money. You sharpened our wits and our commercial practices if we would survive. You set us outside of your social fabric and made us outcasts. We had no legal rights, no rightful place. And because we had no rights, we could only live by your pleasure, caprice, or charity. We are forced to curry favors and plead for privileges so you could both condemn us for fawning and take our monies for granting us what should have been ours by right.

"Of course, when you need us, to build your commerce, your trade, to teach you and to conduct for you the arts of taxation and banking and finance, you invite us into your countries and, after a fashion, permit us to live. We were useful in those pursuits because we had become experts. We were useful because we spoke many languages. We were useful because we had our coreligionists in other countries, and we could move easily between the Christian and Muslim worlds. And we were useful because those areas in which you permitted our endeavors were ones of great risk and danger, so that we were able to preempt them because so few were eager to risk their lives and fortunes.

"No sooner had you learned our skills, or decided that you no longer were in need of them, than you offered us only three bleak choices: annihilation, expulsion, or conversion. Sometimes, temporarily, there was a fourth choice, segregation. And sometimes, of course, you offered us no choice at all."

"In building a Christian commonwealth," Thaddeus commented, "there are only small corners where your people can cower, only fringes where they can be permitted to exist."

Meisel ignored the friar and addressed himself further to the Cardinal. "You forbid us intermarriage and cohabitation with Christians on pain of death; then you criticize us for being clannish and holding ourselves superior. You bid us wear yellow discs and hats and scarves, the same ones with which, ironically, the Muslims had long ago marked Christians with shame—then excoriate us for being different. You forbid us to live together with you as neighbors, pen us into ghettos, then condemn us for keeping to ourselves. If you twist an arm long enough, you may strengthen it, you may make it more cunning, but you will surely also warp it."

"Yet you survived," the Cardinal observed, "even prospered."

Meisel's smile was sardonic. "*Some of us survived.* A remnant only was saved. And only a remnant of that remnant has prospered. But most Jews have been able honestly to echo that plaint one of our poets, Ibn Ezra, made long ago in Spain:

If I sold shrouds, no one would die;
If I sold lamps, then in the sky
The sun, for spite,
Would shine all night."

Everyone except the two friars laughed. Pokorny's chuckle
from the door echoed and drew the Cardinal's attention. With a
gesture he summoned the Count, whispered in his ear, then
peremptorily announced, "We have explored our differences. If
we have reached no agreement, we have managed to define our
conflicts. Perhaps further discussion should await another occasion."

"Your Eminence," Thaddeus began, half-rising from his seat,
but the Cardinal's cold stare stopped him, and he sat back. The
burggraf and council members made their obeisances and departed. Then the Dominicans knelt before the Cardinal and kissed
his ring before they walked together toward the door. "*Domini
canes*," the Cardinal remarked, deliberately before the friars were
quite out of earshot. "*The Dogs of God!* A good phrase for
them, don't you think?"

Neither Rabbi Low nor Meisel answered. They too rose to go,
but the Cardinal's outstretched arm detained them. "There are
still a few things we must talk about, Rabbi," he said. "I thought
it better to do so privately. You, too, Reb Meisel," the Cardinal
added when the financier bowed and walked toward the door.
"Please sit down."

Wearily the Cardinal rested his face in his hands, the sound of
his breathing heavy in the room. When he shook himself erect
again, he said, "We old men tire too quickly. Now when we have
enough wisdom to be useful, we sometimes lack the strength."
He laughed ruefully. "I can see that you both understand.
Pokorny!" he called. "Bring some wine." Pokorny brought a
decanter and three goblets. "Gentlemen, will you join me?"
Pokorny filled the three goblets before the Cardinal caught their
reluctance and sighed, "I forget. You do not share food and drink
with us. Too bad. You will excuse me, then. Your health." He
toasted them, then lingeringly sipped the wine until he had
emptied the goblet.

"I am sorry," he continued, "that Reb Meisel argued your

case so convincingly. Sometimes it pays to lose a skirmish in order to win a war."

The Rabbi and Meisel exchanged glances and Meisel burst into sardonic laughter. The Cardinal was nonplussed.

"That was precisely what Reb Meisel was trying to persuade me of before we arrived," Rabbi Low explained.

"The Emperor assured me that Reb Meisel was an astute diplomat," the Cardinal said, "as well as a clever banker."

"Rabbi Low's plain speech moved me to speak more plainly than I intended, Your Eminence," Meisel apologized, recognizing the Cardinal's comment for the rebuke it was. "As did Friar Thaddeus' fervor."

The Cardinal nodded. "We get carried away. And that is what we must *not* do now."

"Or be swept away," the Rabbi added.

"Yes, yes, that *is* your dilemma." The Cardinal paused, staring vacant-eyed beyond them. His hand reached blindly for the wine carafe, but Pokorny was there before his groping hand found it, and poured the goblet full once more. "I see no true reconciliation between our faiths. Any more than I see reconciliation now between the Mother Church and its children of Huss and Wycliffe and Luther. Toleration, perhaps, but only after long bloodletting." The Cardinal brought the goblet to his mouth, his lips barely brushing the wine. "We are on the verge of a great war in which the Church and Empire will be rocked by the Protestant powers and princes. Unless you are very careful, you Jews will be caught between the hammer and the anvil."

"Are you suggesting an alliance, Your Eminence?" Meisel inquired.

The financier's question interrupted the Cardinal's train of thought. "Such an alliance is impossible for us both," the Cardinal said. "We are like two sons born of the same father struggling for his patrimony. You are the eldest and insist on your privilege and primacy because of primogeniture: You are the Chosen. We are younger, yet maintain that we are superior, that we have outdistanced you: We are the Choice."

"Whose voice is Jacob's," the Rabbi asked softly, "and whose hands Esau's?"

The Cardinal seemed not to have heard. "As once you transcended the pagans," he continued, "so now we have outgrown you and our Jewish origins, as Saul of Tarsus who became Paul outgrew Jesus of Nazareth. We Christians understood men better, we saw their needs more nakedly and honestly. You believed men were created in the image of God and holy, capable of knowing and keeping the way. But we knew that men were flawed from birth with sin from which there was no escape, stones by the builder rejected, yet the only stones upon which the Church could be built. Men were weak and uncertain, stupid and superstitious, full of fraud and illusion, violent and self-willed, whose towering ambition set them stumbling blindly in the morass of their own making. Man was his own worst enemy, the worst enemy of civilization, perhaps the worst enemy of God. Because we perceived man's weakness and folly and evil, we knew what had to be done to save him.

"With one hand we held out the carrot of mercy; with the other we threatened with the stick of eternal damnation, hellfire and all its torments. Mercy was what they cried out for, not the rigors of justice. The yoke of the law was too heavy for them. In the arms of Mother Church we assured them of mercy everlasting, of the certainty of forgiveness; we abandoned the law.

"We humanized your faceless, nameless God, incarnated Him, gave Him a Father and a Holy Mother, made Him understandable to even the most ignorant, troubled, and humble by making Him a poor carpenter born of obscure parents in a manger. We made Him a God of love, of Divine and Infinite love, not of Divine justice, because only from Divine and Infinite love could come Divine and Infinite mercy. We went further. We knew that men could not imagine what they could not see or touch, could not imagine God, so we gave them the cross and the lamb and the fish. We showed them the Passion, the Incarnation, the Birth. We painted Golgotha, Gethsemane, and even the Manger, sculpted them, carved them, set them into colored mosaics. We did not insist on His absolute unity because we remembered the power of men's pagan allegiances to Ishtar and Tammuz, to Isis and her son Horus, and in order that the people should not revert to paganism, we gave them merciful Mary the Holy Mother and Merciful Jesus her Son.

"We knew how hard this world is for most men so we told

them that His kingdom was not of this world as theirs was not. We promised them the kingdom of heaven, the kingdom of the next world. The world they would inherit. For the bread of affliction that you proffered, we substituted the Host of hope, the partaking of the wafer and the wine. We let them raise the chalice of salvation to their lips with His blood and let them partake of the consecration of His flesh in the bread so that they would be chastened and uplifted by a new eternal covenant of unending forgiveness and life eternal. We joined the sinful imperfect victim to the pure, the holy, the all-perfect Victim, *Hostiam puram, Hostiam sanctam, Hostiam immaculatam.* We went beyond Abraham's symbolic sacrifice of Isaac to the real Crucifixion with its blood and nails, vinegar and crown of thorns, and His Infinite suffering by comparison made their finite miseries, however grinding, smaller and more bearable. For the suffering they had to endure in life, we told them of God Who so loved them and the world that He gave His only begotten Son to be crucified for them. What human being could be asked for more, for greater sacrifice, could suffer more than that?

"Like sheep they huddled together against the cold winds of life, so we joined them into a single great flock where they might find comfort in numbers, and we became their shepherd. The True Church relieved them of the terror and anxiety that is human unhappiness. They would not now have to think or ask or dare. Everything was explained, simply, clearly, miraculously. Our infallibility provided them with certainty, confidence, forgiveness, peace, so they would be, could be happy. Only they must have faith. All of them—except those of us who knew."

He stopped and drained the goblet. "Let this cup pass from my lips?" the Cardinal asked, grimacing. "The few of us who have tasted this bitter cup and, like our Lord, must drink it, cry out in the dark hours before dawn, *Eli, Eli, why hast Thou forsaken me?* but in the bright days we smile and frown and guard the people against themselves."

No one spoke for a very long time, then Pokorny coughed and once more woke the Cardinal from his torment. "We chose the power of the world and seized the Roman sword to take it. It meant strife and warfare, but we remembered Jesus' admonitions: *Do not think that I have come to send peace upon the earth;*

*I have come to bring a sword, not peace. Suppose ye that I am
come to give peace on earth? I tell you, nay; but rather division.
The father shall be divided against the son, and the son against the
father.* We became bringers of death that we might be the bringers of life, that at the last we might yet bring the kingdom of
David to the people and make them a perfect society, a Messianic
brotherhood of man under the fatherhood of God with the Holy
Church their all-embracing Mother.

"But you Jews denied that the Messiah had come at all. You
looked for signs and symbols and portents, and could find none.
The wolf had *not* lain down with the lamb. Swords and spears
were *not* beaten into plowshares or pruninghooks. We did *not*
yet love our neighbors as ourselves. But *we* knew it could be
worse yet; just as we hoped we could make it better.

"So we went beyond you and in doing so made you our enemy
—and our victim. We left you behind and went instead to the
heathen to convert them. We gave up being the Chosen to become the Choice, but in our persecution we preserved you. We
took your book, made it ours, and so saved it for all mankind. We
made you an accursed and outcast people, but we saved a remnant of you, as we shall continue to save a remnant of you, for
you are witness to our miracle and our meaning."

Rabbi Low listened, painfully intent, his old hands on the table
still shaking because he could not stop them. "You have saved us
as a witness people," Rabbi Low said softly, "but we believe it is
the Almighty Who saved us. And Who shall save us unto eternity.
We have survived and we shall somehow contrive to survive in
spite of your persecution, *not* because of it. Even if you kept us
alive only as witnesses to your passion, should we be grateful
therefore? Perhaps the future belongs to the victims, to those who
are persecuted, for the presence of the Lord is always with the
persecuted, even with the justly persecuted.

"You say we Jews have misjudged men and perhaps you are
right. Yet neither your baptism nor our circumcision has sealed
the redemption of men. Neither your people nor ours show the
signs that the Messiah has arrived or that his arrival is impending. The human race has not been regenerated either by your
faith and love, or by our justice and mercy.

"But at least we have laid no claim to earthly power and so

we do not accept any responsibility for its evils. Once you were persecuted as we are, but you abandoned the byroads of gentleness for the highway of violence. You took up Caesar's sword, but at what price? In ruling the terrestrial kingdom you have committed the most grievous sin of pride by seeking to bring the perfect society here on earth with the sword, without the Messiah, without the regeneration of man, perhaps even without God. From this sinful pride has followed inevitable disaster. Are you not chastened by a thousand years of seeing whole peoples beggared and ruined, the fields of Europe devastated and blood-soaked? All in the name of Jesus and with the blessings of the church.

"You proclaim that men are all alike, or mostly alike, and want only bread and certainty, a happiness that means freedom from hunger and fear, but also freedom from responsibility and truth. Men are *not* alike. Men are more various than the beasts of the field. They cannot be made alike. And if they could, would that universal Christian commonwealth be anything more than the tyranny and order of the beehive or anthill?

"Law and justice may prove rigid and sterile, but your stressing love above all else is morbid emotionalism, a sickly sentimentality. Your praise of love and faith alone as redeeming leads to the deprecation of reason and free will, to superstition and an unhealthy desire for the miraculous, and finally to blind faith, the *Credo quia impossibile.* In spite of our own Maimonides, we believe that life is a mysterious process in which God performs acts which man's mind can never comprehend or explain, so that we are not without faith. But we are also convinced that reason is the voice of God in man, part of the *tzelem Elohim,* the image of God in man, that cannot be dispensed with; and we are persuaded that your original sin, combined with the primacy you give to faith and love, deprives man of his intellectual and moral birthright as a child of God.

"Your disparagement of the body, your stress on mortification of the flesh, on virginity and monasticism, on asceticism, we find wrong and unhealthy. The body too is the Lord's and the flesh and all its functions are creations of the Almighty and as perfect therefore as the soul. The Lord's *Be fruitful and multiply* is a saner and holier commandment than Paul's *It is better to marry than to burn* We may not be able to promise our flock the bliss of heaven as you do, and it may be more difficult and painstaking to earn our share of the world to come, but the joys of the flesh, the earthly comforts of marriage, children, and home are not yet to be despised.

"However incomprehensible to the mind of man, we insist at last on the absolute unity of God: *Hear, O Israel, the Lord our God, the Lord is One.*"

The Cardinal poured his goblet full once more, this time too quickly for Pokorny to do it for him. He only wet his lips briefly before he replied. "If men would have peace and bread and serenity, then they must endure the tyranny of the beehive and anthill. There is no other way to cope with the problems of men. And it will be a universal tyranny, for all nations, for all mankind to endure alike. In the bosom of the Church it will at least be a benevolent tyranny. If men are forced to lay down their freedom and their individuality, they will be freed of hunger and anxiety and that terror which comes in the night."

His voice was tired, yet now it rose powerfully. "We speak with different tongues and voices, perhaps with an altogether different language, Rabbi, but I am grateful to you for speaking to me with such candor."

"The languages of our books are Hebrew and Aramaic," Rabbi Low commented, "the languages of yours Greek and Latin; yet truth may be spoken in any language."

"But now," the Cardinal continued, setting his goblet down and putting his hands on the table so that his rings flamed light, "we must understand each other very precisely. In three days you must appear for a public disputation with Brother Thaddeus where you will *not* be able to speak so well or so clearly as you have to me here."

"You mean, Cardinal, that you wish me to lose the dispute to Thaddeus."

The Cardinal nodded gravely. "It makes matters simpler. When you have lost, he and some of his friars and seminarians will go through the ghetto and you will have your people let them collect some of your holy books to be burned."

"I cannot permit that."

"You have little choice, Rabbi. Is it not better for paper and scrolls to go to the pyre than the flesh and bones of your people. If you refuse, the Dogs of God will lead the people in sacking the ghetto and I shall not be able to stop them. They will plunder, burn, rape, and kill. Once they have begun, who can tell where they will stop? The mob is a wild beast with a lust for blood."

"I cannot cooperate with the enemies of my people," Rabbi Low said. "I will not."

"The Emperor requested that we proceed in this manner," the Cardinal explained. "He is under great pressure."

The Rabbi turned on Meisel. "You knew!" he accused.

"I did not know *exactly* what would be proposed," Meisel said.

"So that was why you talked of losing to win."

"Now you *must* lose to win," Meisel reiterated.

"And if I refuse?" Rabbi Low asked.

"Thaddeus has told the Emperor Rudolf that the Jews pray for the 'downfall of the unrighteous kingdom,' and he has talked darkly of Jewish dealings with the Turks," the Cardinal reported.

"We do pray for that, but our prayers are for the downfall of the whole world of secular powers, our prayers are for a world of justice and peace to be proclaimed when the Messiah does come. Secular power is a tower of tyranny and Babel. All the kingdoms of men are unrighteous; only the Kingdom of God is just and holy."

"If you know that, Rabbi, then you will understand what the Emperor and the Church require of you now, what your own people need."

"That I betray them?"

"No, that you save them. When Thaddeus speaks of the downfall of the unrighteous kingdom in the disputation, you can reply that your prayers applied only to those ancient kingdoms that slew or persecuted the people of Israel—Egypt, Medea, Assyria. You will also say that you pray for Emperor Rudolf, for Bohemia, for the Holy Roman Empire, that you wish for the peace of the realm, for the prosperity and happiness of the people, for the Emperor's protection and well-being," the Cardinal advised.

Rabbi Low stood up abruptly. "Cardinal, we have lived in Bohemia for seven hundred years. . . ."

"Yes, Rabbi, I know." The Cardinal waved him to be seated. "But the mob neither knows nor cares. When the friars are through haranguing them, when the words and the wine have together done their work, they will be eager to save your souls with fire and sword, by destroying your lives and property."

"Then all things are legitimate in converting men to brotherly love," the Rabbi said.

The Cardinal threw up his hands and turned to Meisel. "Perhaps you can reason with him, Reb Meisel."

"We are grateful to you, Your Eminence," Meisel said, "for letting us speak our minds and hearts freely, and to know your advice and concern. We understand that it was in order for us to feel free *not* to speak them publicly three days from now."

"Exactly," the Cardinal agreed.

"We are very grateful," Meisel repeated.

"But we would be more grateful," Rabbi Low interjected, "if you did not throw us to the mob."

"Not you, Rabbi, nor your people, only a few of your books. They can be replaced."

"The word of God."

"Ink on paper, writing on scrolls," the Cardinal corrected. "It is a small price to pay."

"The *leibzoll*, once more, still, always."

"There are always prices to pay, Judah," Meisel said. "That is the way of the world. Give us a day to think this over, Your Eminence. We shall send word tomorrow."

"You have only two days, Reb Meisel. The disputation is on the third," the Cardinal said. "There is no need to send word, only to behave intelligently."

"I know, but the Rabbi must consider. We must speak to our people. Even a little time will help."

Pokorny showed them out and, as he helped the Rabbi into the carriage, he asked, "Would not a dirk under the ribs have been better?"

"No," Rabbi Low replied emphatically. "*Seek not to revenge yourself upon the man who has abused you. Be thou rather the man who is abused and humble of spirit.* Better our holy books be burned by his hands than Thaddeus' life taken by our hands." And then Meisel's carriage drove off.

XIV

They met in the "garden of the dead" because it was the only place they could think of to meet unobserved. Each day when she brought him food and drink, the top of her golden head rose like a sun above the forest of tombstones and, his heart lurching within him, his breath trapped in his throat, he would rise from his hiding place to meet her. This day when her slender figure emerged from among the graves, he remained hidden, watching her, moved by her grace, touched by the look of puzzlement that gave way to alarm when she did not see him coming to meet her, touched by the rise in her voice from a cooing whispered "Joseph?" like a dove to an almost despairing "Joseph, where are you!" When he could not bear her anxiety for a moment longer, he stole up behind her and lifted her into his arms. She almost leaped from them with fright until she saw his face and then relaxed laughing against his chest. "Joseph, you'll make me drop the food," she cried, but she held him and burrowed her face into the hollow of his neck, her silk hair caressing, her nose cold. Nothing would give him more pleasure than to be greeted this way every day when he came home to her, to spend his life with her, yet he knew his life was not his own to spend, only the Rabbi's to wager as he saw fit.

He set her down and she looked him over appraisingly. "Are you well?" she asked.

"As well as I can be without you," he said softly, moving strands of her hair away from her eyes, back from her forehead behind her small ears.

Her fingers touched his cheek, traced his features. "You grow thinner each day." She dropped to her knees, spread a cloth, and put out his food in swift, sure movements. "Come, eat. You must be starved."

"*Let all who are hungry come and eat,*" the Golem mocked himself, but sat beside her and began to gnaw the chicken she had brought.

She watched, eyes full of concern, then asked, "Why don't you come back? He watches for you all the time, turning to see if you are at his elbow, always as if he were sure you would be there. At night he sits at the window looking down at the *Judengasse* as if at any moment he expected you to come striding down the street."

"How can I come back and sit at his table when he has taken you from me, given you to—Jacob Nissan?"

"I am his to give—"

"As I am—"

"Since I was a little girl. He took me in when no one else would, made me his ward, treated me like a daughter."

"But he does not treat me like his son!"

"God forbid! Bezalel is dead, poor soul, from the way the Rabbi treated him. Differently from everyone, from his daughters, from me. He had such high hopes for his only son, too high for Bezalel to reach."

"Why, did he not understand the boy?"

"Neither the boy nor the man." Kaethe shook her head sadly.

"Bezalel was a fine scholar, they say, a skilled teacher, a sweet boy, and a good man, but not his father, not the great Rabbi to lead a community, fight with the elders, restrain the unlawful and impious, contend with the *goyim*."

"Why did the Rabbi not let him teach then?"

"He could not. He was, after all, the Rabbi of Prague and Bezalel was his only son. He believed Bezalel should follow in his footsteps and so he commanded."

"All must follow *his* commands: Bezalel, you, me," the Golem objected. "Is he the Lord that all must do his will?"

"He is a wise and good man who has saved his people time and again."

"Is he wise and good to us?" the Golem asked. "To drive us to this?" Angrily he gestured at the tombstones around them, then turned gently to her, pleading, "Let us leave here, Kaethe. Let us go away from this whole miserable ghetto and its people."

Kaethe took his hand between hers and rubbed it against her cheek, silent, sorrowful.

When he had finished eating, she asked, "Where would we go, Joseph? We are Jews. Who would take us in? How would we live?"

"I don't know, but we would live." He looked around again. "I hate all this. There are other, better places to live." He remembered the sun-spattered green lake where he and Jitka had swum in the mountains, and he began to tell Kaethe about it, describing the blue, pine-covered, rolling hills, the smell of balsam and fir, the small animals swift with fear but beautiful in the brush, the flit of brilliant birds in the trees, the stars at night like glowing pebbles in the riverbed of heaven.

"Was that where you went with her?" Kaethe asked, dropping his hand into her lap.

"Her?" the Golem asked, abruptly recalled from the dream of Kaethe by his side in the shimmering shade of the abandoned shepherd's hut.

"Jitka Myslikova," Kaethe said. "I heard her name. The girl you brought back to Prague for Meisel's trial, the one who ran off with that Hungarian ostler."

He hung his head.

"Did you love her?" Kaethe asked softly.

He shook his head. "No. She was kind to me."

"Only kind to you?"

"I don't know what 'only' means. Kindness was a great deal to me, not 'only.' "

"You know what I mean," she replied impatiently. "Did you . . . make love to her?"

His green eyes filled with tears. "She was kind to me," he repeated, "very kind to me."

"Kinder than I am?" she asked.

It was some time before he answered, solemnly, "No one is kinder to me than you are."

"You are making fun of me."

Slowly he wagged his head. "No."

"Joseph, do you love me?" Her fingers pressed his hand for a reply, for reassurance.

"I love you, Kaethe," he said.

"Then why are you not kind to me . . . as you were to her? Why do you not let me . . . be kind to you as she was?"

With his finger, he traced the blond arch of her brows, the pursed lilt of her lips. "I cannot."

"Why not?" Her nails bit into his palm.

"Because I love you," he said.

"Is that a reason?"

"The best, Kaethe, and the only."

"You will not change your mind, Joseph, not even if I must marry Jacob Nissan?"

He remembered the apple sweetness of Jitka Myslikova's breasts, the wet earth of her thighs, and shuddered. "Not unless he will let you marry me."

While he buried the remains of the food, she picked up what she had to take back to the kitchen, hiding it under her skirts, as she said, weeping, "It will never be."

"It will never be," he echoed.

Blindly she pressed herself against him and then turned and made her forlorn way through the gravestones back toward the *Altneuschul* and the Rabbi's house.

XV

At morning prayers members of the *Altneuschul* congregation were already aware of the disputation, quarreling so loudly about what should be done that Rabbi Low reprimanded them sharply for disrupting prayer and violating the dignity of the service. Afterward, they besieged him with questions until he retreated to his study. Even there, all through the day Jews came from the Meisel and *Höhe* Synagogues, from the Klaus, from the Jewish Town Hall, from the *Chevra Kedisha,* from off the streets, to inquire, to plead, to advise, to threaten. Some, like Isaac, came to comfort; a few, like Jacob, came to counsel resisting with all their might any incursions into the ghetto. But most entreated him not to anger the authorities or provoke the mob, to give in this time, on this issue, so that there would be no bloodshed. The

Rabbi listened, hoping that some might show him a way, but none did.

How the people of the ghetto all knew what had transpired at the Cardinal's, the Rabbi could not discover. When taxed with having spoken, Meisel denied that he had even mentioned it to Frumett, and since Rabbi Low himself had told no one, he could only conclude that the Cardinal had seen to it that rumors were deliberately and accurately circulated in the *Judenstadt* so that Jews would bring pressure to bear on the Rabbi to submit.

"Don't underestimate Johann Silvester," Mordecai Meisel said late that night when he arrived at the Rabbi's study to disclose that he had gone to the Castle to see Emperor Rudolf. "He is a man of subtlety and skill and, where possible, of compassion."

"He swims with the tide," Rabbi Low insisted.

"How else can anyone swim," Meisel asked angrily, "against it?"

"You have done so, Marcus. Often. With me and with others. With the Jewish community, with the elders, with the *goyim*. Even, I suspect, with the Emperor."

Meisel refused comment. Instead, he revealed that the Emperor had told him there was nothing the monarchy could do to help. The pressure from the Pope, from the Holy Office, from Jesuits and Dominicans, was very great, and although the Emperor and Cardinal had resisted long and stubbornly, they now had to offer some token act of compliance. Burning books had been the best compromise they could arrive at.

Meisel took a pinch of snuff, sneezed heartily, then said, "I reminded him how we had earlier, reluctantly, had to submit to expurgating the Talmud, how this was one step further along the road of persecution. I asked how far we had to go, how far he had to go, to appease the Pope and the Holy Office."

"And he said?"

The Emperor had assured him that they must make this further step. They must also continue to believe that the Emperor was well-disposed toward the Jews as a community and individually, for Meisel himself knew how complicated were the religious, dynastic, economic, and territorial conflicts in which they were involved, how difficult relations were with the Papacy and the holy orders. The overwhelming majority of Bohemia remained Protestant, and the issues that had come down from the time of Huss and Žižka were still unresolved. The German Protestant princes were fulminating conspiracy after conspiracy. Though the Bohemian nobles and gentry favored the Jews, the burghers and the people did not. The Pope had issued a bull declaring the Talmud accursed, and both Dominicans and Jesuits continued to proclaim that the Talmud blasphemed God, vilified Jesus, and distorted the Bible itself: It must, they clamored, be burned.

The Emperor had hesitated a long time before concluding, but when he had, his words were iron. The Emperor did not think he would have to appeal to Jews to consider the consequences of their refusal. Did Meisel not remember the great ghetto fire of 1559 when the rabble, instead of helping the Jews to put out the flames, had thrown Jewish women and children into the inferno and then sacked the ghetto? Did he not recall Emperor Ferdinand's expulsion of the Jews in 1561? Meisel had told him more than once that the whole Meisel family had been driven from Prague then. Did he not recollect the royal decree that made it mandatory that Prague Jews attend a Jesuit sermon once a week in the Salvator Church and also send their children? Were those things preferable? As if that were not enough, Meisel knew as well as any man in Europe that tens of thousands of Huguenots had perished in the massacre of Saint Bartholomew in 1572 on the command of the Papacy. Did he for a moment believe that the Pope loved the Jews more than French Protestants or Swiss Calvinists?

Meisel was an astute man, a man of the world: He should know better. Would it be happier if the Jewish community were wiped out altogether or expelled from Prague?

Unless Rabbi Low agreed to lose the public disputation with Friar Thaddeus, so that the cutting edge of the people's hatred was dulled, the Emperor could not prevent what bloody consequences would ensue.

"Our people, too, have raged against me, threatened and cajoled, begged me to give in," the Rabbi told Meisel. "All have accused me of arrogance or selfishness, of every sin but venality." For a moment his voice became younger and mocking as he imitated those who belabored him. "You are too old, Rabbi. You are soon to die and you are not afraid. But what of us? We *are* afraid. We are young and have children. We do not want to die or to be uprooted once more." In his normal voice, he added, "How frightened they are!"

"Would that you had more fear," Meisel declared.

"Do you really want that? If I were that kind of man, that kind of rabbi, would you have troubled to bring me from Posen? Would you have gone through the difficulties and expense of making me financially independent of you, of the community elders, so that my integrity could not be impugned or my judgment swayed by the need to feed my wife and children?"

Meisel sat, opening and closing the snuffbox. "I sought you out, Judah, because Prague needed you, because I needed you to help me here, because you were a man above other men, close to God yet not too far from men. Though you were proud and intelligent, your tongue did not flay the hide off a man's back for asking stupid questions, as Solomon Luria's did. You had a compassionate heart, but . . ." His voice faded away.

"But?" the Rabbi insisted.

"You are a different man since the community refused to make Bezalel your successor," Meisel said, then gently, "since Bezalel died."

"Bezalel. My beloved son," the Rabbi lamented. His eyes filled with unshed tears. "Bezalel would have carried on what we had begun, Marcus. He would have stood fast against the discord and the selfishness of the ghetto, against its divisiveness, against the greed and violence of the *goyim* outside.

"Bezalel would have insisted on teaching Bible and Talmud to build character, to preserve our traditions, instead of sending students off on the crooked paths of sterile hairsplitting and useless, showy disputation," the Rabbi said. "But when the community rejected him, Bezalel was so embittered, so crushed, he couldn't understand what had happened to him. I told him of the years I had spent in Nikolsburg and Posen, how they had rejected me too, before you brought me back to Prague to the Klaus. I explained how the community elders preferred Isaac Hayyot as rabbi in 1583, how I was forced to work in the schools instead, how I waited five years in Posen before I was able to return again to Prague, and how I was an old man when finally I did. But he couldn't hear me. Bezalel had lost all patience, Marcus. He could not endure their scorn."

"*He who publicly offends his fellow creature foregoes eternal life; an offense in public is the desecration of a man created like all men in the image of God,*" Meisel proclaimed.

"Ah, Marcus, you flatter me by speaking my own words back to me now, but you would flatter me more if you had heeded them," the Rabbi said.

"You mean that I might have kept Bezalel in Prague, don't you, Judah? You have never before spoken of it to me, nor reproved me; but I have sensed your disappointment, and your anguish."

"No, Marcus, I meant that about the disputation with Thaddeus the day after tomorrow. . . . *Could* you have kept Bezalel in Prague?"

Meisel shook his head. Finally he took his snuff again, breathed it in deeply before stifling a sneeze. "Bezalel was too young, too impatient. He did not understand the people, the vying for power in the ghetto. He was not strong enough to stand against our sins and our selfishness, as you have."

"He *was* too young," Rabbi Low admitted. "That was why I wanted him to be my deputy for a while, to learn, to mature."

"Bezalel was not built for the task, Judah. He belonged in his school in Kolín. He was a fine teacher, but not man enough to be Rabbi of Prague. You are convinced that Bezalel died of a broken heart, but I don't believe that people die of broken hearts. Of broken heads, of broken bones, yes; but not of broken hearts. If they did, Judah, I would have died after I buried Eva. But you told me then that it was sinful to mourn further, that I had to go on with my life and my work. You bid me marry again, perhaps even have children. You encouraged me and I went forward."

"*Enjoy life with a wife whom thou lovest*, Ecclesiastes counsels. Was I wrong, Marcus?"

"You were right. Frumett has been a good wife. She has filled my life, and, if . . . if I have never quite forgotten Eva, if sometimes in the night her face, the smell of her fills my head like snuff so powerful that I am unable to sneeze her away, yet the day does finally come and Frumett is with me then. My work has been good. I have believed my life to be worthwhile, that I was building more than my own personal fortune, that I was helping to build a better future for our people, for all the people of Bohemia."

"And so you have, Marcus. Few men can boast of such good works."

"I did try to keep Bezalel in Prague, because of you. But the elders took their own course and opposed me. Not, as you know, for the first time. Had I considered the issue urgent enough, perhaps I might have been able to override them, but I didn't. He was your son, so I did try. I do not regret that I went no further, nor do I think I did wrong."

"You have not had a son, Marcus, you cannot know what it means to see your flesh and blood turned away like that."

Meisel made no reply.

The Rabbi rose and put his hand on Meisel's shoulder. "I am sorry, Marcus. I spoke out of my private pain, without thought. Forgive me."

"The Lord has deprived me of children and I shall never know why. Both with Eva and with Frumett, so that I must assume the fault is mine, not theirs."

"Only God can tell."

"I want no consolation. My nephews have been almost like sons to me."

"The two Samuels are fine men," the Rabbi avowed.

"However fine they are, they too are unequal to our tasks. However good a man and a teacher Bezalel was, he was not the *Höhe* Rabbi Low."

"And now the *Höhe* Rabbi Low must walk low."

"Pride, Judah, pride. If you persist, the consequence will be blood."

"Will it come to that?"

"I believe what the Cardinal and the Emperor have said. Theirs was not an idle threat. Circumstances will produce it: the greed and hatred of the rabble, the ambitions of the burghers, the fanaticism of Thaddeus."

"So you would have me violate a principle I have defended all my life, a principle I have judged and penalized others for failing: Do not cooperate with Christians in persecuting and oppressing Jews."

"Pride or principle, Judah?"

"Can you separate one from the other? To hand over our holy books to the rabble is a profanation of God's name, *Chillul Ha-shem*."

"Does that profanation require *Kiddush Ha-shem*? Will martyrdom to sanctify God's name do more than have our people killed?"

"Will this mock combat avoid the consequences or merely inflame the real combat to come, Marcus? Or is this all simply the outgrowth of the all-consuming fear of wounding the feelings of Christian dignitaries?"

"Offending them may consume us. It does not take too much affront, or what they fancy to be affront, for their rabble to reach for sword and torch, for their priests to invoke the rack and the wheel and the stake," Meisel said softly. He rose. "I can tell you no more than you already know as well as I do. You will argue all sides of this question with yourself better than anyone else. What is being asked of you *is* distasteful. A demanding and demeaning task. But remember, Judah: Whosoever shortens life even for an instant is a murderer."

"The Talmud is as a thing alive for us. If I turn it over to them for burning, that too is murder."

"Judah, Judah, your good sense has deserted you. The Talmud cannot be destroyed by fire nor besmirched by ignorant riffraff. *A synagogue retains its holiness even after it has been desolated.* Remember, they have burned our books before, but have not succeeded in wiping them from the scrolls of our memories. And shamefully we have burned our own books. Did we not burn the great Maimonides' *Guide to the Perplexed*, and were we able thereby to extirpate it from our hearts?"

"Marcus, I cannot. It is not the Talmud alone, but working with those who afflict us."

"You must, Judah. The other way bloodshed lies."

XVI

Never before had the Rabbi entered the Cardinal's palace. There, in the great hall, in spite of himself, he was momentarily dazzled. High, vaulted Gothic ceilings were beamed, spandrels carved with the arms of the city's guilds. Pillared walls were decorated with sculptured white reliefs of Jesus, the apostles, and the saints. Great round-arch windows soared from floor to ceiling and huge wooden doors, massive and somber, were set in all exits and entrances. The hall was packed with thousands of people. All Prague seemed to have come to watch the spectacle of "the defender of the faith" vanquish the Rabbi of "the accursed tribe." Nobles caparisoned in rich furred capes rubbed shoulders with merchants in heavy velvet mantles and with smiths and butchers, wainwrights and carpenters, whose leather jerkins proclaimed their guild marks.

Ladies of the nobility, their wasp waists tightly corseted, looked askance at burly peasant women from whose skirts children hung in clusters, at some who held infants at the breast, but the peasant women seemed unconscious of their disapproval. Stationed at the doors and windows, halberdiers and pikemen, in buff coats, stood guard. Around them were the only empty spaces, little clearings between those who carried arms and those who did not.

The serried ranks of the dais led up to the high seat on which the Cardinal sat, flanked by bishops and attended by deacons and acolytes. Below were the *burggraf*, the town council, the city magistrates, their uniforms weighted down by medallions and the heavy gold chains and keys of their office, which clanked on their chests when they moved. Scarlet and gold, silver and purple, they were an imperial panoply. All carried arms—swords, dirks, poniards.

On one side of the dais, where Thaddeus stood, a host of priests, monks, friars, and seminarians prayed and told their beads. Crucifixes and banners held high, they made a pool of darkness in the sea of color. On his side the Rabbi saw the group of Jews who had accompanied him from the ghetto being jostled away from the dais by the nobles and merchants. Yellow discs, hats, and armbands marked them and they stood crowded together, all except Mordecai Meisel who, refusing to relinquish his position at the dais and unmarked by the yellow badge, stood steadfast.

All except the Jews knelt when the Cardinal blessed the people and the proceedings, then briefly proclaimed that the disputation between Friar Thaddeus and Rabbi Low should be attended with respect and silence. Thaddeus was to speak first and he raised his arms and waited until a hush had settled. "Why," he asked, his voice silken and powerful, "does the Rabbi Simon ben Yochai say, *The best among the Gentiles deserves to be slain?* Why does your Talmud call for Jews to hate and do injury to Gentiles, to steal and plunder our possessions, even to kill us?"

It was the same charge the friar had leveled in private, and Rabbi Low set out to deny it. He tried to explain the difference between the law itself, *halakha*, and those legends which over the ages have collected around the law, *aggada*. The latter was only interpretation that expressed individual opinions; it was therefore neither authoritative nor binding. Among such *aggadic* materials were comments like those of Simon ben Yochai that Thaddeus had quoted.

The rumble from the audience, the satisfied look on the faces of the Dominicans, and Meisel's sardonic grimace all told him that his explanation had failed. Forced back on another interpretation he knew to be only partly true, the Rabbi tried to make clear that when Talmudic law spoke of Gentiles it referred not to Christians but only to the ancient pagan idol worshipers, Moabites, Edomites, Amorites. "*The righteous of all nations have a share of the world to come*, the Tosefta Sanhedrin tells us. And elsewhere we are enjoined to respect the righteous heathen. Even more so are we required to respect those non-Jews who believe in God. *He who honors the Divinity in any righteous manner*, the Otiot of Rabbi Akiba commands us, *even if his belief is different from ours, should be treated exactly the same as a Jew.*"

He saw that now he had at least neutralized the effect of Thaddeus' initial assault. Yet, in doing so, Rabbi Low knew he was conceding, giving ground, despite himself.

"Why do the Jews exalt themselves as 'the chosen people,' a people superior to others and special to God?" Thaddeus asked. "Or is it only as the prophet Amos said of you, *You only have I known of all the families of earth; therefore will I visit upon you all your iniquities?* Your same Rabbi ben Yochai boasts, *You are called men, but the other nations are not called men.* What are we then, beasts?"

Laughter and applause greeted his sally. Some in the audience called out, "Arrogant swine!"

"If we are stiff-necked," Rabbi Low replied, "it is because the Lord has placed a heavy yoke on our necks, the yoke of the Law. God chose us to bear that burden to be an example to the nations. *If ye will hearken unto My voice indeed and keep My covenant, then ye shall be Mine own treasure among all peoples. . . . And ye shall be unto Me a kingdom of priests and a holy nation.* God accepts all men who abandon idolatry and cleave unto Him. On our holy days we pray that *all created beings may unite into a single covenant.* All mankind is descended from the Lord's creation, Adam, and all are equal in God's sight. The prophet Malachi has said, *Have we not all one Father?*"

Pointing his finger at the group of Jews, an island in the crowd,

Thaddeus roared, "The Book of Leviticus says, *For the life of the flesh is in the blood*. Is that why your people require Christian blood for their Passover, for their unleavened bread and ceremonial wine?"

Sadness and sudden nausea overcame Rabbi Low. For four and a half centuries over all Europe the accusation had endured without a shred of evidence. Christian ignorance of Jewish law and lore permitted them to believe what any vicious apostate or demagogue asserted was true in Jewish religion, custom, and language. Yet ignorance in no way reduced the efficacy of such charges; quite the contrary. He remembered Pliny's account that Egyptian Pharaohs, when stricken with elephantiasis, had bathed in the blood of Jewish children every morning and evening. The Egyptians had, therefore, slaughtered one hundred and fifty children each day and night so that their Pharaohs might recover. Had Pliny's tale, too, been completely untrue and had the Jews then also been misled?

"Leviticus also ordains," the Rabbi said calmly, "*You shall not eat with the blood*. Our people have long had an aversion to blood. The commandments prohibit us from killing, remind us that life is sacred, so that we do not shed blood lightly even to eat. Our dietary laws order us to let the blood drain away from the meat we eat. The Talmud reinforces the charge of Scripture, prompting us to recall that he who destroys a single life, it is as if he had destroyed all creation; while he who saves but one single life, it is as if he had saved all creation."

The disputation continued in the same vein, the identical questions the church had been asking for four hundred years, questions ferreted out by fanatics and apostates, scholars and priests, which called into question foolish and ambiguous points in the Talmud and the liturgy, which discovered equivocal, contradictory, or illogical phrases that might be construed as defaming Jesus or questioning some aspect of Christian dogma. He gave Thaddeus the same replies Nachmanides had given to Pablo Christiani in Barcelona in 1263 or Rabbi Yehiel had proposed to Nicholas Donin's accusations in Paris in 1242, the same responses Judah Ha-levi had so poetically composed for enlightening his legendary monarch, the skeptical yet credulous Al Khazari—and they were worse than useless. Such replies had not helped his ancestors in

Spain or France, in Germany or Italy, any more than they would now avail in Bohemia. Humiliation was certain; despair unavoidable—but blood?

After a time Rabbi Low answered almost automatically, with only half his mind, knowing hopelessly that nothing he said could change the outcome, not certain whether he had deliberately decided to give up the contest or had been overwhelmed. Before him the faces of the crowd swam, faces of nobles and gentry amused, haughty, and occasionally even sympathetic; of burghers calculating and competitive; of outraged priests, frightened guildsmen, and uncertain women and children; but the worst were the peasant and priest faces, eyes wide with hatred, anger-twisted mouths self-righteously roaring: Kill! Kill! Kill! The faces of the Jews were pathetic, terrified by the roaring of the crowd, dismayed when his rejoinders seemed too effective, crestfallen when Thaddeus or his Dominicans seemed set back by their own clumsiness or ignorance. Only Meisel's countenance and the Cardinal's seemed urbane, altogether masked and supernal in their disdain, but by no means disinterested: observant, waiting falcons. At the very last Rabbi Low caught a glimpse of the Golem. Standing way back in the hall, head and shoulders above even the tallest in the crowd, his face was full of grief as, inexorably, Thaddeus' victory came into view. Even across all those heads he read the love in the Golem's eyes. "My son," he thought dizzily, as the face of his beloved Bezalel flickered over the Golem's coarse features, replaced them, was there and gone. Rabbi Low rubbed his eyes, the delirium hot in his mind and cold in his loins, the bitterness like the taste of metal in his mouth. All at once he knew that he had accepted defeat and degradation as inevitable. What shall a man do to live? He shall deaden himself....

The verdict was unequivocal, announced by the bishop who stood at the Cardinal's right hand. After the long hours of the disputation, it came almost as a relief.

In the name of the Father, the Son, and the Holy Ghost, the Jews are declared to have been defeated in this disputation, carefully weighed, and in strict judgment found wanting.

The bishop's face grew red, the veins in his neck stood out as in a loud voice he proclaimed in Latin, then in German, and last in Czech the verdict and the sentence.

Fortified against the madness of those who repeat with a perverse mouth that Christ our Savior is not the Messiah, Friar Thaddeus has been declared victorious over those intolerably proud Jews whose habit is seeking protection of their iniquity by defending their sins and error, who accumulate damnation and perdition by despising and opposing truth, and who subject themselves to the burden of the devil by refusing to be among Christ's sheep.

Though he spoke at the top of his voice, the bishop's words carried only a little way into the crowd. There they were picked up by the people and relayed back, wave on wave, word on word, trough and peak of sound, until they had rippled to the most distant limits of the crowd.

The Church is the ark of salvation and those who refuse its sanctuary perish in eternal damnation with the prince of darkness who is king over all the sons of pride.

The Golem stood near the exit farthest from the dais. Watching him, his eyes straining to see that distance, what he saw blurred by tears, Rabbi Low wondered if the Golem had put his hands to his ears to shut out the tidings announced, or merely cupped his hands the better to hear them.

The condition of suffering that one undergoes as the ungodly is very often the last trial. Letting the Jews pass through a time of persecution is a useful probation. On the morrow, at noon, in the square of the Judenstadt, *therefore, they will be required to comply with our edict to burn all the copies of the Talmud and the holy books in their possession.*

He had lost, or won and lost, or lost to win. Did his intention matter now? Whatever the superiority of his scholarship, his logic, his skill in argument, his probity, how had he deluded himself that there was even the remotest chance that he would triumph? The Cardinal had warned him and there had been genuine kindness in the warning: Lose with grace a battle already decided, the Cardinal had advised, in which victory can bring you and your people only grief. The Cardinal had been prophetic. Once more the Almighty had turned His face away.

Two hours' walk, perhaps three miles, but it might have been an eternity. He had not anticipated how defrauded and degraded he would feel. Down from the heights of the Malá Strana, where the Cardinal's palace had been left behind, they trudged through the middle of the cobbled streets, through narrow arcades and shadowed loggias, and everywhere the stream of people parted before them like the waters of the Sea of Reeds, but not without curses, kicks, and blows, stones flung. Rabbi Low was glad to suffer such mortification, but angry with those of his companions who flinched or fawned to avoid a blow. He did not rebuke them; instead, he spurred them on, and he and Mordecai Meisel, arms linked, went ahead to lead the procession, heads high, not deigning to take account of those who harried them. Out of the corner of his eye, the Rabbi saw the Golem wading through the crowd on a course parallel to their own, but he did not come into the street to accompany them, and the Rabbi did not beckon.

They walked across the Moldau on the Charles Bridge and turned toward the ghetto, when Rabbi Low stumbled and fell to one knee. Meisel bent to help him. A churl leaped out of the crowd, but before he could smash his stave down on the Rabbi's head, the Golem had seized it, broken it, and sent the knave reeling. From then on, taking the Rabbi's other arm, he walked with them.

When they were in sight of the *Judenstadt*, most of the Jews broke and ran for the protection of the *Altneuschul*. The crowd let them go, pelting them with stones, hurrying them with sticks, then closed ominously around the Rabbi and the small group that remained clustered defensively around him. Hands pounded them, tore their clothes, and spattered them with muck and dung.

The Golem struck out. Bodies fell backward, noses spurted blood, mouths spat out teeth, until, without warning, Pokorny's hussars were charging into the crowd. Sword in one hand, dirk in the other, Pokorny leaped from the saddle to a position next to the Golem. In minutes they had cleared a small circle around the Rabbi, Meisel, and the other Jews, and in the face of the hussars' lances the mob retreated sullenly down the street.

"You see"—Pokorny laughed—"the Cardinal is a man of his word."

Before anyone could reply, he was back in the saddle, weapons sheathed and, with his horsemen, escorting them to the safety of the *Judenstadt*. When the Rabbi turned to lean on the Golem's arm, the Golem was gone; once more he put his weight on Meisel and went limping with him into the ghetto.

From the *Altneuschul* Rabbi Low gazed down the length of the *Judengasse*, the synagogue at one end and the cemetery at its side. A short distance and the long journey he must soon make. He felt his years more heavily than ever, yet his heart was gladdened because Joseph Golem had claimed them as his own, had at the last come forward and taken his place beside them, beside him. That imperfect creature, the creation not of his loins but of his hands, was not Bezalel, yet the Golem was as much of a son as he would now ever have. A veritable *kaddish*. He had lost the disputation. In doing so he felt besmirched. He knew the consequences would be even more demoralizing when they came, but in the Golem's fight for them, for him, was the only small victory out of that great defeat that he could accept.

XVII

All morning the Dominicans and their seminarians had led the great wooden-wheeled carts through the ghetto. Crucifixes held high, they went from house to house, from synagogue to house of study to school and library, to print shop and store, until they had filled the carts to overflowing. They were prepared. They knew where to look, which households contained volumes either for study or prayer, and when they did not find as many books or scrolls or manuscripts as they had been informed they would, they beat the owners with sticks and staves and often with their wooden crucifixes until a bloodied Jew produced a hidden prayer book, revealed a secreted Torah scroll, unearthed an ancient manuscript. It was the Talmud they sought, but because they could not read Hebrew and did not in any case care, they took every Hebrew writing they could find.

The marketplace had a holiday air. In the center of the square a circle had been formed by the Dominicans and their seminarians where on a raised platform like a catafalque sat the bishop who had announced the verdict of the book burning. At his right, triumphant, towering, Thaddeus stood, and as each cart brought its burden of precious books and dumped them on the ground, his face glowed like a small fire. On the cobblestones before him was a growing mound of holy books, sacred writings, priceless Hebrew manuscripts, Scrolls of the Law, fed by the carts that continued to bring their loads through the crowds of people until the pyramid was thousands of volumes. The Cardinal was not there and Rabbi Low did not know whether to respect his considered absence.

The people danced and sang around the great pyramid. Urged on by the friars and seminarians, the rabble tossed books high into the air and let them smash against the ground. Others ripped volumes into shreds and scattered them over the cobbles. A peasant loosed his codpiece and made water on a scroll and soon dozens of others, laughing uproariously, followed suit. A few went so far as to bare their bottoms to defecate on the writings.

The salvation of Israel was in the hands of the mob, Rabbi Low berated himself. Trampled, spat on, defiled, the legacy of the Lord was befouled. They had not expelled the Jews from Prague. But they were trying to expel them from the kingdom of their minds, the sanctuary of their hearts, which had sustained Jews in exile for fifteen centuries—and would sustain them until the Messiah came.

When the carts had finished, the seminarians circled the great pyramid, crucifixes and torches in hand, to light the bundles of twigs. At first only the smoke of smoldering parchment and paper arose, but soon the twigs burned and, whipped by the fresh morning breeze, the flames leaped skyward. Rabbi Low looked at them, the peasants and shepherds, the drovers and draymen, the goldsmiths and cobblers, none of whom could read, celebrating that roaring inferno, jigging and prancing, drinking wine and mead, making foul gestures and roaring filthy curses while others genuflected, told their beads, or knelt and prayed—and he was overwhelmed.

Among the crowd Rabbi Low recognized other Jews, cautious

without their yellow discs and headgear, who watched as the flames leaped up and bits of ash from what had once been holy —scroll, manuscript, and book—sifted down to whiten their beards and sting their eyeballs. The conflagration raged now, the mound was a pyre, the green fields of the Law were being burned to stubble—and the Rabbi could not contain his rage or his tears. "O Lord!" he cried out. "Why, O Lord?" but his voice caught in his throat, the words choking him, so that not even Mordecai Meisel, standing next to him, heard his anguish.

The bishop on the platform raised his arms and spoke above the inferno:

"This Church, though scattered over the whole world, diligently observes a single faith. It is as if it occupied but one house and it behaves as if it had but one mind and it teaches as if it had but one mouth. We therefore consign these pernicious instructions of the Jews to the flames because those nefarious wretches and their abominable doctrines cannot find eternal life in the single-minded house of the Church, and we condemn their books to perdition. To prevent their poisonous and serpentine wiles from afflicting the faithful, to destroy the contagion of their blasphemy, to prevent them from wreaking heresy and schism among the fellowship of the Church, we offer up these scrolls to our Savior Jesus Christ.

"We exhort and admonish all of you before God to beware all impious Jews who seduce the unwary, wrapping themselves up in the expressions of divine law, as it were with their sheepskins"—he gestured toward the blazing scrolls—"to hide their wolfishness and to prey upon the Lord's flock. We shall fight them to the death to preserve unspoiled the heritage of the Fathers, to safeguard this solid apostolic rock upon which Christ built the universal Church, to maintain us all safe and hallowed disciples of the true cross.

"May the Almighty God and His Son, our Lord and Savior, grant you His grace forever in recompense for your marvelous and abiding faith."

Rabbi Low heard the bishop's malediction, saw the transfigured ecstacy on Thaddeus' face, the vulgar cavorting and obscenity of the mob, and did not wait for the fire to burn itself out.

In the study, when Meisel opened his snuffbox, the Rabbi leaned over and took a pinch, sneezing uncontrollably. The acrid odor of the tobacco did not wipe the harsh smell of books burning from his head. He still breathed that stench and saw the cloud of smoke and ash that hung over the *Judenstadt* like a pall.

"Did you see him?" Meisel asked.

"Who?"

"Joseph Golem. In the crowd. Watching with such a pained expression I thought he might burst into tears."

"Torah, Talmud, and Megillot burning, Marcus. Enough to wring the hardest heart, to bring tears to the coldest eye."

"Better by far, Judah, than flesh burning, better than men, women, and children on the funeral pyre."

Rabbi Low said nothing. He stood staring out of the window into the empty *Judengasse*. Not a soul walked the streets. The Jews of the ghetto were barricaded in their houses, or in the synagogues, hoping that the mob, satisfied with burning their books, would not now turn on them with fire and sword.

In the *Altneuschul* someone had draped the Ark in black and covered the Scrolls of the Law with black cloth, no doubt one of their Spanish "refugees" whose custom that was in mourning destruction of the Temple. No prayer books were left, but none were necessary. Those who were there chanted the *Lamentations* and *Kinot* by heart, repeating with special fervor the dirge that Rabbi Meir of Rothenburg had written to lament another public book burning, in Paris, on June 17, 1242: "O Law that has been consumed by fire, seek the welfare of those who mourn for you . . . of those who gasp as they lie in the dust of the earth, who grieve and are bewildered over the conflagration of your parchments."

Standing before the congregation, chanting the *Kinot*, Rabbi Low still smelled the burning parchment, saw the holy books defiled and the Hebrew letters, graceful as blackbirds, flying up to the heavens. In mid-prayer, he saw the Golem and caught his eye; but the Golem turned his head and slipped silently out of the rear entrance. "The Lord has forsaken us once more," the Rabbi reflected.

Spring was in full blossom and Passover only weeks away when Meisel returned to Prague. He had been away since the book burning and, for an instant, when Pearl brought him into the study, the Rabbi did not recognize him. His features had so drastically changed in the month that he looked like an altogether different man. "Marcus," the Rabbi said, rising to greet him. "*Shalom!* I am happy to see you home in Prague."

Seating himself and taking a long breath of snuff, which brought on a weak spluttering sneeze, Meisel responded, "It is good to be home."

"Yes, Passover will be here in a few weeks," Rabbi Low said. "How I wish we could have our Seders together this year!"

"I too. How many times have we promised ourselves that pleasure, but each time . . . This will be our last chance, Judah."

"We shall have many more opportunities yet, Marcus. We are not so old."

"The change is remarkable, is it not?"

"What change?" Rabbi Low asked, but his tone betrayed him, tears gathered in his eyes, and Meisel awkwardly reached out and touched his hand. "There is no need for mourning, Judah. You do not have to console me—or tell me how well I look." He smiled. "The Lord has vouchsafed me more than my three score and ten, a long life. It is coming to an end. I can feel it, I can see it in my glass, but I am not afraid."

"You speak into the mouth of the Lord," Rabbi Low exclaimed.

Meisel heaved a sigh. "No, Judah, the time is near. My bones will no longer carry their burden. My limbs ache so that no sleep refreshes them. The taste in my mouth is already the taste of earth—"

"A passing indisposition. You work too hard, Marcus. You travel too much and too far. You need rest. The Passover will restore you."

Meisel shook his head. "Do not talk like Frumett. We are men, both of us old men. We know the way of life. The time for all arrives. When I returned and went to her room, Frumett looked at me and did not know me. For that moment, one of the longest and bitterest of my life, I saw myself a stranger in her eyes, an intruder she had never seen before. It was like being already dead.

It was only a moment, a flash of revelation, before it was past. But I knew, I knew. She had only confirmed the testimony of my glass.

"I want to make a will, Judah. And I want you to help me with it."

"I shall do as you ask, Marcus."

Meisel changed the subject. "I have been to see Emperor Rudolf. He was very jolly, for him, feeling clever and wanting me to feel grateful for the way in which he and the Cardinal had managed to save us from Thaddeus' worst. He reported, too, that Pokorny's hussars had seen to it that the rabble was dispersed after the books were ashes, though by then many were wild with drink and ready enough to put the ghetto to the torch. I told him how very grateful we all were and presented him with an antique ruby I had bought in the Levant, which I said the community had sent him for a gift."

"Was he pleased?"

"I had the feeling he thought it was not enough."

"Is there ever enough for an Emperor?"

"Probably not for any human being, emperor and goatherd alike. He reminded me of all the privileges he had granted my house, of all the kindnesses he had shown my people, as if he wanted me to know that he had done more for me and mine by far than could ever be repaid."

"Has he truly done so much?"

"He has let us live. In his way he has defended us from harm. He has let me, personally, grow rich and powerful."

"For a great price, Marcus."

Meisel nodded. "Surely. There is a *leibzoll* for everyone, everywhere, for those who sleep on the ground as for those who sleep on goosedown.

"The Emperor even hinted that if the Jews should bring some new prayer books and Torah scrolls to Prague, he would not be averse to it but would cast a blind eye on the smuggling. Only we may *not* bring any Talmuds."

"We might bring books from Vienna or Frankfurt," Rabbi Low murmured, "especially for the school and the children."

"I have seen to it," Meisel said. "The first shipment is already at my house. Most of it is for the school and the children, but there are also some prayer books, Passover *Haggadah*s, and many other books."

"You are Prague's most eminent and difficult Jew. You try to think of everything."

"Miška Meisel, the Emperor Rudolf's court Jew, the Prague ghetto's *shtadlan*." Meisel grinned, his face looking young again, even boyish. "What a strange way to be remembered. Not the way I think of myself at all. Or like to think of myself."

"Prague will *not* remember you as Rudolf's court Jew. Rest assured, Marcus. It will have mementos of you wherever it turns: two synagogues, the Jewish town hall, the Klaus, ritual baths, a hospital, a house of study, the cemetery enlarged—"

"That at least will soon be useful—"

"You have touched numberless lives. You have ransomed Jewish prisoners from the Turks, given dowries to impoverished brides, charity to widows and orphans. You have even contributed to many Christian charities—"

"The Emperor reminded me that *he* was to be my favorite Christian charity." Meisel smirked. "Why else had he permitted me to dispose of my own estate? What greater gift could he bestow than to allow me to pass all the property I have accumulated over my lifetime to my heirs?"

"I thought you had given him considerable monies he has never repaid."

"Nor ever will. That, Judah, is the Emperor's due. How else could he keep his Tycho Brahe and Johannes Kepler gazing up at the skies without my gold? Did you know that once, when Rudolf was hard-pressed, he locked up all the alchemists on Alchemists' Lane and ordered them to transmute base metals into gold?"

They laughed together.

"How sad, Judah," Meisel said, "that we have no sons to take up our burdens after us."

Again, Rabbi Low saw Bezalel's face, that last deathbed face, full of agonizing disappointment, and felt the pang of his son's absence. Yet he had had a son, he reminded himself, and Meisel had never had one. Bezalel had grown to be a man, a good man, and a scholar and teacher. Could he ask for more? He knew he could, but must not.

"Now I have the two Samuels and you have Joseph Golem," Meisel said, macabre humor in his tone. "And we must make do with them."

"We shall make do."

"We always have, Judah, haven't we?"

"With the Almighty's help, we have tried our best."

Together they began to work on the will. Meisel had brought a list of his assets and bequests, among them ten thousand florins as a gift to the Emperor, five thousand florins as a donation to the Cardinal Johann Silvester, another twenty thousand florins for a hospital for poor Christians and Jews alike, and many more. Meisel consulted the Rabbi on each bequest, its merits, its relative importance, and when they reached an agreement on the amount and how it was to be paid, they discussed the phrasing before inscribing the bequest on a sheet. Although the major portion of his fortune was to go to his wife and his nephews, so large and complex was the estate, so diverse the properties, that great precision had to attend each bequest. There were houses and land, jewels and promissory notes, gold and silver, and all kinds of currency: ordinary ducats and florins, Salzburg turnip ducats and Styrian gulden, English rose nobles and Portugalese florins, silver thaler and kreuzer, all amounting to more than a half million florins in cash alone, not counting the monies owed Meisel on notes.

They worked all through the night, considering and reconsidering, writing and rewriting, until at last the will seemed just. With the first light of dawn, they leaned back in their chairs and Meisel sighed, "A good night's work, Judah." For the first time in all the years he had known him, the Rabbi saw Meisel disheveled, his face and body limp with exhaustion, his limbs shaking.

They washed their hands and made the blessing, then donned their phylacteries and together said the morning prayer. When they intoned the *Elohey Neshomoh*, their eyes met and locked:

"O Lord, the spirit which Thou hast breathed into me is hallowed; Thou hast created it, Thou guardest it, and Thou wilt after a time take it from me, but wilt restore it to me in the other world. As long as my soul is within me, I will praise Thee, and will give thanks unto Thee, O Lord of the universe. Blessed art thou, O Lord, who restorest the spirit unto the dead."

XVIII

———•————•◄•►•————•———

A few days after Mordecai Meisel's will was formally witnessed, Isaac once again brought news that he had seen Joseph Golem with Kaethe Hoch in the old cemetery. "Why did you not rebuke them?" Rabbi Low asked sharply. He was sharper than he had intended to be because, though he was grateful to learn what was happening, he was as always distressed by those who, however well-intentioned, were talebearers. The habits of childhood die hard; he preferred some of them to what men thought to be the ways of maturity.

"I did not think it fitting," Isaac replied.

"Is it fitting that Kaethe should see Joseph when she is betrothed to Jacob Nissan?"

"Because I knew she was betrothed and because Jacob is my

friend, I came to tell you. But I do not relish carrying tales," Isaac said stiffly. "And was it for me to rebuke them?"

Rabbi Low shook his head apologetically. "No, Isaac," he replied, "that duty is mine. You were right not to interfere."

"And, Rabbi, I was afraid," Isaac continued bravely. "Joseph Golem seems to have grown more imposing, like a Goliath on the horizon about to battle all the hosts of Israel, as if he disdained everything about him. Yet something more human and gentle also moves in him, something imploring that might burst into tears or change into a caress." Isaac's voice shook. "I don't know, Rabbi, but I have been afraid of him ever since we . . ."—he stammered —"you . . . the Lord brought him forth from the Moldau clay."

"There is nothing to fear, Isaac. Joseph Golem is the Almighty's creation. The Golem will return to do His bidding in our behalf; he will be *our* David, not *their* Goliath," the Rabbi said.

Kaethe Hoch had changed too, the Rabbi saw. First the Golem, then Mordecai Meisel, and now, in his own house, his ward. People changed overnight, it seemed, before your eyes, but he knew that to be an illusion: All the tiny changes, the daily wounds were suddenly one day there in the face and posture, the changes that had for so long been burrowing beneath the surface were abruptly confirmed in the flesh. The untutored had their own way of marking it: *We are always unprepared for death, yet each day the Angel of Death sends us his little reminder of our mortality, a wrinkle, a sag, an ache, a pain, a scar.*

Kaethe was no longer the fifteen-year-old he had spoken to less than two months before, a child to be scolded and commanded. She was now a grown woman and such chiding was no longer appropriate and would no longer be effective. She had lost in the growth, but gained too. The fine glow of her skin, hair, and eyes had dimmed, her dancing walk had sobered to a stride, but new determination informed her. "You sent for me?" she asked, her face full of foreboding, her posture rebellious.

"Sit down, Kaethe," Rabbi Low said.

Unwillingly, gathering her skirts slowly around her, she sat.

"Have you been meeting Joseph?" he asked.

"I have been meeting him," Kaethe responded. "It is no secret. It is not forbidden. And it is not a sin."

"We have betrothed you to my most gifted student, a scholar and a fine man, a man who will make you a good husband. Yet you make public mockery of him and of your betrothal by seeking out Joseph Golem, displaying yourself with him for all eyes to see and for all tongues to wag about," the Rabbi upbraided her.

"I have not deliberately sought to mock Jacob Nissan, or you," Kaethe said. "I have simply wished to see Joseph while I could. And there was no other way."

"Joseph has disobeyed me. He was not to see you—and he has. His duty was to remain here—and he has run away."

"You ask too much of him, Rabbi, and of me." Kaethe bowed her head. "He loves me and I love him."

"You are Jacob Nissan's betrothed!"

"Must I be?"

"We have given our word and plighted your troth. We have set your dowry aside, to which Reb Meisel has contributed generously."

"At least in that he has acknowledged me!"

"Why should Mordecai Meisel *not* acknowledge you? Your parents, may they rest in peace, were his most cherished friends, and you their only child."

"Are you sure?"

"Of what, my child?"

"I am not a child! And if I were a child, *your* child, would you force me to marry Jacob Nissan?"

"Only a child would ask such a question!" he exclaimed scornfully. "There is no difference in the way we married our own daughters and the way we wish to marry you. Even the dowry is the same, more for you because of Meisel." He turned his back and stalked to the window, looking into the courtyard quiet to calm himself, angry for having lost his temper with her.

Her question clung to his mind like a briar. Were she his daughter, would he? He knew the answer: Law and custom were to be obeyed and preserved by all. He had given his daughter Leah to Isaac, and when she had died in childbirth, young and without issue, he had given their youngest, Sarah, in marriage to Isaac because Ruth, their second daughter, was already spoken for.

There had been no talk of love, no consideration of anything but a lasting and fruitful marriage. He knew the power of passion, knew it still though his flesh had failed him, knew it not as an old man remembers a rainy-day ache but as the powerful thrust of youthful desire, knew its need so intensely that he felt it insupportable and unmasterable though he had a hundred, a thousand times supported and mastered it. As Kaethe would have to do. As Joseph Golem would. As all men every day everywhere had to do.

Abruptly, Kaethe's first question stung him. "What did you mean," he asked, "about your being the Hochs' only child?"

"People have told me," she began hoarsely, "I have heard . . ." She could not continue. Rabbi Low waited. "They have called me bastard," she said finally. "Meisel's *momzer* cast off conveniently into the Rabbi's fold like an errant lamb. Another *nadler*. No one can say that the banker Meisel did not provide for his own. If he could not bear to acknowledge me publicly, or take me into his house to have me a living reprimand daily before his eyes, at least in the Rabbi's house his sin would become a *mitzvah*, the bastard merely a poor orphan."

Compassion flooded him, swept his anger away, shook him. "How long have you thought such things? Who has misled you with such slurs, maligned you with such vile gossip?"

Kaethe bit her lip, but did not speak.

"Will we never be through with this *momzer, nadler* misery?" he expostulated. "You are the daughter of Joachim and Malka Hoch. You are not a bastard, nor were your parents wayward. You are their only child, and without parents. Nor are you related by blood either to Mordecai Meisel or to me. Does that set your mind at rest?"

Kaethe nodded, then shrugged, and finally, hopelessly, helplessly, threw up her arms.

Rabbi Low saw her mien was just like Joseph's: I will do, I will obey; but what you do to me, what you make me do, I hate. It almost said as well: and I hate you for making me do it. He saw now what bound them together. In each other they had discovered a refuge from the world's oppression and rejection. Together, *momzer* and *golem*, they were outcasts. What mortar more fast for love? But not for marriage, for if they were arrayed together against the world, it was in their case their own Jewish world they opposed, and that could not be.

As if Kaethe had heard him thinking, she said, "I shall obey. I shall marry Jacob Nissan because you command it, because you and your wife have cared for me as if I were your own daughter, because even if I am not a . . . *momzer*, I am an orphan and a woman, and I would have neither dowry nor place to go were it not for you. But I shall marry Jacob Nissan with a dead heart, without love, without joy."

But with loyalty and restraint, respect and affection. Perhaps not so much, perhaps not even enough, but more than most received. "Joseph Golem is not a proper husband for you," the Rabbi said. "His tasks are not those of ordinary men, nor his pleasures."

"*You* say that! *You* make him what he is, what he is not!"

"The Lord has made him what he is, Kaethe, not I. He cannot avoid the Almighty's outstretched arm."

"I am a simple woman. Yes, a woman! Joseph is a poor woodcutter, but I do not care. I want to be his wife. Isn't that enough?"

"No, it is not enough. You are not suited. You must walk your separate paths."

"You are too old to know the wisdom of the heart. You have forgotten."

"You are too young to know the wisdom of the years. You have not lived long enough to see men and women and marriages."

She lifted her tormented face to him. "I beg you, Rabbi, let my heart live. Let me marry him."

Wearily, Rabbi Low put his hand on her fair hair and silently blessed her before he spoke. "Even if there were no other reasons, I could not permit the marriage because Joseph can have no children. Could I, however indulgent my heart, permit you to marry a man who cannot give you children?"

"No children?" Her lips trembled. "You are sure, Rabbi?"

Rabbi Low nodded, twice.

She fell to her knees, her fists beating the carpet.

He bent to stroke her head, then his hands dropped away. He straightened up and went to find his wife. Pearl needed no urging or instruction. She hurried to his study to share Kaethe's sorrow and to bring her what solace another, older, and barren woman could.

Now everything was visions of desolation. His days were full of apprehension and his nights of terrifying dreams. Invariably he was yoked like an ox to the plow of the Angel of Death, who drove him unmercifully across fields full of Jews who cried out their hope that the furrow he plowed would not be their grave. Earth's night lightened with faces turned up to him from the tomb, full-fleshed faces bright with blood that masked bone-white skulls: his son Bezalel's, Mordecai Meisel's, Kaethe Hoch's and, over and over again, that of Joseph Golem. As he strove wildly to avoid cutting them down, tearing at the traces, twisting the blade so that he would not sever the lines of their lives, the plow bucked like a wild beast with a life of its own and a joy in death.

Unable to sleep through the nights, the Rabbi walked the streets of the ghetto to exhaustion, as if he were himself the Golem, as if an old man laden with years might stand between his people and their fate.

At dawn, a week before the Passover, trudging wearily up the *Judengasse* back to the *Altneuschul* and home, he saw, like a mirage in the desert night, Joseph Golem carrying Kaethe in his arms. Limbs dangling, hair in disarray, the bodice of her dress torn so that part of her breast like a separate shy face was exposed, Kaethe crooned meaninglessly in a distant soprano.

Rabbi Low ran toward them, but his legs gave way and he braced himself against the wall of a building damp with dew and waited. As Joseph came abreast, the Rabbi hastened with him to the house. In the kitchen, the Golem placed Kaethe in a chair, but she collapsed and slumped to the floor. He propped her up, but she crumpled again before he held her upright by bracing her shoulders against the back of her chair.

Pearl came into the kitchen completely dressed. With no more than raised eyebrows and turned-down mouth, she covered the shivering Kaethe with her shawl, brought a bowl of hot water and a cloth, and washed the clawed, dirty, tormented face, stopping only when a wince became a whimper. Kaethe swallowed the small glass of wine Pearl gave her, gasped and coughed color back into her white face. Then Pearl took her shoes off, chafed her feet, and wrapped a blanket around them. During that time, Pearl spoke not a word, but every one of her movements admonished them all. Finally, she brought cups of broth and they sat silently around the kitchen table watching the tongues of steam rise from the pewter.

When Rabbi Low asked what happened, Kaethe's head lolled as if it were no longer her own. She tried to answer, then burst into hysterical sobbing, and Pearl, lips thin, led her from the kitchen. The Golem's face worked, his fists clenched, as he groped for words. "Kaethe came to where we meet, in the old cemetery. There is a tombstone, near a special grave. At sunrise, before the day begins, we meet there so that each day . . ." He stopped, then began again. "They must have followed Kaethe from this house, watched us. They knew how we met, when, and where. Usually I am first and wait just to see her in the distance, her yellow hair coming up through the gravestones like the morning sun, but today . . . I was delayed. Four tavern hooligans had thrown her to the ground when I arrived, were holding her. They were . . ." He could not continue.

"Joseph," Rabbi Low asked, "did they force her?"

The Golem stood dumb.

"Joseph," the Rabbi persisted, "did they rape her?" He hated even to speak the words, but it was necessary to know.

"They struck her, shamed her!" The Golem rose to his full height, lifting his arms to the heavens, his fists grazing the ceiling. "I shall kill them," he said very softly.

"You know them?"

"I shall remember their faces. No corner of Prague, no village in all Bohemia is too small for me to search them out."

"You must not kill them," the Rabbi warned.

The Golem's eyes were contemptuous, then stony. "To protect the Jews of the ghetto, you bid me kill, made me free to kill. Is Kaethe not worthy of such protection?"

"In such a matter it is wiser to let the bailiffs find and punish."

"No." His voice was almost a whisper, lost.

"Joseph."

"No!" The roar was outrage, protest.

"If they have violated Kaethe, they will be punished, without their blood on your hands."

"If! They touched her, Rabbi! They spoke such words to her! They tore her garments and beat her, kicked her and threw her to the ground! And you say *if*."

"But they did not force her," the Rabbi reminded him.

Pearl returned then and the Rabbi's inquiring look brought only an angry shake of her head to his unspoken question. But the Rabbi was not content. "Well?" he asked her.

"They tried," she replied reluctantly, "but Joseph Golem arrived too soon for them. Hooligans! Riffraff! *Goyim!*"

Spasmodically the Golem's great hands choked the air, his fingers strangled the morning light.

"You must not kill them," the Rabbi warned. "It is evil."

"When *you* tell me to kill, it is good. When *you* think Jews are threatened, killing is an exalted destiny."

Sadly Rabbi Low shook his head. "When killing is the only recourse, you are permitted, even enjoined to kill."

"The only hope?"

"Blood for blood is the way of the nations. We may kill only to avoid the most profound horror, the destruction of the spirit, the community, the body."

"To stain my hands with blood to save someone I love—yes"— he turned fiercely on Pearl's scowling face—"someone I love— that is evil. To spill blood when you command me to save Jews, to save people who scorn and fear me, who walk to the other side of the *Judengasse* when I approach—that is good."

"However understandable your hatred, however"—the Rabbi hesitated—"human your desire for revenge, that is not our way nor your mission. If we have no better way—"

"Or better Golem—"

"Then you must defend us. To obey the Lord's command to kill to save His people is good; to disobey the Almighty's edict to kill is evil and sin."

"To obey is good; to disobey, evil?"

Rabbi Low nodded.

"Then I shall do evil." With only the briefest glance at the door through which Pearl had taken Kaethe, the Golem left the way he had come.

XIX

He dreamt that he was running down the slope of a hill leading to a bridge, the wild longings of his soul shrieking in his
ears. Two long rows of exalted linden trees arched over his
head, the canopy of heaven turned to a bower of luxuriant green
leaves. When he came to the bridge, his legs turned to wooden
wheels that ran of their own accord and would not slow or re-
spond to his command. They wobbled this way and that, turned,
veered, until he crashed through the side of the bridge down
into the waters. The wheels weighted him and plunged him down
into the cold, green, hostile deep. Though he struggled for the
surface, for light and air, he breathed chill streams of water into
his lungs, felt them fill, and in the depths began to drown.
When he awoke, eight of them stood in a semicircle around

him, the four who had seized Kaethe and four he had never before seen, panting, pacing, almost prancing, unable to stand still, like wild dogs after a long chase who had run their prey to earth and were now ready to kill. When he had gone to seek Jitka, he had seen such dogs run even a bull to earth.

"He's awake," one of them called. Tall, powerfully muscled, with great black mustaches and side-whiskers and a head of tight black curls, he was the last of the four who had fled the cemetery that morning. "Well, you big Jew bastard, I heard that you were looking for us. Well, you found us—and we found you."

The Golem struggled to get up, to talk, but he was bound and gagged. The leader looked at him, laughed, and kicked him sharply in the head.

When they had left him, the Golem, head ringing, eyes closed, tried to remember how he had come there. He was following two of them he had recognized in a market stall near the ghetto to a tavern on the edge of Prague. A tavern in a small village just beyond the city. He sat and drank mead and listened to someone playing the zither, but that was all he could remember. He saw that he was in a great barn, lying between stacks of fodder and mounds of manure. Nearby he smelled and heard cows, pigs, and chickens and then heard the voice of one of the men outside saying, "Let's finish him before they come looking."

"In a little while. It's not dark yet," the leader's voice answered.

The Golem heard them quarreling, some calling for him to be killed and buried there, beneath the barn, but the leader at last convinced them that drowning him in the well was a better plan. They would soak his clothes with wine, take his bonds off, and throw him into the well. He would seem to have fallen drunkenly into the well and drowned there. After all, others must know about the girl and the cemetery, the leader reminded them. They would be natural suspects for the murder if anything happened to him that seemed suspicious.

"Let's prepare then," another advised. "That big bastard won't be easy to handle awake."

"Lucky that Alois had Jiri put that potion in his mead," another voice said. "That big man won't be easy to handle, awake or groggy."

"He's so goddamn big we need six to carry him," another complained.

"All right," the leader assented. "Bring the cart, Jiri. We'll drive him to the well."

While they brought the creaking cart around, the Golem loosened the cords that bound him so that he could free himself in an instant. He remembered Samson and the look on Isaac's face when they had been studying and he had told Isaac that because he felt Samson's great strength and passion for women, he understood the Nazirite. Now he would not have the jawbone of an ass to smite these men with, but they were only eight, not a thousand. He closed his eyes and prayed, "O Lord, give Thy servant deliverance by Thy hand. Do not let me fall into the hands of the uncircumsized." Virtually free of his bonds, he let the cords remain on his limbs so that it should seem he was still bound.

Soon thereafter, they came for him, in two groups of four. He kept his eyes slitted, his head askew so that they would imagine him unconscious. One stooped, his face close and reeking of beer, and said, "He's still out. Still bleeding too. Who kicked him in the head like that?"

"I did," the leader acknowledged. "Into the cart now, quick!"

They lifted him and threw him into the back of the cart. Six of them sat with him, the leader and one other up front handling the team. The Golem heard them drinking. Each time they passed the jug across his body, they splashed a little on him, and each time the same whining voice complained that they were wasting good wine.

They drove over rutted roads and occasionally, when the Golem peered out of slitted eyes, he saw the rising moon so that he knew they were traveling westward, toward Prague. Finally, the wagon stopped and they rolled him onto the stony ground.

"That was some kick, Alois," one of the men remarked. "He's still out cold."

"Get him to the well," Alois barked.

Six of them carried him and laid him against the stone brim. Through narrow eyes the Golem peered down the long shaft and, deep below, saw the dark glitter of water.

"Jiri, give me the wine," Alois called.

"Why waste wine?" Jiri grumbled. "Stink him up with ale."

"The wine!" Alois repeated.

With one fervent prayer, the Golem threw off his bonds, seized the two men closest to him, and slammed their heads together. But Alois had already leaped out of his reach, yelling to the others, "All together, knock him into the well! If he gets loose . . ." The six of them came at him together, and though they had staves and clubs, he fought them off, again and again, until by sheer weight of numbers they toppled him back over the stone rim of the well. He fell, holding fast to two of them, hoping that one of them might be Alois. When he struck the water, he thrust them from him and with pleasure heard the crunch of bone against the walls.

Faces up there looked down, which at that distance and in the dim light the Golem could only see faintly. Alois' voice called, "Get rocks and stones. He's still alive down there."

From below, next to him, another voice cried out, "No, Alois, it's me, Jiri, down here in the well too. No stones!"

The faces looked over the rim again, then disappeared.

"Throw me a rope," Jiri called.

From above, silence.

"Zdenek, throw me a rope!" Jiri bawled.

No answer.

"Vaclav, don't let me die down here! I'm your friend. Get me up!"

Still no reply.

Jiri began to sob. "Zdenek, save me. Don't let me drown. Vaclav! Alois? Alois! Alois!" Neither rope nor comfort came from above. The Golem felt sorry for him, but when he reached out to help him stay afloat, Jiri blubbered in terror, "Don't touch me! Don't hit me!" Then he blustered, "If you lay a hand on me, my friends will kill you. They'll kill you!" Then, like a dog baying the moon, he raised his head and wailed for help.

The first stone came like the whirr of wind and the Golem dived, Jiri's voice in his ears pleading, "No, Alois, no!"

When he came up, there was silence. Jiri floated nearby, eyes staring, his forehead crushed. The face lay just under the surface, rippled, then turned and sank from sight just before another hail of rocks rained down.

"Get a torch so we can see if he's still down there," someone called.

"Idiot! Do you want to bring every farmer for miles around?"

"What can we do, Alois?"

"Leave him. He can't float forever. He'll drown, never fear."

"What if someone hears him bellow for help?"

"Who's to hear him? You can see a torch for a long way, but no one's close enough to hear. Let him bawl. By morning he'll be with Gustav and Jiri."

The cartwheels creaked, traces and whip snapped and strained, but smaller, rustling sounds told the Golem that some had remained behind. Anxiously, he waited in silence and soon the light of heaven was being blocked out. In rage and fear, he cried out, "O Lord, let Thy mercies come to me that I may live," and dived as deeply as he could, flattening himself against the well wall. The boulder buffeted his shoulders, back and buttocks, pounding by him to sink still farther into the depths. Even before his head broke the surface of the waters, his heart beat with joy. "Blessed art Thou, O Lord. Thy hands made me and fashioned me. Teach me Thy way that I may ever walk in Thy truth." But he kept noiselessly pressed flat against the well, his face to the wall.

"That one worked," Alois' voice said at last. "Can't see him, or anything else down there."

"That stone was enough to kill a bear," someone exclaimed.

"Probably block the spring at the bottom of the well too," another voice observed.

"No one drinks from this well anymore anyway," Alois declared.

Leaving this time they made more noise than they had in their ruse. As sounds of cart and horses and men's voices died away, the Golem, cold and bruised, but elated to be alive, prayed once more that the Lord would allow him vengeance against them for having hurt Kaethe, for having tried to kill him—and, deep in the well, he continued to tread water.

Rabbi Low woke with a start, the dream so vivid he could not extricate himself from it. Down the slope of the ghetto wall, precariously balanced because his legs were infirm, he walked beneath a forest of high pine and cedar grown so dense that they shut out the stars and the sky. Each step he took in the darkness that closed off the *Judengasse* from the main street of the Old Town seemed endless, and when he had taken another, he realized that he was falling. He fell without fear, standing erect as he normally stood, conscious only that he was plummeting down a long shaft with irregular stone walls overgrown with thin green layers of lichen. Not until that depth bottomed out into a clay bank on which he was abruptly jarred and so perilously perched did he know he was searching to reclaim the Golem because the stone walls became mirrors that distorted the outlines of his frame as they welled blood from deep unstanchable wounds. Looking closely about him, he saw a meadow rise in the moonlight, a waist-high circle of stones that might have been an asherah in the Judean hills, but that was only a wall around an old well. From it, the echo of the Golem's voice boomed: *"He that planted the ear, shall he not hear? He that formed the eye, shall he not see?"* With that he knew surely what had befallen Joseph Golem.

It was fully two hours before they reached the meadow outside of Prague, though Rabbi Low led them unerringly to it. The time had been taken with traveling, with summoning Jacob and Isaac, with borrowing Meisel's coach and coachman. Not a sound emerged from the well until the Rabbi shone his lantern down into its depths and called, "Joseph Golem, it is Judah ben Bezalel, come at your call."

"Peace be with you, Rabbi," the Golem's voice ascended from the depths.

They lowered the well rope and pulled the Golem up. Bleeding, the Golem fell exhausted on the ground and lay there. The Rabbi covered him with his own cloak, which Isaac soon replaced with a warm blanket from the coach. Isaac gave the Golem some wine, which he drank in small sips until Petr Singer mutely brought him dry clothes. All three helped him to his feet while the Rabbi watched; but when the Golem stripped off his wet clothes, they modestly turned their backs on his nakedness.

Riding back to Prague, the Golem haltingly described how the men had tried to kill him, and why, how Jiri and Gustav died, how the giant boulder had narrowly missed him, how he had prayed. Though his strength had been as twenty, though the Lord had sustained him, he could not climb the smooth walls of the well, had only been able to stay on the surface of the water and pray for rescue.

"Your prayer was heard," the Rabbi said, "and answered."

"You are here," the Golem acknowledged.

"And you."

Petr Singer drove them to the Rabbi's house. After Rabbi Low descended from the coach, he beckoned the Golem to follow, but the Golem did not move. Awkwardly, Jacob spoke for the first time, saying, "Thank you, Joseph, for rescuing my betrothed."

The Golem's powerful arms rose above him, clutched the velvet-lined roof of the coach, then dropped to his sides. "Is she well?" he asked.

Jacob nodded. "Better—though not yet well."

"I would be avenged of her violators," the Golem swore.

"Go, Joseph," Isaac urged. "Rest. Sleep. Tomorrow will be time enough for vengeance."

Unwillingly, the Golem stepped from the carriage to follow the Rabbi into the house. In the kitchen Pearl dressed his wounds as thoroughly as she had Kaethe's, but she spoke not a word to him. She set a hot bowl of thick gruel on the table for him, and when he had eaten, wrapped him in quilts and left him near the hot stove to sleep the night.

Early the next day, when Rabbi Low came down from his study after morning prayers, all that remained was a pile of neatly folded quilts, some breadcrumbs on the kitchen table, and a half-filled mug of water: Once more the Golem had gone away.

XX

The first Seder night was blue-black with a benign moon and winter's brisk gustiness tempered by the sweet soft air of spring. Looking out on the *Judengasse* from his study, Rabbi Low was grateful for the peaceful dark of the streets: Passover had come and *they* had not. Everywhere in the ghetto, behind curtained and shuttered windows, Jews prepared to celebrate the ancient festival: candelabra sparkled, candles glowed, linen shone, and families sat down to repeat the age-old ritual of the emancipation of the Jewish people from Egypt. Once more the Jews of Prague would only eat the symbolic bread of affliction and be spared the bitter taste of contention; once more they would share the manna of being God's firstborn, of having been liberated from the bondage of Pharaoh by the power of the Almighty's hand.

Not altogether free, for now they were dispersed in many distant lands, strangers in the earth; but if the Jews were in exile, they knew that the very presence of God lay with the persecuted and would therefore be with them. They were a desert people and even in the desert of the exile they would somehow survive. In the Diaspora wilderness each of their holidays was an oasis where they might pause to be refreshed and reminded of their greatness, where they could gather new strength and courage to journey onward toward the day of the Messiah when all would live in peace under their own vine and fig tree, when on all God's holy mountain none would do harm.

In the darkness below, street shadows moved, first the shape of Bezalel, then that of Joseph Golem, but neither materialized, and he knew they were figments. How different the Seders had become since Bezalel's death. Now Marcus, too, was dying, his last, oldest friend. He had always hoped for a long life, but he wondered if that hope fulfilled had been a blessing. The price of aging was in some ways more grievous than death itself. One endured the deaths of those one loved most, children, friends, colleagues, students, until one's memory was like a field of graves to which one went gingerly and not too often to leave a rock of remembrance on the tombstones.

Pride and passion died too, yet his passion to do good, to save his people, had not died, nor even been diminished by age. Age brought the knowledge of how the *yetzer* hid in such ambition to do good, like a worm in a rose, grew swollen from the pride of having done good. That wisdom he had not arrived at as a young man. Yet one could never drive out the evil propensity altogether, and the Sages had observed that one should not, for without the proclivity for evil "men would never build a house or take a wife or beget a child or engage in commerce." Yes, the *yetzer* remained a driving force subtler than the serpent, which snared man's most honored intentions, wound itself around his conceit, and provoked his obstinacy until, blinded by the majesty of his motives, man was moved to deception, delusion, evil.

Those soul-darkening considerations about the Lord's command to create the Golem never left his mind. By absence the Golem had become an intimate, jostling part of his consciousness and calling his whole world into question. Though Rabbi

Low prayed for some sign, the Lord vouchsafed him neither dream nor vision, neither symbol nor portent, and he despaired. He had not imagined that his creation would so estrange him from God; he had presumed that it would bring him closer to the Almighty, yet now he could not hear his own voice truly, nor did he hear the voice of the Lord. He had hoped to profane a single vessel to keep from profaning many men, as Jacob wished to do. Jacob was more adamant and fiery than ever. To all who would listen in the ghetto he cried out, "Prayer shawls are no armor, nor phylacteries a sword!" So passionately did Jacob plead with the people to arm themselves that he frequently moved himself to tears. Many, especially among the youth, were already armed and prepared to walk in the ways of the nations, to lose their Jewish souls and perhaps their lives.

None paid heed to the Almighty's words to Zechariah, *Not by might, nor by power, but by My spirit.* Did that offer a truly holy alternative, or did one only serve the Lord in peace— and man in war? And was that not what Scripture meant by the choice of serving the Lord or serving idols? *Even when you shall offer many prayers, I will not hear because your hands are full of blood.* Of one thing he was certain: He had prayed and listened and obeyed the voice of God in creating the Golem. How else would the vessel of clay have risen sensate from the river's bank? But the Golem had fled and now he despaired of Joseph, yet a part of him rejoiced in Joseph as well: The Golem's clay had become flesh, his stumbling, seeking spirit human and recalcitrant. Had the Lord, too, despaired of His creation in the same way, or was such thought blasphemy?

The Seder table instantly restored his repose, its linen, silver, and glassware a sanctuary; and the old familiar rituals, blessing wine, washing hands, displaying those fragile matzos, to whose purity Joseph Golem had attested with the agony of his flesh, were the land of promise. Eyes closed, Rabbi Low spoke the hallowed words, moved by them as he always was: *"This is the bread of our affliction, which our ancestors ate in the land of Egypt. Let all those who are hungry enter and eat thereof; and all who are in distress, come and celebrate the Passover."*

The intake of breath opened his eyes to see Joseph Golem

slip quietly into the empty chair set before the Prophet Elijah's wineglass. Ignoring the others, Joseph nodded to him, his green eyes shiny and menacing. As if he had spoken aloud, Joseph's voice echoed Pharaoh's words in his ear, *"Who is the Lord that I should listen to His voice?"*

The Rabbi's own sharp unspoken rejoinder transfixed the Golem:

Shall the potter be esteemed as the clay;
That the thing made should say of him that made
    it: "He made me not";
Or the thing framed say of him that framed it: "He
    has no understanding"?

The Golem's reply remained silent, but powerful. *"Then I heard the voice of the Lord saying, 'Whom shall I send? Who will go for us?' I answered, 'Here am I, send me.'"*

The Lord had turned the Golem's heart, yet there was no rejoicing in the Rabbi's heart, not even relief when, together, their silences spoke to each other once more, *"All that the Lord has spoken we will do and we will obey."* Among the puzzled faces, they nodded, a covenant shared, extended and received without a word spoken.

Pearl filled another wineglass for the Golem, ostentatiously moving the one reserved to Elijah out of his reach. The Golem then turned his face to Kaethe, who was sitting next to Jacob. They smiled at each other, shyly, in painful radiance.

Bezalel's only son, soon to be *bar mitzvah*, asked the Four Questions and in the boy's changing face and voice, Rabbi Low saw the beginnings of the man to come and was uplifted by the continuity of generations: Bezalel lived; they would persist; the Jews would survive, or at least a remnant would be saved. The Almighty's arm had not waxed short.

The Seder went on, with only the occasional glimpse of what pulsed beneath the ritual. While they ate, there was talk and laughter, Talmudic disputation and gossip of the town, argument about whether now that Passover was here *they* would come at all, joking and play as the children searched for the hidden matzo to gain their rewards. Joseph Golem took no part: He ate; he drank the cups of wine; he shared the bitter herbs and the bread of affliction; and he prayed with them, his Hebrew clear and classical, with exactly the same lilt as that of Isaac who had taught him.

When they read the powerful lines from Leviticus, *"The stranger that sojourns among you shall be to you as the native and you shall love him as yourself; for you were strangers in the land of Egypt,"* the Rabbi saw the tracery of tears on Kaethe's cheeks. And when the door was opened for the invisible arrival of Elijah the Prophet, Jacob's voice rang over all the others while the Golem sat silent: *"Pour out your wrath upon the heathen who will not acknowledge you, and upon the king-doms who do not invoke your name, for they have devoured Jacob, and laid waste his dwelling. Pour out your indignation upon them and let your fierce anger overtake them. Pursue them in wrath and destroy them from under the heavens of the Eternal."* The Golem, eyes fixed on Isaac, saw that he too sat solemn and tight-lipped, also refusing to read those wrathful words.

Moments before, the Golem, green eyes focused on Rabbi Low, had paid him the tender regard of praying aloud, "May He who is most merciful bless *my honored father,*" instead of chanting the usual *head of the house,* which one normally said when at the Seder table of someone other than one's parents. Again, shared, unspoken thought flashed clearly between them: the Golem, *"He who has not shared the suffering of his community can never be a part of it";* Rabbi Low, *"In every generation it is each man's duty to look upon himself as if he personally had come out of Egypt."* They were joined, but no closer together.

Not until the very end of the ceremonies, when, drowsy with wine and food, they began to sing the final three verses of the very last Seder song did Rabbi Low foresee what would come:

Then the slaughterer came and slaughtered the ox which had drunk the water which had extinguished the fire which had burnt the staff which had smitten the dog which had bitten the cat which had devoured the kid which my father bought for two zuzim; one only kid, one only kid.

There was no mistaking the look in the Golem's eyes as they sang the two verses that told that the Angel of Death then came and slew the slaughterer, and that finally came the Most Holy, blessed be He, who slew the Angel of Death. The Golem's lips moved and shaped the words, but no sound emerged, no song. He knew he was the slaughterer to be slaughtered; he knew that Rabbi Low was his Angel of Death. For just the blink of an eye the Rabbi was sure there was a gleam of satisfaction, of revenge on that grim face—had Bezalel also looked that way on his death bed in Kolín?—which bespoke that the Lord would at last take His vengeance of the Rabbi too. And that last could not be very far off.

In the middle of the night, the Rabbi, unsleeping, heard whispers in the courtyard and through the shutters saw Kaethe and the Golem standing next to the wall, close together but not touching. She had thrown a robe around her nightdress, but her bare white feet, innocent on the cobbles, and her long blond hair, furled over her shoulders, seemed more nakedly revealing than flesh. The Golem was fully dressed, in the same clothes he had worn at the Seder. Clearly, he had not gone to bed at all, but had instead made his rounds of the ghetto, for he still carried his ax, which he now leaned carefully against the wall.

"Perhaps," Kaethe was saying, "*they* will not come."

"*They* will come. They have not yet exhausted their hatred," the Golem replied.

"What will happen then?"

"I don't know. I am uneasy. I would run and shout and fight and . . . I don't know what. I must live so much for others that I am a stranger to myself. My mission is to guard the ghetto."

"What will happen to me, Joseph?"

"You will be the wife of Jacob Nissan, a scholar and a rabbi. You are betrothed and at the end of the year, when Jacob's studies are finished, you will stand together under the canopy. Later you will be the mother of his children."

"Could you not take me away so that I could be Joseph Golem's wife and the mother of his children?"

"Everything is too late, and perhaps was too late from the beginning. The darkness falls. No sun will come up for me."

"Prague is not the world. Let us leave it, now."

"Prague is my world. The hand of Rabbi Low that is the hand of God holds me here. I must do and I must obey."

"We can go to Vilna or Cracow, anywhere. I want to be *your* wife, Joseph, bear *your* children."

Joseph hung his head. "I can have no children, Kaethe."

She stepped back. "Then what the Rabbi said was true!"

The Golem nodded. "So I was created. So I am. A lump of earth, a flawed clay vessel, a golem."

"Joseph!" She put her hands on his arms.

"Jacob is better for you. He will give you children. You will be the wife of a scholar, not of a woodcutter. He is slender, handsome, and I . . . I hate my size, my awkwardness, my ugliness. I detest my own flesh. I should not even want any children. What for? To make others like myself?"

Kaethe put her head against him. Her voice was almost lost. "You will not go?"

"I cannot." He paused. "You cannot. We have given our words."

Kaethe was crying. "I love you," she sobbed.

He lifted her up as if she were a child and pressed her to him. He kissed her cheeks, then set her feet gently back down on the cobbles. "Your feet are bare," he said. "Go inside, you will be sick."

"I don't care. I don't care," she cried, then fled into the house.

The Golem watched her go. With one great smash, he brought his ax down against the cobbles and broke the haft in two. Savagely, he kicked the two pieces to the ends of the courtyard, then, after a long wait, went hunch-shouldered to pick them up, put them under his arms, and stalked from the courtyard.

XXI

Rabbi Low was in the *Altneuschul* by himself, wandering up and down the aisles, aimless but driven. In the night's dark flesh the eternal light shone like a wound. The Torah curtain of shorn velvet and black silk damask was richly embroidered with the golden spread fingers of the *Kohanim* blessing a wisdom well. Beneath was emblazoned in letters of flame *Draw water carefully*, while overhead a circumcision knife, the blade bright, the mother-of-pearl haft blazing with precious stones, dropped toward it like a falling bird. At the entrance to the main aisle two pale stone outstretched hands projected from the walls, begging—for alms? mercy? justice? love?—but were so importunate that he turned his back on them. The clock struck twelve, time to recite the midnight lamentation, but he could not remember it. He concentrated his resolve on recalling the lamentation because he knew the souls of the dead were assembled there with him in the darkness of the empty synagogue, but his resolve drained away with his memory.

Imposing gates of twisted metal were set with filigreed tablets of stone at their hearts, the halves joined where the gates locked. On them, burning, were only two Hebrew letters: *Lo—Thou shalt not!* As he raised his hands to open the gates, the tablets turned to clay, cracked as if they had been too long in the kiln, the letters burned to ashes, the gates crumbled to dust.

The altar stood before him and on it a man whose blind eyes and nostrils were filled with blood. His hand reached up for the circumcision knife, which was now a ritual slaughterer's. A long line of young men and old stood waiting, each turning his face to look at him before lifting his throat to the knife. Swiftly, in succession, the slaughterer cut their throats, without an outcry, without a grimace from any of the slaughtered, his eyes and nostrils swelling with blood until they concealed his entire face.

Again and again the Rabbi tried to call out, but no voice rang from his throat. What was there churned like the blood of an animal in his chest. The slaughterer went on, methodically, not hurrying, secure, until, mustering all his strength, the Rabbi struck the knife from his hand. Then he was able to find the voice in his lungs and cry out, "Stop, thou destroyer of men!"

The figure stooped to retrieve the knife, his hands disappearing into the great pool of blood at his feet, wallowing, bathing, soaking, then reappeared holding the knife, which spurted blood.

A light was lit in the darkness behind the Rabbi, but he dared not turn from the slaughterer to face it. The eternal light above the altar melted into waxen blood that began to drip like tallow, then to rain down, first on the slaughterer, then on him. Though he twisted and turned he could not escape; it clung to him, soaked his hair and his clothes, worked its way into clots under his fingernails. But the slaughterer turned his face up, kicked and cavorted under the bloody rain as if in delight at a summer shower.

On the reading stand he stood once more, the bloodied knife in his right hand, in his left a scroll of names written in blood curving away into the infinite distant dark. Livid lips moving, he read name after name, monotonously, as if they were Biblical chronologies, but instead of Adam begot Seth and Seth, Enosh, who begot Kenan who begot Mahalel who begot Jared, it was always killing instead of begetting, murder instead of birth. He read the names soundlessly—*And Cain rose up against Abel his brother, and slew him*—but the Rabbi heard each name as a clap of thunder against the synagogue rafters.

He listened, knowing the familiar names, Abraham and Isaac and Jacob, Moses and Joshua, David and Solomon, Isaiah, Micah, and Jeremiah, but the last name at the very foot of the list was his own, booming in his skull as if the thunder were trapped there, a ram in a thicket: *Judah ben Bezalel*; and he understood that he was in the presence of the Angel of Death.

With a lunge he tore the scroll from that bloodless hand, but the Terrible One did not move. Instead, he looked down almost benignly, amused, tolerant, without resistance or resentment, imperturbable.

Holding tightly to the scroll, guarding it with his very life, Rabbi Low ran blindly up the main aisle, past the importunate stone hands, which now clutched and tore at his clothing, and fled the synagogue. In his study, again and again, he read the names inscribed on the scroll. It seemed like the list of all the adult males in the ghetto, and many women and children as well. Joy rose in him like wine because he had saved them from the *Malach Hamoves*, all, Jacob and Isaac, Marcus and Abraham, Frumett and Pearl.

He placed the scroll on his table and watched as, like an animal, it curled up. Only then did he notice that one corner of it had been torn away, a jagged remnant on which some names had been written, but whose names he did not know. And those remained in the hands of the Angel of Death. *Whose names were they?*

XXII

At dawn the first day after the Passover holidays, Petr Singer woke him with a note from Frumett telling that Mordecai Meisel was dead. Even before he opened the envelope, Rabbi Low surmised from Singer's red-rimmed eyes what had occurred, and he sent the man back promptly to his mistress. When he had dressed, his weakness told him that he should eat, but he could not. The Golem was nowhere to be found in the house, but the Rabbi discovered him in the cemetery stretched out on the ground between two tombstones, moss-covered and ancient, one carved with a female figure, a rose in her raised left hand, which told that it was the grave of a virgin bride, the other inscribed to a man:

Here lies a man, faithful and true, slain.
May the Lord avenge his blood—
His blood which was shed like the blood of a bull.

"Joseph?" the Rabbi called.

The Golem nodded his face into the ground, then turned it up from its burrowing, his thick eyebrows full of earth, which he brushed impatiently away. "I am here, Rabbi," he said in a stifled voice.

"Is this where you met?" the Rabbi could not help asking. The Golem nodded.

"Meisel is dead," Rabbi Low announced.

"A good man," the Golem said.

"A man to whom I could speak my heart."

"It must be good to have such a friend, to whom one can speak one's heart," the Golem observed evenly, but the Rabbi felt shamed.

They walked together toward Meisel's house, the morning so full of spring sunlight and birdsong that the face of death seemed only an illusion, yet he could not shake his mind free of that vision of the Angel of Death, which now returned nightly to haunt him. Marcus' face, almost corpselike, swam before his eyes, looking as it had the night they worked on his will; and then that same face during the morning prayer, illumined, when together they had affirmed, *Praise be to Thee who restores the spirit to the dead.* Marcus' name had been on that corner of the scroll the Angel of Death had held in his hand. The way was not long now for himself, and with Marcus dead, it would be shorter still.

Frumett was dry-eyed, composed. "The Lord was merciful," she said. "He died in his sleep, just as dawn had begun to lighten the sky."

"You saw him?"

"He could not sleep, so I made him some hot broth and spiced wine. I sent the servants to bed, then I sat and read to him. He asked me to read the Song of Songs." She turned her face away. "He fell asleep after a time, his hand in mine, and I must have dozed myself, for when I woke, his hand, which had clasped mine, lay open and limp but still rested in my palm. I knew at once he was gone."

"Love is as strong as death," the Rabbi said, and then, too late, saw the Golem's face.

"Stronger than death," Frumett affirmed, tears starting in her eyes. "I have known that every time Marcus and I went to pray in the High Synagogue."

Without asking, Rabbi Low knew why. Set into the High Synagogue wall was a votive plaque that read: *And Mordecai built the synagogue in honor of the Song and in honor of the Torah with the help of his wife, Eva, the pure one, the daughter of Moses of blessed memory.* Love *was* stronger than death, jealousy too. And, remembering Pearl and Bezalel, hatred and resentment too. Was that why Frumett and Marcus had built the new synagogue now called the Meisel? And was it the only reason?

"Have you sent for the two Samuels?" the Rabbi inquired.

Frumett nodded. "Everything is prepared—according to the will. Marcus planned so there would be no disturbance." Her voice broke, recovered. "What will I do without him?" she asked.

"What will we all do without him?" the Rabbi said.

Though they were the separate sons of Meisel's two younger brothers, the two Samuels might have been twins. Stocky, powerfully built, looking even shorter than they were, they were not at all like the tall, lean, and elegant Marcus. When they emerged from the bedroom where Meisel lay and where the members of the burial society were preparing his body, they were altogether unnerved. The elder Samuel said, "I thought he would never die. Like the *Altstadt*, old, but always there."

"And always active, performing good deeds," the younger Samuel added, almost ruefully.

"He knew better than anyone that his was not to complete the task," the Rabbi reminded them, "nor may you desist from it. That is why he made you his chief heirs."

"We shall take up his burdens," the younger Samuel vowed, "but we shall not be equal to the task."

"One is never equal to the task when one begins. But with God's help, with man's intelligence and continual striving, one becomes superior to it," Rabbi Low said, feeling suddenly so weak that he tottered and would have fallen had not the Golem led him to a chair. Frumett sent one of the servants to bring a cup of broth and bread. After he had made the blessings and eaten, his faintness faded and he felt stronger.

"You think His Majesty will be as good as his word about disposing of my uncle's property?" the elder Samuel inquired.

Rabbi Low shrugged. "Long ago, in Spain, a Jew named Samuel Abulafia lived in Toledo. Like your uncle, Don Samuel ha-Levi was a man of God and the commandments, learned, skillful in finance and diplomacy, an advisor to the king, who was well-named Pedro the Cruel. Pedro granted Samuel ha-Levi many privileges of the kind that Rudolf has given to your uncle —tax exemptions, personal concessions, the right to carry on banking and commerce that few Christians of that time possessed. And then, one day, the wind changed, for kings are capricious as the wind. They took Samuel Abulafia from his house, stripped his privileges from him, converted his own synagogue into a church. They drove him out of Toledo, imprisoned him and all his relatives, confiscated their fortunes, and then tortured him to death—a man not yet forty."

Frumett and her nephews exchanged glances. "We are prepared," the elder Samuel began, but under his aunt's stare he quailed and fell silent.

The day of Mordecai Meisel's funeral it seemed that the flowering earth would only give forth bloom, would accept no death, would refuse those who were to be buried. But in the Jewish cemetery, which Meisel had cared for and in which the Golem seemed more at home than anywhere else, the freshly dug grave accepted the coffin. Swiftly Rabbi Low spoke the prayers over the grave while the words he had read earlier at Meisel's house echoed painfully in his mind: ". . . *from everlasting to everlasting Thou art God. Thou turnest back man to dust. The Rock, His work is perfect . . . just and right is He. . . . For a thousand years in Thy sight are but as yesterday when it is past, and as a watch in the night. If a man live a year or a thousand years, what profits it him? He shall be as though he had not been. As for man, his days are as grass; as the flower of the field, so he flourishes. For the wind passes over it, and it is gone. . . . The Rock . . . who can say to Him, What workest Thou? What doest Thou? . . . Have mercy upon the remnant of the flock of Thy hand and say unto the destroying angel, Stay thy hand.*"

The prayers were too brief and exalted; eulogy was what the crowd had come to hear, praise of the *befreiter Hofjude*, Mordecai Marcus Meisel, counselor to kings and emperors, rich man and philanthropist. Other speakers made up for his brevity, fulsome, long-winded, some sincere, others servile and self-serving, all aware of the new grave and Frumett and the two Samuels standing before it. Words came easily to them, Rabbi Low supposed, yet none had really known Marcus as more than a name, a haughty, elegant, rich, and powerful man who was one of the *parnasim*, who could and did intercede in their behalf with the powers, who sometimes had stood between them and their fate.

In late afternoon, when they returned from the cemetery, the street outside of Meisel's house was crowded with half a dozen carts. Men were carrying furniture, clothes, carpets, boxes, loading them into the wagons. The gates and doors of the house had been forced and there, inside, they found Johannes von Sternberg, President of the Bohemian Chamber, supervising the looting. "Good day, Dame Meisel, Rabbi Low," von Sternberg said, bowing slightly. Then he went on directing his men, who were collecting Meisel's silver plate and cutlery.

The two Samuels rushed to stop them, but were forcibly restrained by bailiffs. The younger Samuel roared, "What are you doing here! Do you know that you are violating the house of Mordecai Meisel, the Emperor Rudolf's friend and advisor!" The elder Samuel struggled silently to free himself while next to him Frumett, grim and stiff, said, "The Emperor will know."

Von Sternberg smirked. "The Emperor knew his court Jew when he was alive, but now . . ."

Several men, led by a bailiff, returned still laden with their burdens. "Herr Vorstand," the bailiff complained, "a crowd of Jews will not let anyone pass. And they are emptying the carts."

Jacob and his young guards had unloaded all Meisel's possessions from the carts and piled them on the cobblestones. With linked arms they formed a human chain that did not permit the bailiffs and draymen to reload the carts, but neither would the bailiffs and draymen allow the Jewish lads to carry Meisel's goods back into the house. Von Sternberg cast one startled glance at the young Jews, then sent the chief bailiff hurrying off in the direction of the Castle.

The Golem made his way to Jacob's side and said softly, "Soon there will be many others, more than—"

"I know," Jacob interrupted grimly.

"What will you do then?"

"We shall have others too," Jacob replied.

Arms majestically folded on his chest, von Sternberg stood on the threshold of Meisel's house, his face full of haughty assurance. The rest waited in the street. There were flare-ups, shoving, a face slapped, a few heavier blows, someone thrown to the ground, but neither bailiffs and draymen nor young Jews gave way—nor did any resort to the weapons they all carried. It would not last long that way, the Golem saw. It was stalemated because the Jews wanted to avoid violence and the others were certain that they would shortly be able to overwhelm this thin line of Jews that stood between them and their booty.

"Where is Isaac?" the Golem asked Jacob, surveying the scene without seeing anywhere the bright thatch of red hair.

"In the *Altneuschul*, praying," Jacob growled. "Your teacher wants no violence."

"Did you ask him to come here with you?"

"Ask him?" Jacob laughed. "I begged him."

"But?"

"But? Your teacher did not want any Jewish blood to be shed for Mordecai Meisel's fortune."

Reinforcements came. Pokorny's hussars from one side, the imperial guards from the other, down opposite ends of the street so that Jacob's young men were hemmed in. Bailiffs and draymen, grinning and puffed-up now, began to shove harder against the chain of Jews, trying to force them away from the wagons, back against the walls of the houses.

There was a surge of the horses, jammed together as they were by twos in the narrow street, before Pokorny, his mount rearing, waved hussars and foot soldiers back. Directly, the Golem moved into Pokorny's path. The Count recognized him immediately. "Ah, my great friend," he said in a low voice, so that only those around them heard, "this time you are against us. I wondered when it would come to that."

The Golem, legs braced, contested his passage in silence. Pokorny rose in his stirrups to survey the scene just as Rabbi Low emerged from the open door and stood at von Sternberg's elbow. "Herr Vorstand," Pokorny called loudly, "what's happening here?"

It was Rabbi Low who answered. "Herr von Sternberg has forcibly entered the house of the widow Meisel to seize her properties."

"Those are the Emperor's orders," von Sternberg announced.

"So the President of the Chamber tells us, but he refuses to show us his orders," the Rabbi said.

"I have them," von Sternberg declared, "and I do not have to show them to you—or to anyone."

"The Emperor promised the honorable Mordecai Meisel that he might dispose of his estate without interference. I do not believe that His Majesty would break his solemn word to an old friend and loyal counselor on the very day of his burial."

"That is the Emperor's share of the estate," von Sternberg blustered, indicating the properties on the street.

"The Herr Vorstand knows that to be untrue," Rabbi Low said. "Reb Meisel, may he rest in peace, left His Imperial Majesty a gift of ten thousand florins in his will."

The intake of breath and whispering among bailiffs and draymen, soldiers and Jews, was testimony to the generosity of the bequest.

"And Reb Meisel also left thousands of florins to the hospital for poor Christians and Jews," Rabbi Low added, "and tens of thousands more for charity to the poor."

"How can you know that?" von Sternberg demanded angrily.

"Because I helped to draw the will, I was a witness to it, and I am one of its executors," the Rabbi stated.

There was a hum of talk until von Sternberg declared, "I have my orders. These properties of Mordecai Meisel are to be confiscated in the name of the crown. Pokorny, see that they are loaded on the carts. If any Jew stands in your way, cut him down!"

Weapons were bared, swords and dirks, halberds and clubs

and staves lifted and brandished. At the raising of Jacob's right arm, armed young Jews appeared abruptly on the roofs and in the windows of the houses. The forces were now more equal, with some strategic advantage to the Jews overlooking the street. Pokorny took it all in, including the Golem's having seized the bridle of his horse. "So, it shall be blood!" he said between his teeth, but the Golem could not tell whether he spoke with appetite or apprehension.

"Let no blood be shed!" a woman's voice shrilled. Frumett Meisel stood in front of von Sternberg and Rabbi Low, her face white, stiff. "Let no Jew die here to save my property. If we must do battle and shed our blood and the blood of others, let it be only to save our lives."

No one moved. Not a sound was heard. It was as if a stone had been dropped into a well.

"Let no blood be shed," Frumett Meisel repeated in a more controlled voice. "The properties are mine." Her manner aristocratically dismissed boxes, furniture, carpets, bolts of cloth. "They are only things."

"But," someone called from the crowd, "he who deprives a man of his property, it as if he were depriving him of life, of sons and daughters."

The Golem recognized the Talmudic quotation, even acknowledged its partial truth. It was Isaac who had taught it to him, but even in the crush of bodies, he knew the voice had been Jacob's.

Sternly, uncompromisingly, Rabbi Low intervened. "*He who destroys one soul in Israel, it is as if he had destroyed the whole world.*" It was not commentary; it was command.

Slowly, out of the silence, movement came. Pokorny sheathed his sword, the Golem released the horse's bridle, the linked arms of Jacob's young Jews reluctantly separated, and those on the roofs and in the windows vanished. Bailiffs and draymen began to load Meisel's properties onto the carts, and at a signal from Pokorny both hussars and imperial guardsmen returned the way they had come. Gradually the street emptied until only von Sternberg's bailiffs and draymen, Pokorny and a few hussars, and the Rabbi and the Golem were left. Meisel's door had closed on Frumett and her nephews, Jacob and his young guards had left, and von Sternberg had driven off on the first loaded cart. Pokorny slid from his saddle and, smiling, said to the Golem, "Well, my big man, perhaps next time. We shall yet test our mettle in the field."

Rabbi Low spoke. "Next time and next time, but never justifying the last time or the next time but one."

"The battle, Rabbi, is endless, the fighting forever."

"The Messiah will come, Count Pokorny. Men will not go on like this forever. They *will* change."

"Several Messiahs have already come and gone—and nothing has changed," Pokorny replied. "Men are men, power is power."

"The image of God in man will emerge. In the name of the Almighty they will yet make a Holy Mountain of the world."

"How?"

"By good deeds. By law. By reason."

Pokorny snorted. "You Jews are fools to appeal to society's sense of decency, to man's reason. Society knows only the dirk and the cannon. Man's reason!" He burst into sardonic laughter.

The Golem spoke harshly. "Rabbi Low believes that the Lord will not forsake him—or us. He has faith in God, in man, and in the Messiah."

"*The Messiah comes like a thief in the night,*" Rabbi Low said.

"Thieves in the night are caught—and quartered," Pokorny commented shortly. Then he turned on his heel, remounted, and at a signal, rode off with his remaining hussars.

XXIII

On Sabbath, just after morning prayers, Jacob came to Rabbi Low's study. It was the first time that they had spoken more than in passing for a long while. At prayers Jacob avoided him, they no longer studied together, and although Jacob continued to come to the house to visit Kaethe Hoch, he did not enter the study. "They have taken the two Samuels and are torturing them to discover where the remainder of Reb Meisel's fortune is concealed," Jacob said. "That is what the promises of kings are worth."

"We put our trust not in kings but in the King."

"And what will that trust perform for the two Samuels while the Emperor's inquisitioner breaks their bones on the rack and tears their nails from their fingers with his burning tongs?"

Jacob began to pace. "They will not let us live. Reb Meisel left the Emperor ten thousand florins. It was not enough. His Majesty sent the Vorstand and his bailiffs to seize the value of another forty-five thousand florins that day when you and Frumett Meisel kept us from fighting them. Forty-five thousand florins at a time when five florins can buy a whole ox! Now, that too is not enough; it is never enough."

"Would your fighting have forestalled that, Jacob, or changed it?"

"I don't know. But is our inheritance only to wait for the Vorstand's bailiffs to seize us, as they did the two Samuels, and then to endure torture and death?"

"Our inheritance is Israel, our legacy the Lord. We endure and we shall continue to endure. We may not surrender our inheritance for any other inheritance, for the work of hands, even for the wealth of such worthy hands as Mordecai Meisel's."

They stood there, each of them trembling, both feeling that they had traveled a long road together where once they had a common goal before them, where they could both read the signs; but the roads had diverged. In Jacob's eyes he saw tears melt anger, then rekindle rage, and to avoid further quarreling, the Rabbi sent him downstairs to wait.

Rabbi Low wanted to pray, hungering for the nourishment of prayer as his body hungered for food; but the words cleaved to the roof of his mouth and only the harrowing utterance of Micah jarred his teeth:

> The godly man is perished out of the earth,
> And the upright among men is no more;
> They all lie in wait for blood;
> They hunt every man his brother with a net.

Try as he would he could not summon the presence of God. The longer light of spring outside his window, the noises in the kitchen below, where he heard voices, his own fear, his trembling reverence stood in his way. Though he strove to see, to reach, to imagine the other side, the timeless world beyond, he was only distracted by the torments he knew the two Samuels were undergoing. Then, in the night of his mind, lightning flashed and forked. *Thou canst not see My face. . . . Thou shalt see My back parts, but My face shall not be seen.* Had the Lord for a moment lifted the curtain to reassure him, to say that if he could not see the Almighty's face, His purpose for the future, then at least he might be reassured by what God had wrought in the past? The presence of the Lord had been with them, driven though they were. A remnant *had* been saved. And thus far the Emperor and the Cardinal had kept Thaddeus and his fanatics from ravaging them. Blood had not been spilled. They had endured much; but still they endured.

By the time he had descended the stairs, the sense of uncertainty and doom were more chokingly a part of him than before. He was not reassured and could offer no reassurance to Jacob or to Kaethe who stood near him, or to Pearl, who, although she was as usual silent, cried out for words from him that would set her mind at rest. Only the Golem, though his eyes never left Jacob and Kaethe, seemed suspended in some place where neither wanting nor worrying afflicted him. If he could offer them no comfort, yet his duty was plain: He would go immediately to the Chamber to see if he could persuade von Sternberg to release the two Samuels from the torments of the inquisitioner.

It was late afternoon before von Sternberg had them ushered into his office. He had let them wait for hours in his anteroom until the Rabbi was weak with hunger, but he had refused to depart to eat and also refused to allow the Golem to go to bring him food. He was content too that he had denied Frumett Meisel permission to accompany them, though she had pleaded that since it was her property at stake, and because the two Samuels were her nephews, she should go with them to the Chamber.

"Well, Rabbi Low," von Sternberg said, looking up but not rising from his chair. "And Reb Golem."

"We have come to see you on a matter of grave importance, Herr Vorstand," the Rabbi began. "Mordecai Meisel's nephews were seized during the night and spirited away. We have been reliably informed that they are being put to the torture."

"And who told you that?" the Vorstand inquired, looking at his nails. "And you come to me to conduct negotiations on your holy Sabbath, Rabbi? For shame!"

"Though the Sabbath is holy, Herr Vorstand, we are taught that it is better to profane one Sabbath so that we can observe many Sabbaths. Had you not seen fit to take those two men on the Sabbath, we would have had no need to profane the Sabbath to save their lives," the Rabbi replied. "We demand that the two Samuel Meisels be released. I wish to see them and to have their families permitted to see them."

"Demand?"

"Very well, request."

"Better, Rabbi, much better."

"Those men are innocent of wrongdoing. Why should they be tormented?"

"Who are you to judge their innocence or guilt? His Majesty, Rudolf II, judges, and he has judged that the two Samuel Meisels have attempted to defraud the crown of Mordecai Meisel's estate."

"Mordecai Meisel bequeathed his estate to his wife, Frumett, and to his kinsmen, of whom the two Samuels are his closest relatives."

"The Jew Meisel's will is illegal. Dame Meisel was very generous that day I came to her house. 'Let there be no bloodshed!' she cried. 'Not for property!' How generous! How humane! How easy to talk that way because she had already hidden the greatest part of her husband's valuables. Her husband had willed the Emperor a mere ten thousand florins. And that day we put another forty-five thousand florins on our carts and into His Majesty's treasury; but we knew there was more, much more, and we also wanted that. For it belonged to us, not to the Jew Meisel. He had taken it from the people and the earth of Bohemia; it was ours and not his."

"Mordecai Meisel and his family have lived in Bohemia for three hundred years. He is as much of this country as any of you. He was banker to the court, the Emperor's esteemed advisor. He took nothing from the people of Bohemia and gave them much. His advice, his skill, his knowledge created trade and prosperity for all Bohemia."

"Banker?" von Sternberg spat. "Usurer!"

"Is this to be the reward of faithful service to the Emperor and the country? You will take all that Mordecai Meisel created in a lifetime of work?" Rabbi Low asked.

"The crown claims the entire Meisel estate by right of escheat," the Vorstand declared.

"Escheat! Meisel has a wife, kinsmen. The two Samuels you have taken prisoner are his nephews."

"Where there are no heirs, the property is forfeit to the crown. Mordecai and Frumett Meisel were childless, without *direct* heirs. They are therefore enjoined from bequeathing their properties, which, instead, pass to His Majesty, Rudolf, King of Bohemia," von Sternberg proclaimed.

"The Emperor himself guaranteed Meisel that he might pass on his estate."

"The Emperor does not recall making any promise to Meisel," the Vorstand insisted. "Besides, the Jew Meisel exercised privileges in his commerce denied by law to Jews. Since the means by which he acquired his properties were contrary to law, *ipso facto*, his property must be confiscated by the crown."

"Such tortuous reasoning to deny a man his rights."

"Jews in Bohemia have no rights, Rabbi. Those of you who are permitted to sojourn in our kingdom do so only by the grace of the Emperor and under His Majesty's protection. You are not his vassals, as we are, with defined rights and duties; you are his prisoners, without any rights at all."

"If you have established all this, why must you torture those two poor men?"

"We must know where the rest of Meisel's monies are hidden."

When he returned from von Sternberg, Rabbi Low continued his fast and was surprised when the Golem remained in the study with him after Pearl's slammed-door departure—"It will take none of the anguish from the Samuels' torments for you to starve yourself" ringing in the room behind her.

"So, Joseph, do you, too, think me a stubborn old fool?" the Rabbi asked.

"No, Rabbi, but I do not see how your fasting will help."

"Perhaps the Lord will relieve their anguish to relieve mine."

The Golem shook his head. "I do not think so, though it may relieve *your* anguish."

"Perhaps it will persuade Frumett Meisel to tell them where Marcus hid his wealth."

Again the Golem shook his head. "She will not tell, but one of the Samuels will. Had they tortured her, she might have died without speaking, because she is old and she knows the value and power of property. That is why the Vorstand did not take her. The two Samuels are young. They want to live. They have children." Pain flickered across his face. "They will choose life over property."

The Rabbi stared at him for a long time before saying, "You have grown wise, Joseph."

"Suffering makes for wisdom, Rabbi."

"And wisdom for more suffering?"

"That, too, Rabbi."

"Is not our suffering the result of the *yetzer*, which our reason cannot master? Frumett's *yetzer* for Marcus' wealth and power will not permit her to reveal where the bulk of his legacy is hiding."

Rabbi Low remembered what Marcus had told him soon after they had finished and certified his will. Frumett was infuriated because he had tried to persuade Marcus to distribute large sums to the poor before he died. She had upbraided her husband for having fallen prey to such rabbinical foolishness. Now, instead of helping the poor while Marcus was alive, it would all go to Rudolf's imperial extravagance.

"Perhaps, Rabbi," the Golem said, "but what is the two Samuels' *yetzer*? Do they suffer torture out of greed for their share of the inheritance, or because they choose not to betray his trust and their aunt's? Or has the Lord abandoned them to their suffering as . . ."

The Golem did not complete his sentence, but the Rabbi finished it for him silently. "As He has abandoned me."

The Rabbi slept fitfully, conscious that his hunger was part of his spirit, which sought to seize the hidden connections in the events that plagued them. He dreamed of the Sanhedrin tractate of the Babylonian Talmud that told of the fourth-century,

Common Era, Rabbi Rab who created a golem and sent him with a message to his colleague, Rabbi Zera. When the golem arrived and could not speak, Rabbi Zera exclaimed: "You are one of those vessels of clay! Begone! Return to the dust!" And the messenger had crumbled into dust.

When he awoke, it was the middle of the night, the moon outside his window a bent needle of light, the stars remote pinpoints in the night sky. Careful not to rouse the Golem, who slept on the floor next to his couch, he rose and went to his desk. The moonlight was too faint to read by, so he lit the lamp and began immediately to write as if his hand were impelled:

"God and man are divided as by a curtain. Although God is one, the powers originating in and deriving from Him are multiple and various, and those powers the beings in this world acquire do not emanate from the true name of God. Our world does not know His name because it belongs to a world entirely different from our corporeal one. His name consists of four letters, but it is not pronounced as it is written; the writing points to the true Name, but the reading of it is human.

"Order is God's plan inherent in all happenings and mutual relations, but it is beyond our comprehension. The material world is a curtain that forever hides the eternal so that only a fragment is accessible to man. Only study of the Law lifts the curtain and permits one to approach God on the other side. The Law is God's charter upholding the world; it teaches order and informs man how to arrange his conduct. Man is not created in final perfection; he must realize perfection himself. So, too, is his world not created in final perfection; man must realize and create the world's perfection himself. The way of true conduct lies in keeping order in daily life and in recognizing order in the occurrences of the world around us. Sin is disorder. To put order into the world is man's messianic task."

As he wrote the last word and his hand, of its own volition, dropped limply to his side, the Golem sighed deeply in his sleep and clearly spoke: *"Let them be ashamed that persecute me, but let me not be ashamed; let them be dismayed, but let me not be dismayed.*

The knocking at the outside door was uncertain, but the gravel against the window was a hailstorm. The Golem was instantly awake and looking out. In the well of darkness below they saw only shadows, but the voice that mounted to them pleaded in Yiddish, "For the sake of charity, let us in."

The Golem hurried down, and moments later the elder Samuel Meisel staggered through the door of the study, stumbled, and fell at the Rabbi's feet. He lay gasping for breath like an exhausted swimmer on a beach, his body shaken by waves of chill. The Rabbi tried to help him to his feet, to a chair, but he was too feeble. The Golem soon followed with the younger Samuel Meisel in his arms and carried him to the Rabbi's couch. Then he went to help the other Samuel, who waved him away.

It was Kaethe who scratched on the study door and, when the Golem opened it, stood there, long hair over her nightdress, sleep-filled eyes staring horror-struck at the two Samuels. Without a word she ran down the stairs and soon returned with a bottle of wine, a pitcher of water, and clean cloths. She handed the wine to the Golem, who poured some into a cup, knelt and, lifting the elder Samuel's head, helped him to drink. Coughing, the elder Samuel let the wine run over his chin.

Kaethe knelt next to the younger Samuel, whose arm hung over the side of the couch, his fingertips trailing a pool of blood. When she lifted his hand to wipe it clean, she saw where the nails had been torn out and shuddered convulsively. "Let me," the Golem offered, reaching for the bloodied cloth.

"No," Kaethe refused hoarsely. "Help me to undress him."

The younger Samuel's clothes were pasted to his back by blood and filth, and the Golem had to use a knife to cut the coat, shirt, and ritual fringes from him. He had been lashed and his back, arms, and waist were bleeding furrows and raised black welts. His blood-soaked shoes and stockings also had to be cut away because the soles of his feet had been bastinadoed into lumps of lacerated flesh. "Why?" Kaethe asked the room, "why?" But no one answered. She dressed each wound with unguent, loosely bandaging his entire back with soft cloths. She showed no embarrassment when the Golem cut the younger Samuel's breeches away and she had to wash the urine and excrement from his body, but when she came to the flayed feet she retched so convulsively it seemed she would not be able to continue. Yet she did not turn away until the feet were bandaged and she had covered the younger Samuel with the bedclothes. "I have done what I could, Rabbi," she said. "His back will heal, I think, though he will be badly scarred. He must have a doctor to treat his feet, but even then I do not believe he will ever walk on them as he used to."

The elder Samuel, his face against the floor, gave an animal yowl, "Samuel! Samuel!" and they could not tell whether he was weeping for himself or for his cousin. After he had drunk more wine, the elder Samuel tried to pick himself off the floor but his knees and elbows buckled until the Golem lifted him into a chair. Only then did the Rabbi see that two fingers of his left hand dangled broken, that his eyes and head had been badly beaten. Words tumbled from his mouth as though his split lips had lost all control. "They came in the middle of Sabbath night. We were all sleeping. How they got into the house, I don't know, but when I awoke, they were in my bedroom. My wife screamed and they knocked her down and gagged her. I rushed to help her, but three of them beat me unconscious.

"When I revived, I was in the cellar of a strange building, shackled, lying on a filthy floor. The first face I saw was Vorstand von Sternberg's, the second was that of the friar Thaddeus who stood next to him with two hooded torturers. He told me they were executioners from the Holy Office of the Inquisition. The third face was my cousin Samuel's, and when he saw that I had recognized him, he called out, 'Tell them nothing!' before they knocked him puking to the floor.

"It was the Herr Vorstand who explained what they wanted. Because Uncle Marcus had no direct heirs, His Majesty claimed the entire Meisel estate by escheat. Everything my uncle owned was now crown property. But they couldn't find his money and they wanted to know where it was hidden.

"I said I didn't know and they laughed and battered my face with their fists. Then the torturers began to break my fingers, one at a time." Wincing, he held up his left hand to show the fingers.

"After they broke the second finger, the friar stopped them. He drew von Sternberg aside and they talked in whispers until the Vorstand nodded his agreement. Then the torturers picked my cousin up from the floor and chained him to the wall. They began to flog him, and with each lash, Samuel roared, 'Tell them nothing, Samuel!' as if he were talking to us both. But they asked him nothing: They only asked me. If I turned away, they made me watch. If I closed my eyes, they pried them open or held my nose and mouth so I couldn't breathe. And they flogged him, lash after lash. Each time he fainted, I was ready to tell them everything to make them stop, but Samuel would recover and moan or yell that I was to say nothing, and I did not want to mock his suffering by surrendering what he refused to surrender. Finally they bastinadoed him into unconsciousness and then I could tell them everything, because I could no longer bear his torment." The elder Samuel hung his head. "I thought they would kill him, or cripple him for life."

"They may have crippled him," Kaethe whispered, as if to assure him that he had done the right thing.

Painfully the elder Samuel shrugged and continued, "I remember nothing after that until they rolled me out of a cart onto the street in front of your house."

"They left you here?" the Rabbi asked. "Not at your house, or his, or your uncle's?"

"Here," the elder Samuel said.

Covering her face with her hands, Kaethe sobbed steadily, like rain on a roof. The Golem moved to comfort her, caught the Rabbi's eye, and stopped. Rabbi Low tried to lift their spirits and found himself despairingly repeating the words that had welled out of the Golem's sleeping mouth, "*Let them be ashamed that persecute me, but let me not be ashamed; let them be dismayed, but let me not be dismayed,*" though he saw that they were all, himself included, both ashamed and dismayed.

Early the next day the Golem took the two Samuels to their homes. People noted their passage in the *Judengasse,* and in some of their faces the Golem saw hatred and anger against their tormentors, compassion for the tormented; but in the eyes of others he saw only satisfaction that some of the rich Meisels had at last been brought low.

When he returned to the Rabbi's study, Frumett Meisel sat weeping in the chair that only a short time before had held her nephew. "They have taken it all," she lamented, "all, transferred all the monies to the Chamber. More than half a million florins!"

"Remember what Marcus always said, Frumett," Rabbi Low reminded her. "With such things we pay our *leibzoll.*"

"They tax us excessively, they expropriate our properties," she raged, "they even deprive us of our lifetime's work."

"But they let us live in peace, more or less, most of the time," the Rabbi said.

"Is there no way to oppose them?" Frumett sobbed.

"We shall lodge a complaint with the Privy Council. We shall begin proceedings against von Sternberg. But you know that none of it will help. None of it will bring back a single florin. It is the Emperor who is behind it all. We cannot oppose him."

"And my nephews! They have given away five hundred and sixteen thousand florins! A king's ransom!"

"What could they have done, Frumett? They were tortured."

"They could have died," she said spitefully. "They could have gone silent to the grave, as I would have gone, to save what their uncle had taken a lifetime to build."

Three days later, an official imperial proclamation was read in the squares and handbills were distributed and prominently posted on many buildings in the Old Town. It praised "the faithful and fruitful services of the esteemed counselor of the Emperor and the Supreme Governing Body, Mordecai Meisel," and expressed "the profound grief and sense of loss felt by the Emperor Rudolf and the entire kingdom of Bohemia" at the great financier's demise.

XXIV

Hidden on the roof of one of the houses on the ghetto wall, they could see for a good distance. "It is impressive," Jacob said.

"There are many people singing and praying," the Golem agreed.

Not turning his head, Jacob remarked sharply, "Sometimes, if I forget and am not looking at you, I think it's him speaking to me. And with Isaac's accent and intonation, because . . ."

"Because he taught them to me?"

"But what did *he* teach you?"

"He?"

"Rabbi Low, the *Höhe*."

The Golem did not reply. Instead, looking at the processional, he asked, "How many times during the year?"

"Once only, at Easter. A most solemn processional. Priests in vestments and monks and friars in their habits, all carrying crucifixes and candles and chalices. It *is* impressive," Jacob repeated, "for the townspeople, but especially for the peasants who come from the countryside at Easter to celebrate the passion."

"The passion?"

"The crucifixion of Jesus and his resurrection."

"Is that why we are here?"

"No. They say we crucified him, so this is the time things happen and this will be the place." Their roof overlooked the main gate to the ghetto.

"Look! There's Thaddeus." The friar, in black and white, was near the head of the procession, holding before him a cup that blazed in the sun.

"What is he carrying?"

"A chalice with a tiny piece of unleavened bread."

A thousand voices chanted powerfully so that even at that distance they could hear the words: "Brothers, pour out the old leaven that you may be a new dough, as you really are without leaven. For Christ, our Passover, has been sacrificed for us. Therefore let us keep the feast, not with the old leaven, nor with the leaven of malice and wickedness, but with the un-leavened bread of sincerity and truth."

"Is it their Passover, Jacob?" the Golem asked.

"Because of the unleavened bread?" Jacob shook his head. "No, they believe that the little wafer of unleavened bread—they call it the host—is miraculously transformed into the body of Jesus. It is the miracle of their mass. Because they believe it, they think we are always scheming to steal their wafer to torture it and mock it, as if we believed it to be the real Jesus."

"Why would we do that?"

"I told you. They think *we* were responsible for Jesus' cruci-fixion. And on Easter Jesus is supposed to be resurrected. In the taverns Thaddeus' seminarians are saying that we bribed an old woman to steal one of those sacramental wafers so that we might stick pins in it, drop it into boiling oil, pound it with a mortar— desecrate their host, torment their god once again."

The Golem squinted into the spring sun. "Do you think they will pass around the ghetto, or through it?"

"Through it."

"There are thousands of them."

"That's what I am afraid of."

"Perhaps they are only marching to the great church." The Golem pointed to where twin Gothic spires soared over the slate roofs.

"What does the Rabbi think?"

"He did not say. He told me only to go with you and to take my ax." He lifted his woodcutter's ax a few inches off the roof. "But I know that he prayed and fasted through the night."

"And your teacher, the scholar Isaac? Where is he?"

"He remains in the *Altneuschul*, praying."

"That's where he belongs."

"Why do you hate him?"

"I don't hate him. I despise him."

"Because he refuses to shed blood?"

"Because he is willing to let them shed our blood. He and his friends, they will stand there in the synagogue, white and holy in their shrouds, crying out to the Lord, but doing nothing."

"You question Isaac's sincerity?"

"No, his intelligence."

"He asked me to remain with them in the synagogue."

"And you refused?" Jacob turned to look at him.

"Rabbi Low said I was to go with you."

"But you didn't want to?"

"I would rather have stayed with Isaac."

"Like teacher, like pupil."

"Then who taught you, Jacob?"

Jacob grinned and jerked his head toward the processional. "They did."

The procession moved slowly through the streets, the slight wind carrying the chanting over the rooftops: "*O Lord, remove not Thy help to a distance from me, look toward my defense; deliver me from the lion's mouth. . . . O God, my God, look upon me: why hast Thou forsaken me?*"

"How much their words sound like ours," the Golem remarked.

"Many *are* our words," Jacob said, "but what they have made of them! *Eli, Eli, lomo azavtoni. Our fathers trusted in thee:*

*they trusted, and thou didst deliver them. But I am a worm, and
no man; a reproach of men, and despised of the people. For dogs
have compassed me; the assembly of the wicked have enclosed
me. But Thou, O Lord, be not far from me: O my strength,
hasten to help me. Deliver my soul from the sword; My only
one from the power of the dog. Save me from the lion's mouth."*

"The twenty-second Psalm."

"You remember," Jacob said, a small smile lighting his face,
as if the reward of Isaac's teaching were his own.

"I remember. And this morning, when Isaac brought me to
the synagogue to see his people standing there in their shrouds,
they were reciting that Psalm."

"Fools! With the Psalm they surrender to their enemy. And
with our Psalm the enemy glorifies a Jesus who said, *He who
smites thee on the right cheek, turn to him the left also; and he
who takes away thy coat, let him have thy shirt also.* Now they
glorify and glory in using the same floggings and slayings that
once they themselves were forced to endure. Look at them.
Even when they march in a religious processional, they carry
weapons."

The people were armed. "You think they will come?"

"I know in my bones. The memory of the passion, its blood
and torment, are inflammatory. They remind the people that
they were told it was we Jews who betrayed and killed their
god. And when they are reminded, they are possessed by a
blind joyous violence, a *yetzer* to kill and plunder and wreak
revenge."

"I feel such a *yetzer* in myself."

"And so do I," Jacob confessed. "That's how I know what
they will do."

"Perhaps Isaac lacks such a *yetzer*."

"And the Rabbi?"

In unison they shrugged.

Floating on the air the words echoed over them:

> *Kyrie, eleison.*
> *Kyrie, eleison. . . .*
> *Christe, eleison.*
> *Christe, eleison. . . .*

"What language is that?" the Golem asked.

"Greek. It means *Lord, have mercy on us. Christ, have mercy on us*," Jacob explained hoarsely.

Snakelike, the processional wound its way through the narrow streets of the Old Town. Soon the head of the procession was on the street next to the ghetto walls, singing and chanting, priests, monks, friars, and pilgrims holding their crucifixes aloft, candles guttering. Thaddeus lifted the burnished gold of the chalice high so that it shone like a separate sun. When they were at the gate, one of the seminarians cried out and pointed to an ancient, rough-hewn, earth-colored crucifix: On it blood was pouring from the wounds of the broken Jesus. Others began to stare, to point, to push one another so that they might see what the others saw. Then another cry louder than the first and other fingers pointed at the chalice Thaddeus held, its gold sides suddenly stained by blood seeping over its brim and down over the friar's hands. "Our Lord bleeds! The Jews desecrated the Host!" the voices called.

Like a great serpent the processional wound itself around the ghetto. News of the bleeding crucifix and wafer swept through its coils in convulsive waves and a low murmur slowly grew to a great roar punctuated by shouts of "Christ bleeds! The Jews have desecrated the Host!"

Weapons were brandished. Clubs and staves, daggers and pikes, swords and halberds and poleaxes. Voices took up the cries: "Kill the Jews! Put on the armor of the Lord. Kill a Jew and save your soul!" Other voices echoed the cries, and the shouting multiplied into "Kill the Jews and save Bohemia!" The mob surged against the ghetto walls and gates, and from the walls a flight of swifts was startled and soared black into the heavens. Men began to climb over the walls, stones were hurled, and great logs appeared and began to batter the gates. The Golem saw Jacob's stricken face as he lit the signal torch and from the roof threw it high into the air to fall into the deserted *Judengasse* below. Young Jews appeared in the streets, on the roofs, and in the windows of houses, on the ghetto wall—all armed.

The sight of them seemed to inflame the mob further. And then a young Jew, a boy no older than fifteen, stood on tiptoe on the wall to see what that roar of hatred was—and became the first victim. The javelin caught him full in the chest, went through him. The boy dropped his stave and, both hands clutching the haft of the javelin, seemed to be trying to tear death from his body before he fell into the crowd below. A monk held his head high by the hair so that the others on the ghetto wall might see what awaited them. "Soldiers of Christ!" the monk shouted. "So die all the crucifiers!" A roar of acclaim resounded.

In the street Jacob gathered a group of young guards behind the main gate. Barricades had been thrown up all along the *Judengasse.* The gate, already battered, would soon give. Sword in hand, Jacob deployed his young men, who stood determined but uncertain of their powers.

The first few invaders over the wall were soon joined by others who plunged through the gap in the gate made by the battering ram. Young Jews leaped to meet them, the fighting fierce. Yet the Golem could not bring himself to join. His arm seemed held back by Isaac's words, by the Rabbi's, by what he had learned himself. He saw Jacob beset by three men, a peasant with a stave, a soldier with a pike, and a monk with a dirk, circling, waiting for an opening. Still the Golem held back, the surge of hope rising in him that all together the three might kill Jacob and so leave Kaethe to him. Then horrified by his own thoughts, he raised his ax and with a great cry leaped to Jacob's aid. With two strokes he cut down the peasant and the soldier; Jacob killed the monk. "Bless you, Joseph!" Jacob called and, with a leap of his heart, the Golem knew it was only the second time Jacob Nissan had called him by his name.

All morning they fought without respite as more and more of the procession sieved through the breaches in the ghetto walls and through the gates, which had finally been splintered off their hinges. Peasants, friars, monks, pilgrims, priests, soldiers, bailiffs guildsmen, and even a few merchants rampaged through the narrow streets of the ghetto.

A group of hooligans caught two old Jews in the street, forced them to their knees, urinated in their mouths, and cut off their beards. Before the Golem and Jacob could drive them off, the old men's throats were cut and one had his eyes gouged out.

In the *Judengasse* the Golem stood helpless as four laughing peasants hurled an entire family from a third-story window; the peasants threw first the parents and then, giggling insanely, the small bodies down after them.

They found two young women lying naked in a side street under an arcade, ravished and disemboweled. Their breasts bore the dagger-incised sign of the cross.

In the square, among the debris of glass and broken furniture, the air was full of down and feathers from quilts and pillows, like a late spring snowfall. A middle-aged woman, her long black braided hair whitened with down, feathers stuck to her sides, was down on all fours barking like a dog around the bodies of her slain husband and two sons, whose heads lolled on the cobbles.

Every house seemed under attack. In one the Golem, Jacob, and four young Jewish boys fought their way up from the ground floor five stories to the roof. On the first floor two peasants were raping two Jewish girls while a pair of monks held the girls' parents and made them watch. They killed all four, but not before one of the monks had brained one of the young Jews and the peasants had killed the parents. On the second floor a son whose shirt had been flayed into bloody ribbons had been forced to hang his father by a group of wheelwrights who urged him on with a horsewhip. In the skirmish another young Jewish guard and the son perished; the father was already dead from hanging. On the third floor a small boy whimpering "Mama, Mama" ran from corner to corner looking empty-eyed at his slain parents in the center of the room. His mother's head had been crushed, his father's nose and ears torn from his head. When the Golem tried to catch the boy to take him with them, the boy, with one terrified glance at his bloodied ax, wrenched himself free and with a long wail threw himself from the window. On the fourth floor a man was nailed to the door. Blood still trickled over his white beard; his tongue had been torn out. All around him were scattered books, torn and broken. On the top floor nothing had been touched, everything was in order, but not a soul was there. They heard the fire beneath and felt its heat and knew that the building was aflame; and so the four of them who remained escaped over the rooftops.

The rabble seemed drunk and wild, yet it went systematically from house to house, from street to street, killing and looting. A dozen fires raged and smoke hung like a pall over the entire ghetto; walls crashed, shooting up geysers of flame and sparks that endangered the adjacent densely packed houses. Everywhere the shops were broken into and pillaged. In the streets, the squares, the alleyways, the ground was littered with dead and dying, and with the plunder of a hundred homes: linen, clothes, shoes, pillows, coats, furniture. Everywhere there was moaning and weeping, jeering and laughter, swearing and praying.

Gradually the Jews were being driven back from barricade to barricade, house to house, to the ghetto's best-defended strongpoints, the synagogues, the town hall, and the old cemetery. The Golem led the rear guard, holding off the assaulters until the Jews could safely retreat, taking as many of the old and infirm, women and children and wounded with them as they could.

The Golem killed until his arms ached and his head spun. His lungs panted with the joy of fighting, but his stomach turned with the nausea of murder. He killed many who were robbing the dead, including two who were stripping the breeches and boots from a dead old man, and another who was senselessly pounding a dead woman's face to a pulp with a paving stone, all the while tittering, "You're guilty, you're a Jew." He came on a peasant who, having fired a house, was helping his two cronies bar the doors and windows so that the Jews inside were howling as they burned to death. When the flames drove him back and he knew he could not save those in the house, the Golem pursued the three peasants and cut them down. All around him the faces of people had turned into the faces of animals—lynxes, wolves, wild dogs—so that when he killed, it no longer seemed as if he were killing human beings.

The Jews fell back to the cemetery grounds. At the entrance there dogs gnawed at the disemboweled entrails of the dead and ate the half-formed fishlike creature that, ripped from its nearby mother's swollen womb, lay still tied to it by the cord of birth. Nearby, its brother, head crushed, still clutched his mother's breast.

In the cemetery some Jews dug graves for the dead, others for the living. Many, already mad, groveled, crept, and slithered on their bellies. They did not answer to their names, and when their loved ones called to them, one chewed his own clothing and bit his flesh like an animal enraged against itself. Another ran raving, frothing at the mouth, the point of a poleax buried in his skull, its haft mechanically beating his shoulders as he ran; propelled forward, he stumbled, toppled, and fell down dead. Many, heads bowed, wrapped in prayer shawls and shrouds, prepared to die as martyrs, fearfully, numbly, ecstatically sanctifying the Name and intoning the *Shema* and the Psalms.

XXV

A thin Jewish boy not much beyond *bar-mitzvah* age limped
into the cemetery, trying to run but only able to hop on one
leg and drag the other. Blood seeped through his fingers where
his left hand clutched his side, a pike dragged in his right hand.
He brought news from Isaac that Thaddeus was leading the
mob against the *Altneuschul* and Rabbi Low's house. "At least
Isaac is brave enough to send for us to defend him and the
synagogue," Jacob said to the Golem, his face a mixture of triumph and despair. He left men to guard the living, the wounded,
and the dead in the cemetery, then ordered the rest to follow him.

In the narrow streets, jammed together, the Jews formed a
wedge with Jacob at the point and the Golem at the rear, and
fought their way between flaming houses, past piles of house-

hold goods, kegs of wine, bolts of cloth, groups of hooligans looting houses, until they made their way to the *Altneuschul* and the Rabbi's house. There, so intent was the mob on what Thaddeus was saying that Jacob signaled his people to make their way singly through the rabble to join the thin line of Jews who stood holding off the hooligans while Thaddeus urged them on.

"Soldiers of Christ!" Thaddeus cried. "Not to kill Christ's enemies is to be an enemy to Christ. Jews are an accursed race, outlawed by God and the Church. When the last Jew is dead, we, the descendants of the Crucified, shall finally be avenged on the descendants of the crucifiers. The Jew always has a fat goose or fat chicken for dinner while the poor Christian soaks a piece of hard bread in the tears that stream from his eyes. All that is theirs will be ours, yours, when the Jews are dead. Take their silver. Take their belongings. Take their women. Take their lives. Kill them! KILL THEM!"

As the mob surged forward, the Golem threw himself against them, bellowing, "Run, Thaddeus, run! I, Joseph Golem, am coming to kill you!" Though seminarians and peasants stood in his path, the Golem fought through them toward Thaddeus. The friar turned, took a few uncertain steps, then, brandishing his crucifix, stood his ground. As the friar leaped at him, trying to brain him with the wooden crucifix, Jacob emerged from the throng and deflected the blow with his sword. With his other hand he drove his dagger into Thaddeus' chest, then thrust it cruelly home until its haft was pressed against the friar's breastbone. The friar's fingers tore at the dagger as he cried out: "*My Lord God, even now I accept at Thy hands . . . with all its pains and sufferings, whatever kind of death it shall please Thee. . . .*" When Jacob pulled his dagger free, a burst of blood shook Thaddeus to his knees, his luminous eyes turned up into his head, and he cried a great howling cry, then lurched forward on his face and died.

"Amen!" Jacob sobbed.

"Amen!" the Golem echoed.

They fought, the fires from nearby houses burning hot and spraying them with sparks and ashes, the air stifling, the smoke making it difficult to breathe, until, by weight of numbers, the mob split them into two groups, the Golem in one that was gradually pushed out onto the street, Jacob in the second, which was forced farther back into the courtyard toward the Rabbi's house. Jewish defender after defender went down, slain or badly wounded. In twos and threes their enemies penetrated their line and broke into the Rabbi's house. A window burst open from within and Kaethe, trying to fling herself out of it, was caught by her long hair and pulled back into the darkness, but not before she had glimpsed the Golem and shrieked to him, "Joseph! Joseph!"

The Golem heard and saw her, and a maniacal bawl came from his throat. He rushed headlong at the enemy, storming through them into the courtyard first, then into the house.

He found Kaethe on the floor of her bedroom, neck broken, eyes, alive with pain and horror, still open. Her clothes had been torn off and her legs lay askew. Dumbly, the Golem fell to his knees beside her, leaned his ear against her breast, and when he heard nothing, gently closed her eyelids. He turned his face from her nakedness and smashed everything in sight. As he came to break her mirror, he saw his own face, began to weep, and let the ax fall to the floor. Spent, quivering, he took the bedsheet to wrap her in, but when he lifted her in his arms, her golden hair lay shorn like a fallen banner on the floor. He sat on her bed then, cradling her in his arms, her cropped head so small in his hand, and wept.

He heard the horses and the clang of armor, the fierce cries of attack, the hussars' commands and the rabble's defiance, and he knew that once more the Emperor had sent Pokorny, once more a remnant of the Jews would be saved. But not his Kaethe. Not all the others killed and mutilated, ravished and crippled. They could neither be saved nor helped now; for them it was all too late. Too late. He sat there rocking Kaethe in his arms, her head pressed against his shoulder, crooning the only lullaby he had ever heard, one a woman he had passed in the street had been singing to the babe at her breast, "Sleep, my baby, sleep. *Ai lyu lyu*, sleep."

The clamor outside roused, then angered him, and he stood up. He placed Kathe's body in the center of her bed, drew the sheet up to her throat, but could not bear to cover her face. Then he kissed the cold, bruised mouth. He stooped to retrieve the golden train of her hair and wound it like a phylactery around his left arm. Then he found his woodsman's ax and, thus armed, descended the stairs and strode into the late afternoon sun.

Fires still flared, smoke hung heavy over the ghetto, and in the darkening sky sparks fountained like spray. The fighting in the courtyard and around the synagogue beyond still raged unchecked. Hussars, mounted and dismounted, now fought priests and peasants, guildsmen and students, pilgrims and beggars. New forces had also arrived from among the patricians and burghers, who had armed themselves and were fighting both the fires and the mob lest either or both spill over the ghetto walls into their world.

A blinding hatred blistered his eyes. He threw himself into the fray, screaming, "You killed her. You let her die." He rode roughshod over hussar and burgher, priest and student alike. Laughing crazily, he struck his first Jew and the man fell dying, crying out dismayed, "Reb Golem, I am a Jew!" The second Jew died with the surprised words "But you are one of ours" bubbling from his lips with his heart's blood.

Single-handed, the Golem cleared a third of the Rabbi's courtyard, leaving a trail of dead and dying until, sword raised and eyes blazing, Pokorny barred his way. "Are you mad, man?" the Count roared. "You are killing my men and your own people!"

The Golem, swaying, looked down on him, the ax high. "I have no people," he said. "Neither Jew nor Christian, no father or mother, no wife or children. Do you hear? I have no people. *They killed her. And you let her die!*" He swung the ax.

Pokorny evaded it.

"Joseph!" Jacob called. "Pokorny is helping us."

"No one helps me," the Golem roared, charging the elusive Pokorny a second time.

Skillfully circling and holding him off with his sword, Pokorny said calmly, "I have no wish to kill you like this. You are drunk with blood."

"But I wish to kill you, all of you," the Golem shouted. "All men. If you had a single skull, I would split it."

Once again he lunged at Pokorny and now Jacob came to Pokorny's aid. Together, slashing at him with their swords, they strove to force him back toward the wall of the Rabbi's house, but again and again he broke through one of them and narrowly missed killing them both. With a sudden twist he flicked Pokorny's blade from his hand and watched it clatter on the cobbles. "Now!" he cried jubilantly, raising his ax.

A flicker of dying sunlight pierced the smoke and, flaming, caught the red beard and his eye at once. He heard and saw Isaac at the same moment, white and ghostly, standing wrapped in his shroud, ashes and grime all over him, blood redder than his hair trickling down the side of his head. Hands spasmodically clutching the fringes of his *tallis*, Isaac stood as if in prayer. "Joseph," he lamented. "Kaethe. I could not stop them. I tried."

The Golem, ax still high over his head, turned. "You tried?"

Isaac nodded, his tongue wet his lips, his hands were pleading. "I tried . . . to reason with them, to beg them, but they would not listen. When I stood in their way, they thrust me aside and beat me senseless with their staves. They did not even bother to kill me."

"You tried?"

"Believe me, Joseph. I did try . . . and I failed."

Bewildered, the Golem stood there. Then he groaned, *"You killed her! You let her die!"* With a moan and all his strength he drove his ax down in a blow that cut Isaac from head to groin. For a long time, limp and weeping joyously, miserably, the Golem stood shaking over the severed halves of the man who had once been his teacher. He turned to Pokorny, but Rabbi Low's voice thundered in his ears, "Golem, put down your ax!" The Rabbi stood in the doorway of his house.

"He has murdered Isaac," one of the older Jewish guards yelled. "Kill him!"

Jews, hussars, and rabble alike took up the cry, "Kill him! Kill him!"

"Let no one lay a hand on him!" Rabbi Low commanded.

The trio stood frozen: Pokorny, in a crouch, poised to dodge the ax; Jacob, staunch between Pokorny and the Golem's blow; and the Golem, ready to slay, but unmoving.

"Put down the ax," Rabbi Low ordered.

Imperceptibly at first, then in slow stages, the Golem let the ax fall. "You called me Golem," he said to the Rabbi.

"When you are a golem," the Rabbi answered, "there is no Joseph."

"You killed her. You let her die," the Golem declared. "You and Isaac."

"We did not kill her," Rabbi Low maintained. "Nor did you. You could not save her, Isaac could not, no one could."

Then Jacob heard and understood. He turned aside and vomited.

The Golem watched in silence and Pokorny took advantage of the diversion to reclaim his sword from the ground.

White-faced, Jacob looked up and asked, "Where?"

The Golem gestured to Kaethe's window with his ax. As he did someone threw a stone that bloodied his forehead, but the Golem shook it off as if it were a gnat's sting. A hail of stones followed, until Pokorny, roaring commands, charged the mob with his hussars and drove it back. The courtyard was soon cleared; among the living, only Jacob, the Golem, and Rabbi Low remained there.

"I want to see Kaethe," Jacob said to the Rabbi.

Rabbi Low led him to her bedroom. The Golem followed. Pearl was on her knees next to the bed, crooning, "My child, my child." When she heard them come in, she turned her reddened eyes on the Rabbi and her quivering finger pointed at him. "You killed her!" she accused. "You let her die!" The Golem burst into savage laughter.

"They cut off her hair," Pearl lamented, turning back to the bed to caress Kaethe's head, "all her beautiful, golden hair."

From his arm the Golem unwound the bright bracelet of hair and laid it on the bed. Pearl's wrinkled old hands with their parchment skin and prominent blue veins trembled as she took the hair gently between her fingers and kneaded it, sighing, "*Mein kindt, mein kindt.*"

Jacob approached from the other side of the bed, leaned over, and grazed Kaethe's cheek with his fingertips. His forefinger traced the straightness of her nose and the curve of her cheek before his hand fell away and he whispered, "My bride, my bride." Then he ran from the room.

"I shall go with him," the Golem announced.

"You have killed Isaac and shed Jewish blood. They will stone you," the Rabbi warned.

"Jacob cannot go alone," the Golem replied.

When they emerged from the house, Jacob stood at the entrance to the courtyard as if rooted there. Before them the ghetto lay in ruins. Houses still burned, others smoldered, walls crashed and crumbled; the city seemed to be in the throes of death, the *Judengasse* a desolation. Carts carried corpses toward the cemetery followed by wailing mourners. Jews wandered in search of their own, forlornly calling names among the dead and dying. Here and there, dogs in droves attacked the corpses in the streets. From afar cries like those of crazed gulls came from the Moldau where Jews set adrift by the mob were on the river in small boats without oars.

"I have seen a mountain of Jewish dead higher than Sinai," Rabbi Low grieved, "a mountain of cast-off shoes and shrouds and murdered children."

"Higher than Sinai, and holier," Jacob added bitterly.

"I hear footsteps walking on the cobbles through the streets of life," the Golem echoed hollowly. "They walk, they go on walking, their footsteps echoing forever."

"Lord, O Lord, why hast Thou once more forsaken us?"

"It is man, not God, who has forsaken us," the Rabbi muttered. "Even in the millenium we can hope only for the weakening of the evil impulse, not for its total extinction. But God's spirit is with the humiliated, God's presence with the persecuted. *Alenu leshabeach,*" Rabbi Low chanted, "as for us, we must praise."

"Praise?" The Golem laughed wildly once more. "You are a madman. One and all you are mad."

"Silence!" the Rabbi commanded.

"My tongue will be stilled soon enough. Now I shall speak."

"Not blasphemy."

The Golem threw his arms wide to encompass the scene of devastation around them. "Blasphemy? Is this not blasphemy?" Abruptly, he declared, "I shall speak as I will."

"You have already spoken as you will," the Rabbi said, and he pointed to Isaac's corpse.

XXVI

———◆◆▶◆◆———

Why, Rabbi Low considered, must the final decision be mine? Having created him, why now must I also have to decide to destroy him? The Golem is like a son to me, not like Bezalel perhaps, not even like Isaac, but a son nonetheless.

"His hands are covered with blood," Pearl was saying. "He has widowed your daughter."

Jacob held his hands outstretched, unable to hide their trembling. "These hands too are covered with blood."

"Not Jewish blood," Pearl objected.

"Jewish and Gentile blood alike. More than a hundred of those who fought with me are dead, more than five hundred wounded. And more than three thousand who did not fight are dead. Are not my hands bloodier than Joseph Golem's?" Jacob asked.

"But you killed reluctantly," Pearl insisted. "The Golem killed like one of *them*, with joy. To our people, you are a hero and he is a monster. They will stone him for the Jewish blood he has shed."

"They have already forgotten how many Jewish lives he saved, how many of their enemies he destroyed," Jacob answered sadly. "Without him, my companions would have lost heart, and their strongest hand."

"But now his task is done," Pearl said. "He could not save the ghetto by himself, or even with your help."

"Should we therefore kill him?" Jacob asked.

"He is a golem. A golem is neither murdered nor mourned."

"Joseph is as much a human being as you are or I am. Perhaps we violated his humanity so that he was forced to do what he did. Many would wish to stone him, as you say, but there are also many who would only applaud him gratefully."

"It is best that they neither stone nor applaud," Rabbi Low interjected.

"Then there is only one way, to do what I ask," Pearl persisted. "Let him return to the dust from which he was made. Swiftly, tonight."

The Lord, Rabbi Low thought, can save with one as with many. But He did not save and I do not know why. Finally, he said, "Go find Joseph Golem, Jacob, and bring him here to me."

When they were both gone, the Rabbi put his face into his hands and prayed, "On my hands, the blood he shed, O Lord, on my head his transgression, for I created him and thought him Your emissary and our defender. Why else did You give me the power to shape his clay and create his strength, unless Your desire was that we should be saved from the sword? Your mystery evades me. Your presence eludes me. Did You not permit me entry into the other realm only so that I might do Your bidding? Did You not endow my hands to shape the clay and my mouth to breathe Your breath into him that he might live?

"The sin was mine, mine alone. For Joseph Golem, his destiny was a burden that I laid on his shoulders in Your holy name, a collar on his neck from which he struggled to be freed. He did not covet the role of the redeemer, nor even did he find in his superhuman strength more than a burden. He cried out to be left to follow the way of common men, but I insisted and he yielded to what was my command, and what I thought to be Yours."

His head sank to the table. He put his hands over his ears to shut out the sounds of life around him, pressed his eyelids shut so that he might hear the voice, but he heard only the ancient tired beating of his heart, the sluicing of his blood until, behind his eyes, lit up in flame, he saw the words:

> Wherefore then have you devised such a thing against the people of God? for in speaking this word the king is as one that is guilty, in that the king does not fetch home again his banished one. For we must all die, and are as water spilt on the ground which cannot be gathered up again; neither does God show favor to any person; but let him devise means that he that is banished be not an outcast from him.

He knew the passage well, but why had it come to his mind now? Was this the Lord's sign? His words? The text concerned the advice the woman of Tekoa, and through her Joab, had given to King David to restore his son Absalom to the royal presence. But what had come of that? Divisiveness, warfare, and death. Only when Absalom, hanging by his hair, had felt Joab's darts, only when rebellion had been crushed, could the king dom be united, the house of David established, and at last the Temple of the Lord built. . . . Yet, even then, the great King David had been denied the privilege of building God's house because he had shed blood.

Abruptly, Rabbi Low remembered the Radak's comment on the passage. "Mankind must not increase the spilling of blood."

Impelled to lift his face, to take his hands from his ears, to open his eyes, and to speak aloud to the empty room, he knew he was being commanded. "For we must all die, and are as water spilt on the ground which cannot be gathered up again. . . . Mankind must not increase the spilling of blood." The Lord had spoken. While the motions of the heart belonged to man, speech was under covenant: What his tongue had spoken aloud was from the Almighty.

"O Lord," he cried, "did I have a messianic nightmare that I might make an end to this violence without end? Did I imagine a worldly redemption, which cannot be garnered where there is none? Did you move me, out of my pride and desperation, to spill blood through the Golem and yet think to keep my hands clean? In my blind desire to do good, did I commit the very sin I sought to avoid for Your people? Did You tempt me with my dream of salvation that I might be the one to shield Your people from the sword, that I might avoid the rule of man's necessity and Your necessity that we must wait, suffer, endure, have faith in Your providence and mercy? Did I walk in the ways of the nations and thereby lead Your people on that very same path— and not on Yours?"

Jacob returned without the Golem. "Jacob seeks to persuade the Golem to come, but he refuses," Jacob reported, speaking of himself strangely in the third person.

"Why does he refuse?" Rabbi Low asked.

With downcast eyes, Jacob mumbled, "The Golem is afraid."

"Afraid?"

"Afraid to die."

"Does he think that *I* shall put him to death?" the Rabbi inquired.

Jacob lifted his eyes. "He believes that you will put him to death for having shed Jewish blood, for murdering Isaac, for having widowed your daughter."

"And what did you tell him?"

Again Jacob averted his gaze. "Jacob told him that the Lord had even protected Cain and marked Cain so that none should do him injury."

"But Joseph was not reassured."

Jacob shook his head. "He said he knew you. You would act to save him—your own way—from stoning and from himself."

"Did Jacob say nothing?" the Rabbi asked, using the same third-person form.

Jacob was silent for a time before he spoke. "Jacob told him to run away, to lose himself among the *goyim*, to become of them, so that he might live. Jacob even offered to go with him."

The Rabbi's eyes asked the question.

"The Golem said it was too late for that," Jacob said. "Once it might have been possible, but now, having killed Isaac, having spilled Jewish blood, he was altogether an outcast, but still a Jew. Besides—"

"Besides?"

"He could not leave you. You were . . . father to him and he must cleave to you."

"Where is he?"

"When Jacob spoke to him, they were in the cemetery, sitting on the ground together next to Kaethe Hoch's grave."

This time they returned together, the Golem leading, his face grim. Streaks of gray stained his black hair and beard.

"We are here"—Jacob spoke for both—"as you wished."

"Joseph," the Rabbi said, "I have yet one task for you."

The Golem bowed his head.

"Do you not ask what it is?" the Rabbi exclaimed.

"I know my final task," the Golem replied, "and yours."

"Jacob and I will need your help. Come to the *Altneuschul* loft tonight at midnight."

Trembling, the Golem agreed. Jacob, about to protest, was cut off by the Rabbi's gesture.

Jacob went like Lot's wife, looking back.

"And now, Rabbi?" the Golem asked when they were alone.

"And now, Joseph?" The Rabbi motioned for him to sit, but the Golem remained standing.

Several times Rabbi Low tried to begin, but each time he could not pry the words loose. Finally, he said, in a whisper, "I want you to forgive me, Joseph, for the life I made you live—"

"And for the death you will now make me endure?"

"For that too."

"I do *not* forgive you."

"I hoped that you could," the Rabbi said.

"Am I more than human, or less?"

"If you do not forgive me, why did you not run away?"

"Ah, Jacob told you."

"To be afraid is human."

"Though I am a golem, I, too, am afraid, Rabbi."

"Of what, Joseph?"

"Of what is to come," the Golem replied. "If Jacob told you that I would not run, perhaps he also told you why. You brought me out of the darkness; but you would not let me live. You fed and clothed me, sheltered me, you taught me to study and to pray; but you would not let me live. *To be unmarried is to live without kindness, without religion, without peace.*"

"What Talmud Isaac taught you, he taught you well," the Rabbi observed.

"As he taught me, so did I teach him. A man does not know what is in the heart of his neighbor, nor the teacher in the heart of his pupil."

"So you taught him death."

"To kill was my fate. I performed my holy destiny."

"In that was my error—and my despair."

"Despair, Rabbi? The ghetto is saved. For now. Thaddeus is dead. And, at last, the Emperor himself has issued a proclamation exonerating the Jews from all accusations of bloodguilt. Is that not a great victory?"

"Three thousand Jews are dead, hundreds more are wounded. How can that be a victory? Scores of houses and two synagogues in ruins. Thousands dishonored and humiliated. And we ourselves with hands covered with blood."

"Had we not shed their blood, more of ours would have been spilled. You think helplessness would have deterred them? No, Rabbi, that is a dream."

"We would at least not have walked in the way of the nations."

"You created *me* to walk in the way of the nations. Death was to be my life."

"Your life was not to be ours, and my purpose was to keep ours from becoming yours. I would have your forgiveness for that."

"You had my life in your hands. You were father and mother to me—and now Angel of Death. I can neither forgive nor leave you."

"So you remained?"

The Golem nodded. "Kaethe is dead. The ghetto, like a wounded animal, wishes to strike back at someone. At me. At one of its own. For it can only hate itself for its helplessness. And I, awake or asleep, have nightmares of the ax. I dream I am no longer the Golem who kills in defense of the defenseless. Instead, I am a man who kills for sheer joy, to hear with pleasure bone crunching, to see with delight blood spurting. Not for sport, like Pokorny, but for the savage desire to revenge and destroy. Forever before me I see Isaac pleading, and then Kaethe calling to me from her window, and again and again I kill him. I cannot eat, I cannot sleep, I cannot live. I would be at peace, but I am afraid to die."

"I, too, am afraid, Joseph."

"The *Höhe* Rabbi Low afraid?"

"I know what must be done and am afraid to do it, because that which I sought to avoid I precipitated." The Rabbi's voice had the pleading of prayer. "I have devoted all my life to helping our people, Joseph, to teaching, protecting. I sacrificed myself, my wife, my son and daughters to our people's welfare. I went where the Lord sent me and where I was needed—Posen, Nikolsburg, Prague—and I did what the Lord laid upon me to do. I had no hesitation to ask you to do the same."

"You had a wife, children, work, the admiration of all, Rabbi, all a man could ask for."

"For denying you a wife, I also ask your forgiveness. Children the Lord denied you, not I. I thought it the Almighty's intention that you should defend us against our enemies without distractions so that you might be more stalwart in our defense." The Rabbi's laughter was a lament. "How stupid! I forgot that man is more ferocious than any other animal. Yet the more human you became, the gentler you seemed to grow, a reproach to all of us who are merely men."

"You commanded me to kill in your behalf. I did so. And it was you who kept me from a wife, or even a companion, from Jitka as well as Kaethe. Out of my pain and rage for Kaethe's death I killed Jews, and I killed Isaac. To kill the innocent is the way of the world of men. You, Isaac, *they* killed Kaethe as surely as if you had all sentenced her with your own hands. *They* killed Kaethe. I killed *them*. Now it is your turn to kill. Me. I do not feel guilty."

"That is what *I* am afraid of, Joseph."

"The time to have been afraid was at my birth, Rabbi, not now."

"I was full of fear then, but full of hope. Now, too, I am full of fear, but altogether without hope."

"I cannot conquer my fear or despair, nor help you with yours," the Golem said.

"Nor forgive mine?" the Rabbi asked. He covered his face with his hands for a long time before he said, "Go, then, Joseph, to the *Altneuschul* loft. We shall come to you there at midnight."

"The time is short, but there *is* time. I would walk beneath the sun and moon, see the stars, and breathe the night air. And I would say farewell at Kaethe's grave."

"Do what you will now," Rabbi Low said, removing his hands from his face, "but return to the synagogue before midnight."

"I wait with as much eagerness as trepidation," the Golem declared. "*God will redeem my soul from the power of the grave when He receives me.*"

"*When the dust shall return to the earth that it was, the spirit shall return to God who gave it.*" The Rabbi endeavored to make the words a blessing, but the Golem had already turned away.

At dinner Pearl sat morosely picking at her food, watching intently to see that he ate. Rabbi Low could manage only a piece of bread and drink a glass of wine, but her eyes' rebuke nettled him. He bore it as long as he could before he berated her and she started to cry. Then, to comfort her, he asked, "Why do you weep?"

"I have seen such things in the ghetto, such things. . . . Why must it always be this way? The killing, the hatred? And I have seen these things in myself, even at my age, even now."

Rabbi Low said nothing, unable to swallow the wine caught in his throat, warmed sour there.

"I weep for all those people, for Kaethe and Leah, for Bezalel and Isaac, even for Joseph Golem, though he has widowed our daughter, orphaned our grandchildren. Our house is empty. Not a footstep or voice is heard there and the echoes in the *Juden-*

gasse only make the house more desolate still. We are old and alone, and soon . . ."

"We shall die," Rabbi Low finished the sentence.

He put down his wineglass, reached across and took her hand, but she withdrew it.

"You asked me to send Joseph Golem away," he said.

"Not now."

"Why?"

"I have changed my mind. Because he, too, is a son. Your child, not mine, yet a son in the house. He will die like Bezalel who, since he could not be the *Höhe* Rabbi Low, had to die in Kolín." Pearl raised her hand to stop his objection. "You will save Joseph from stoning, but for the sake of the community, you will send him to his death, as you sent Bezalel to his. *Thus will they quench my coal which is left, and will leave to my husband neither name nor remainder upon the face of the earth.*"

Again the words of the woman of Tekoa! The Lord indeed gave him omens.

"Joseph Golem," he said sternly, "has killed three Jews and wounded six others."

"And one of them Isaac, the gentle, red-haired Isaac who was like a son to me, and to you. But if the Golem killed him, it was in an anguish of love and loss, crazed with the killing you made his task. He is guilty, but is he not also innocent? Is there no forgiveness for him for that?"

"My forgiveness, Pearl? Joseph has that. But the law and the community require justice. The law stands above man and I must carry it out impartially."

"Impartially!" she scoffed. "Mercilessly! For that there *will* be no forgiveness, here or in the world to come."

"I asked Joseph for his forgiveness," Rabbi Low said, "but he would not forgive me."

"Like Bezalel."

"Yes, like my own son."

"You have succeeded in much with the community, Judah, but you have failed with your sons," Pearl said implacably. "The Lord, Judah, has had His own ways to punish."

XXVII

———◆—◀◆▶—◆—◆———

Shortly before midnight, Jacob returned carrying lanterns. Rabbi Low met him at the door, already dressed. They did not speak, but walked to the *Altneuschul* nearby. In the soft spring darkness, a heavy orange moon hung low on the horizon like a sodden fruit. As they walked, the debris of the pogrom, wood, coal, glass shards, crunched beneath their heels.

Except for the blood-red eternal light over the altar, the synagogue was dark, great shadows on the walls moving crippled and tormented. When Jacob raised his lantern so they might find the door that led to the stairs ascending to the loft, Rabbi Low thought he saw on the speaker's stand the awesome figure of the *Malach Hamoves* waiting imperturbably, but it was only the distorted shadow of the Ark. Once more, for an instant, he had seen the torn scroll and fragment in the Angel of Death's hands and now he knew that the torn fragment bore both his name and the Golem's. The ancient cry to the Lord, the plaint of centuries to God comparing the Jews' sacrifices of their sons to Abraham's sacrifice of Isaac, rose up in his throat like nausea. "You, Father Abraham, built one altar and did *not* offer up your son, but I have built a thousand altars and offered up my sons on all of them." He tried to fight down the nausea and the rebellion, telling himself that each man to his own *Akédah*; each generation to its own sacrifice: He had had his Bezalel, and now, too, he had his very own Isaac—and his Golem.

In the garret their lanterns drove the darkness back only a little way. All around were strewn a snow of shredded tassels, old, faded prayer shawls, torn prayer books, worn phylacteries. From them rose the musty odor of decay, mournful, lingering.

"Joseph," the Rabbi called into the darkness.

"Here I am." The Golem moved from the darkness into their light. The shadow he cast, gigantic and wavering, loomed threateningly over them. The Rabbi and Jacob held their lanterns high so that they could see his face. Without another word, the Golem bent and cleared a large space on the floor at their feet. "I have done your every task, Rabbi," he said, and with a sigh, he lay down, outstretched.

"You have done well," the Rabbi commended him.

"Who tries to do good can only do well—or badly," the Golem replied.

"But not good?" the Rabbi asked.

"Never good enough, Rabbi," the Golem answered.

"I have but one more task for you, Joseph," the Rabbi stated.

"I hear and obey. I shall go and do," the Golem replied and began to rise.

"No. Stay. There is no place to go from here. Here is the last and hardest task of all."

"To die?"

Rabbi Low did not answer. With gestures he stationed himself and Jacob in their places and began to chant: "Lord, we have not been pure at heart, nor free of base ambition and sinful thought, and we have therefore used the holy name of the Lord

· 2 2 9 ·

in vain. We have desecrated the holy name of the Almighty. Forgive us and forgive Joseph Golem."

A wild gust of wind shook the rafters, the lanterns flickered, and a shudder shook the Golem's frame.

Chanting Psalms, the Rabbi walked around clockwise, Jacob counterclockwise, the full seven times, intoning solemnly:

> Why art thou cast down, O my soul?
> And why moanest thou within me?
> Hope thou in God; for yet shall I praise Him
> For the salvation of His countenance.

Wide-eyed, the Golem murmured, "Rabbi, I am afraid."

Rabbi Low bent to comfort him. "There is nothing to fear now, my son, nothing." He took the Golem's hand in his. "I shall give you back to peace and darkness, and then to the light beyond darkness that is the very presence of God."

"I do not want to go!" the Golem shrieked, struggling to arise.

"Not of your will were you born and not of your will shall you die," the Rabbi declared, feeling the tremor of the Golem's flesh as it gave in to his own and slumped back.

"Help me, Father," the Golem cried out.

"*Your dead shall live again, the mortal being shall rise up,*" the Rabbi sang.

"Death!" the Golem screamed, and as he did so, the Rabbi tore the *Shem* from his gaping mouth, snatched from beneath that great twisted tongue the parchment with the holiest name of the Lord.

The Golem's eyes started, his hair and beard in an instant whitened, his face grayed. On his forehead, first pale as flesh, then scarlet as blood, the word *Truth* shone. *Emes.* With his forefinger, the Rabbi gently erased the first letter to make it *Mes*—"corpse." The Golem's body, so monumental that it seemed to fill the entire synagogue, became a great gray corpse. "*Into Thy hand I commit my spirit; Thou wilt surely redeem me, Lord, God of truth,*" Rabbi Low proclaimed.

The flaming *Mes* on the Golem's forehead disappeared into the crumbling clay and in its place there shimmered a golden שׁ, initial of that holiest name of the Almighty, *Shaddai.* From somewhere in the distance, above and around them, past and present, the Golem's scream whipped the world and flayed their spirits like a cutting night wind. "Do not forget me!" his voice, fading away, pleaded and commanded: "Remember me!"

In a moment more the Golem was only a rough-hewn outline of clay, a clod they had once shaped from the Moldau riverbank.

Groaning, the Rabbi finally rose, staring at his hands. Then, together, they began to chant the mourner's *Kaddish*:

> Exalted and hallowed be God's great name
> In this world of His creation.
> May His will be fulfilled
> And His sovereignty revealed
> In the days of your lifetime
> And the life of the whole house of Israel
> Speedily and soon,
> And say, Amen.

Heads bowed and silent, they stood until the last reverberations of the *Amen* had died away in the dusty silence of the garret. Then Rabbi Low directed Jacob to cover the Golem's corpse with old prayer shawls and with the remnants of old prayer books. When Jacob had finished, all that was visible was a great yellowing mound of Hebrew lettered sheets.

"What shall we say happened to him?" Jacob finally asked.

"A wayfarer he came, a wayfarer he went," the Rabbi replied. "A stranger and a sojourner, he has gone away." He shook himself and continued. "Tomorrow, at services, you will announce that no one is to go up into the synagogue loft. Nor is the garret to be used any longer to store the remains of prayer books or other sacred articles."

"The people will imagine it is a precaution against the risk of fire," Jacob said.

Uncertainly, they waited, neither able to look in the other's face, until Rabbi Low said, "Go, now, Jacob, I wish to remain here a little while."

Jacob bid him good-night and left his lantern on the floor next to the great mound that had been the Golem. When he had departed, Rabbi Low looked at his hands and began to rub his palms slowly together until the bits of clay on them grew finer and finer and were at last resolved into dust. Then he tore his vest over his heart, sat on the floor, and wept.

The first rays of dawn that faintly illumined the darkness of the garret brought Rabbi Low down into the synagogue, where he left his extinguished lantern, and into the street. The late April sun already warmly asserted itself and the breeze from the Moldau blew brisk and clean through the *Judengasse*. It was still too early for morning prayers and wearily he walked through the streets of the ghetto. Men, fish dangling from their bloodstained hands, were coming back from the fish market and from the river. Butchers' boys, their open wicker baskets on their heads, left rivulets of blood on the cobbles as they delivered their meats. Young women hurried toward the bakeries for the morning's freshly baked bread; and here and there young girls selling flowers displayed their bright bouquets in makeshift stalls. Water carts with great vats went from house to house and vied for the way with clumsy, double-teamed peasant carts heavy laden with country produce that, slow and stately, were drawn through the narrow streets. The sunshine and color momentarily transformed the ghetto's winter into spring. It should have been all different, or all the same, yet it was neither. The time of the Golem would remain with them until the coming of the Messiah because everything was fatal propensity and impulse, *yetzer*; in the time of the Golem the brute spirit of man could not be straightened, its crookedness would forever be an affliction.

When he returned to his house, Rabbi Low looked at the carved lion above his door and, reaching up, touched its stone mouth, saying aloud: "Judah is the lion's whelp; from the prey, my son, art thou saved." He laughed, broke into a fit of coughing, and through the paroxysm heard gratefully the measured tread of Pearl's shoes as she walked slowly to open the door to him.